CHILLERS FROM THE ROCK

A COLLECTION OF SHORT STORIES

Copyright © 2018 Engen Books

The CIP data for this collection is available online or by request.

Man on Fire, The Chosen Copyright © 2018 Jon Dobbin
The Culling © 2018 Jeff Slade
Scarlett Ribbons © 2018 Bronwynn Erskine
Leopold's Cherubs Princes © 2018 Michelle Churchill
The Cache © 2018 Anastacia Hopkins
Dark Peaks, Nuckelavee © 2018 Samuel Bauer
Werewolf, Halloween Mummers © 2018 Paul Carberry
The Pursuit © 2018 Eryn Heidel
The Wine Dark Sea © 2018 Shannon K Green
Flickers in the Night, The Lakehouse, Afterword © 2018 Matthew LeDrew
A Friend In Shadow © 2018 Peter J Foote
Extinction © 2018 Lynn Reicker
Grow Gold Together © 2018 Matthew Daniels
Falling Like Flies © 2018 Maggie Carroll
Territory © 2018 Chantal Boudreau
The Deal, The Taste of Copper © 2018 Alison House
Beyond No Man's Land © 2018 Teresita E. Dziadura
Tommy © 2018 Chelsea Bee
Treatment, Sifting © 2018 Kelley Power
Forward © 2018 Dale Gilbert Jarvis
Stephen King & The Dungeon of Nightmares © 2023 Mike Hickey

Distributed by:
Engen Books
www.engenbooks.com
submissions@engenbooks.com
First mass market paperback printing: March 2018
Second Printing: February 2024
Second Printing Cover Image: Mike Hickey

CHILLERS FROM THE ROCK

EDITED BY ERIN VANCE & ELLEN CURTIS

CONTENTS

Foreword
Dale Gilbert Jarvis

Come with me, back into the mists of time. I have a yarn to spin for you.

It is about one Thorvald Erikson, the brother of the more-famous Leif. Alas, poor Thorvald was shot in the armpit by an arrow fired at him by an angry Skraeling. He died of his wound and was buried in Vinland, one of the first Europeans on record to perish in this New Found Land. When his other brother Thorstein heard of his untimely demise, he sailed to Vinland to recover Thorvald's body. Early that winter, a terrible disease broke out amongst the crew. It spread from man to man, and, unchecked, eventually to Thorstein himself. He too perished, and was greatly mourned by his wife, Gudrid.

Things then took a turn towards the supernatural. Much to their horror, the dead body of Thorstein Eiriksson sat up on the bench where he had been laid out.

"Where is Gudrid?" the revenant corpse moaned.

His wife, terrified, said nothing. Three times the corpse spoke; three times she remained silent in fear. One of the crew-members, also named Thorstein, spoke up instead.

"What is it you want, namesake?" inquired the second Thorstein.

At this the corpse spoke, saying that he was anxious to reveal to Gudrid her destiny. Then, having spoken words of prophecy, the corpse thudded back onto his funeral bench. The Vikings packed him up, and sailed him back to Eiriksfjord, Greenland, where he was buried. Presumably he did not speak again.

It is the earliest-known European ghost story in North

America, adding to centuries of pre-existing tales. For as long as people have lived on and visited this Rock, we have been gathering around campfires and kerosene lamps to whisper chilling tales and shiver in fear at what might lie in the lengthening shadows.

One of my favourite St. John's legends involves a man named Samuel Pettyham, who had an encounter with a headless phantom in the 1740s. It is replete with the things I love about a good ghost story: a gradual build-up of strange occurrences into one final, terrifying encounter; an everyday protagonist, caught up by supernatural forces beyond his control; a doomed love triangle; and a spirit so motivated by vengeance that it wanders eternity in search of its unpunished foe. What's not to love in that?

Times and traditions change. The oral storytellers of yesteryear are joined today by the next generation of literary fabulists, who continue to craft stories designed to keep us up at night. The forces of horror, dark fantasy, and supernatural fiction are on the rise in Newfoundland and Labrador, writing a new chapter in our long history of loving a good creepy tale.

But why do we adore stories that chill us to the marrow? Why do we hunger for tales that make us look over our shoulders when walking home in the dark? Perhaps we like tales of this sort because we know that they are not true, that they will end with us still safe and sound. Perhaps we hunger for magic and mystery we lack in our nine-to-five existence. Perhaps it is a biological impulse, a physical craving for that rush of adrenaline, that boost in endorphins. Maybe a little bit of fear reminds us that we are alive… for now.

If you have picked up this book it is because you are one of those souls who seek out the darkness. So, enjoy the stories herein. May the hairs rise on the back of your neck, and may your pulse quicken just a tiny bit. Something is waiting there in the darkness to meet you.

With grim, ghoulish wishes, I remain,

Eternally yours,
Dale Gilbert Jarvis
Storyteller and Author,
www.nlunexplained.ca

Jon Dobbin

Jon Dobbin is an award winning author living in the St. John's, Newfoundland metro region.

He is a father of three, the husband to an amazing wife, an educator, and a tattoo and beard enthusiast.

Dobbin's work has appeared in the all three *Terror Nova* books to date, *Chillers from the Rock, Dystopia from the Rock, Pulp Science-Fiction from the Rock, From the Rock Stars,* and, *Kit Sora: The Artobiography* collections.

To date he has released three novels from Engen Books: 2019's *The Starving,* 2020's *The Broken Spire,* and 2021's *The Risen.*

Man of Fire

The boy sat next to the dog and it began.

"Don't bother me, boy," said the dog, shaking his ears and brown, matted fur. The boy just sat there though, elbows on his knees, a plastic Jack-o-Lantern hanging from his small fist: hardly a bother at all.

"Why are you dressed like a man of fire?" asked the dog when the boy hadn't moved. Might as well pass the time, he thought.

The boy looked himself over. "Fireman," he sighed and his black, plastic coat creaked as he adjusted himself.

"That's what I said," said the dog. "Why are you dressed that way? You're no man, boy, and certainly not a man of fire." The dog sneezed and nodded to himself.

The boy looked into the darkness before him, past the wet pavement, his eyes hardened. "It's Halloween, dog."

The dog perked up his ears and lay down on his elbows, feeling the dampness of the street on his fur. He sat up again and stretched a paw towards the boy.

"Oh. That's a good dog," the boy blinked.

"Did you get many treats, boy?"

The boy nodded.

"Many tricks?"

The boy shook his head.

"Why so glum, boy?" The dog had started to feel

worried for this boy. He was dressed like a man, he had treats, he was out at night, and he was *free*. Everything boys like.

The boy shrugged.

"You're not happy, boy. Perhaps I'll tell you a secret; that should be happy. Do you want to know why you wear costumes on Halloween?"

The boy crinkled his nose and turned up an eyebrow. "For the treats, right?"

Dog laughed, but it came out like a howl. The boy flinched. "No, boy, that's what your mother and father tell you, that's what your schools and your teachers tell you, but Dog knows the real reason." The dog grunted, "Do you want to know too?"

The boy turned toward the dog more now, his shoulders shifted and his coat squeaked. Dog wagged his tail.

"Are you sure you want to know?" said the dog smiling, his tongue lolling out of his jaws.

The boy nodded, his hard plastic helmet bobbing with excitement. Dog was excited too; he stood up, and sat down. He stood up again, turned in a circle twice, sniffed the ground and sat facing the boy. He closed his mouth, his right lip caught in one of his bottom teeth and curled out, but he didn't mind. He perked up his ears and focused his deep, chestnut eyes on the boy.

"Alright boy. The reason you wear a costume on Halloween is," he paused-- for greater effect-- "to trick the devil." The dog nodded to himself, fixed his lip, and turned away from the boy. The boy wasn't done though; suddenly he was a bother.

"There's no such thing as the devil, dog. You made that up." The boy's face cracked with a smile.

Giving the boy a sidelong look, the dog said, "Are you sure about that?"

"Silly dog, you don't know anything about Halloween." A man walked by with a green suit and a black cane followed by a thin, pale girl dressed in leather. He had her on a leash.

Dog growled."You know so much now, boy? Very smart then, very wise? Why don't you take off your man of fire suit and see. Just see if the devil comes?"

The boy turned away from the dog, placed his Jack-o-Lantern between his feet and took off his hat. He squeaked out of his jacket and looked at Dog, daring him.

Dog smiled, his tongue bobbing in and out of his mouth, salivating.

The Chosen

1.

"I say," the lanky Englishman broke the silence around the fire. "It's quite chilly here at night." He huddled closer to the crackling flame, rubbing his hands together. "Not as damp as home though, I dare say." A crooked, mirthless grin spread across his face.

Bill Weston plucked his wide brimmed hat from a sun-creased face. He reclined back and regarded the man with a grimace. "It gets colder. Snow hasn't fallen yet," he said, rubbing the coarse stubble of his chin with a calloused hand.

"Yep." Clancy Fifield nodded from a log he used as a make-shift seat, as he turned his coat collar up against the chill, its worn edge brushed the back of his Bowler.

Weston pushed himself up to his elbows, feeling the coolness of the grass that he was using as a bed as he did. They were hired, Clancy and himself, to escort the stately Mr. Nigel Dolarhydethrough the wilds of Colorado. Dolarhyde proclaimed himself an academic and a gentleman of delicate nature. As such, he required Clancy to do the heavy lifting when the pack mule was at rest. Weston was their guide, having cut his teeth on the Colorado wilderness as a boy and formerly held a job as a scout for the National Railroad Company.

Weston sighed as he sat upright and crossed his arms

over his bent knees. "Rains a lot where you're from, Nigel?"

The Englishman brightened, but only nodded and said, "Rain? Yes, and fog! Fog so thick you could cut it with a knife." Dolarhyde's face sagged, and he retreated back into himself and made a hesitant glance at his belongings, his assorted bags, and of course, the large box.

"Don't know much about your wares, Nigel; what have you got in that box that's been breaking Clancy's back so?" Weston said with a smile, and a chuckle lifted from Clancy's barrel chest. Dolarhyde darkened and withdrew more into himself.

"It's nothing really. A statue, a small thing, for a colleague in Denver." He leaned back out of the firelight, his face darkening as it fell into shadows.

Weston whistled through his teeth, his steady brown eyes burning a hole in the blackness where Dolarhyde's face used to be. "Doesn't seem much like nothing, or a small thing. What do you say, Clancy?"

The big man grunted, and lowered his girth to the ground. Silence followed. Weston peered after Dolarhyde and his mysterious statue encased in a box resplendent in the moonlight.

2.

It was the soft click of gravel under a boot that roused Weston, but it was the cold touch of a gun barrel on his neck that brought him to his senses. Darkness and shadows had crept over the small camp as the fire waned, daylight was still far off, and the night was still and without sound.

"Easy there," a hoarse whisper breathed into his ear. "Easy now or you'll end up like your big friend." A black, leather-clad hand pointed past his eyes. Weston followed the direction, his jaw clenched. In the dim light of the dying fire, Weston saw a sour faced man unfold himself from the ground, wiping a large knife on his dark jeans as the red-hot ash of a cigar glowing from his mouth. At the man's feet Clancy sprawled, a sanguine river flowing from his cut throat.

Weston began to rise, but the steel grip of his assailant forced him to remain on his knees. He craned his neck to try for a glimpse of Dolarhyde. In the low light, he could see the Englishman cower next to his belongings, glasses askew as he hugged the large box, his face pressed against it. Two men laughed as they closed around him.

The man at his back yanked him to his feet, and guided Weston away from his bag and gun, towards the remains of the fire. As he sat, two men dragged a blubbering Dolarhyde to the campground and deposited him across from Weston. The Englishman's long, sallow face was streaked with blood, dust, and tears. The same two men then left to fetch Dolarhyde's belongings while the man who killed Clancy and Weston's captor stayed behind to watch their hostages. They kept their pistols in hand and a watchful eye on their captives; they spoke very little. The man who had slain Clancy maintained a humourless grin behind his dwindling cigar.

"Can't be much work for your sort on this path," Weston ventured, "not many know of it."

"Not sure of that myself, mister, this is our first trip over it," the man who had captured him replied, crossing his hands in front of him, gun barrel pointed to the ground with the hammer cocked.

"Luck then?" Weston chuckled and Dolarhyde's face drained of colour. "Well, friends, there is precious little with us that will fill your pockets and plenty that will strain your backs." He chuckled again, picking at the dirt under his fingernails.

"That a fact?" A smile stretched across the man's face that turned Weston's stomach. "Well, apologies all around, this is quite embarrassing. I'll just gather my friends and we will leave your company with haste."

Clancy's killer bent to stoke the fire and the growing flame lit a toothy smile that Dolarhyde cringed away from.

"You see," the man continued, "we were under the impression that this Brit here was escorting some pretty treasure to Denver. We've been following you since you picked him up in Texas."

Clancy's killer uttered a dry and low chuckle void of levity.

3.

"God dammit!" a deep voice croaked followed by the crash of Dolarhyde's crate on the ground before the fire. The Brit nearly fainted at the sound, and had to catch himself before he lunged forward to check the integrity of the box. "Carlos, you dirty bean eater. You dropped your end!"

"**** you, Vato," the second man said in a quiet, accented voice.

The two men stood across from each other, their long coats thrown back and their hands on their pistols. The bandit closest to Weston, Charlie Vato, had seen more seasons then his companions. His skin was pocked and scarred and his pate stood sparse of hair while which remained was greying. His watery green eyes locked on the much younger man who opposed him. Carlos, with his hazel eyes and chestnut skin, sneered at the older man through a mouth that was heavily scarred, as if it was torn asunder at birth. A tense silence followed. Weston watched with interest while Dolarhyde cowered closer to him, quiet now save for a constant sniffle; he shook all over.

"Idiots," the leader said, breaking the silence. "Keep your hands off your iron unless you want Lazarus to put a bullet in each of you." Both men cast a glance at Clancy's murderer who barked a mechanical laugh. The rivals turned from each other, abashed like children scolded by their father.

Virgil crouched before the crate, and prodded at it where it had struck the ground. He pulled away pieces of wood with his gloved hand and crumbled them between his thumb and forefinger; a frown lined his face. "We'll have to check it," he rubbed his hands together and brushed the remaining wood and splinters away.

Dolarhyde exploded from the ground and landed upon the bandit leader, his slender, pale fists wrapping around the collar of Virgil's coat. "Don't open it!" Dolarhyde practically salivated over the prone Virgil's face. "If your life means anything to you, don't touch it!" His voice had reached a high-pitched squeal that shook Weston's nerves and delivered him from momentary shock.

Lazarus' senses reawakened as well and he jumped forward with his companions to wrestle the half-mad Englishman from their struggling leader.

The scramble was over almost as quick as it started. The bandits began pummelling the delirious Englishman to loosen his grip. Charlie in particular seemed to relish the beating. When he had satisfied himself, he and Carlos dragged Dolarhyde back to Weston.

Virgil rose and dusted himself off, his eyes burned as they locked on the Englishman. He called over his shoulder, "Get the pry bar." Carlos ran off.

Virgil crept forward, coat thrown back and hand on

his revolver. "Do that again and see how fast you enter hell."

Dolarhyde groaned, his wide eyes shut in pain. Virgil gave Weston a warning glance and walked away as Carlos ran out of the trees. He pointed tersely at the crate, and met Charlie and Carlos there. Charlie's hand glided over his balding head, and he began directing the young Mexican. Lazarus stood close to Weston and Nigel, waving his hands absently over the fire.

The box creaked as Carlos and Charlie worked the pry bar and slid the long nails from the wood. They dislodged the cover and pushed it to the ground with a humble crash. Both men stood back from the box and made way for Virgil. The bandit leader tilted his head to the side, studying the contents, before he bent at the waist and began to brush hay out of the box where it was picked up and carried away on the building wind.

Virgil uttered a surprised grunt that made Charlie and Carlos sneak closer for a better look. Their faces betrayed their puzzlement. Lazarus was not immune to the curiosity from his place by the fire and craned his neck for a better look. Weston was feeling quite interested himself and it took a concentrated effort to contain his impulse to jump up for a quick look. Nevertheless, his eyes did not move from the box. Nigel groaned by his side.

"Well?" Carlos moved closer, squinting as if the contents in the crate were hard to see.

"Doesn't look damaged from here," answered Virgil, his voice distant and uncertain. "I guess we better remove it to be sure," he sighed as he reached into the box. A look of pain came over his dark face and he hesitated as his hand passed the threshold of the container. It took an effort, but he finally forced his shaking hand further into the box.

Dolarhyde sat up straight, moving so suddenly as to break Weston's gaze from the scene that was playing out before him. The beaten Englishman's face was serene despite being caked with blood and tears. His eyes watered and tears rolled down his cheeks. "I don't know if you gentlemen pray," Dolarhyde said, his voice barely rose beyond that of a whisper between lovers, "but if you do, now would be a good time."

His words rang out on the wind. The horses had gone completely silent, no insects hummed, no animals scraped or snuffed, and no birds squawked. Weston felt a thick apprehension crush upon him. He no longer wanted to know what was in the Englishman's accursed box; he wanted to leave this place and never return.

Virgil drew forth the black effigy and took it into both gloved hands, turning it over and over, upending it, his face that of disgust. The creature portrayed in the stone was bulbous and without basis in Weston's mind. As Virgil moved it about, the idol seemed to take a different shape, alter itself before his eyes. One moment it had three overlapping mouths each filled with razor-sharp, yellow teeth glistening against a scaled, reptilian skin. The next moment it was dog-like with a rat face wearing a helmet, crouched and clenching man-like fists.

Weston tore his eyes away from the statue. He turned to Dolarhyde who sat wide-eyed and slack-jawed, eyes clasped on the scene before him, froth gathering at the corners of his mouth. Charlie and Carlos closed in on their boss, as did Lazarus, seeming to have forgotten their captives. Weston caught a glance of Lazarus before he moved off. His face was that of a man entranced: he licked his lips under his heavy, brown beard and he began to remove his heavy leather gloves.

"What an ugly piece of crap," Virgil managed, attempting a laugh.

"Put it back in the box," Charlie coughed, his hand furiously rubbing his sparsely haired scalp. "I can't bear to look on it," but he made no move to look away.

"Is it okay?" Carlos chimed, leaning closer.

"Seems so," Virgil said turning it over again. "Weird is what it is. It's solid, and it's heavy, but it looks... liquid." And in a whisper: "It keeps changing."

At that Weston turned his eyes to the bandits, careful to keep his gaze away from the Idol.

"Pass it here, Virgil," Lazarus said, his voice was rough, like rocks grating rocks. He was back on to Weston, his shoulders tense, and his back straight. He stretched one open hand in front of him. Virgil grasped the prize tighter to his chest, the dark leather of his gloves creaking with the pressure.

"I just want to look at it," Lazarus breathed out, effort and pain mixed in equal measure.

Virgil backed away from his compatriot, statue still gripped tightly into him, anger and confusion spreading across his face. As he moved, Lazarus' knife appeared in his hand as if he had conjured it; Clancy's blood still stained it. Reading Lazarus' intention, Virgil whipped back his long jacket and made for his revolver. Lazarus sprung into action with a quickness and savagery of a feral beast. He lunged forward, gripping Virgil's gun hand before he could level it on him and, with one murderous strike, plunged his blade deep into Virgil's belly. Virgil dropped his gun and groaned as he fell back, holding his stomach. Carlos followed him to the ground, his hand putting pressure on the wound along with Virgil's. Lazarus turned away from them and began to walk towards the fire. His face was grim; darkness came over it in the flickering shadows of the fire. He held the statue, slender fingers curled like claws around the smooth ebony surface.

Weston was not a man who scared easy. Yet, at the approach of Lazarus and the statue, the hair on the back of his neck stood on end. It was passed time to leave. Weston hopped to his feet and grabbed the bleary-eyed Dolarhyde under the arm, yanking him to his side, and making a run for his bag. It took no more than an instant to reach his belongings and less than that to grab his revolver. Then the screaming began.

To his side, Dolarhyde began to moan and wheeze; a wet gurgle oozed forth from his jaws. Trying his best to ignore him, Weston holstered his gun and began to move again, grabbing the Englishman's arm as he did. A high-pitched, inhuman wail came from behind them. Weston whirled with fright and instinct, and drew his gun again.

The world behind him had gone insane. Weston's mind reeled at what he saw and a vulgar urge to survive gnawed at his guts. Lazarus writhed before the fire, his features distorted and unnatural screams of pain emanated from his ever-widening jaw. Black tendrils had begun to sprout from his back and sides slick with a molten ebony that dripped and ran like hot tar hitting the ground with a belching sizzle. The statue enveloped Lazarus' hand, smaller tendrils of ebony burrowing under his skin and melded itself with it. More screams flowed from Lazarus, and Weston's whole body began to ache with their reverberations.

Gunfire drew his attention away from the transforming bandit. Weston caught sight of Charlie, one hand still grazing the sparse hair on his balding head, firing two more shots into what had once been Lazarus. Charlie wore a mask of horror and tears rolled over his wrinkled and worn face. His shots slammed into Lazarus' convulsing back, and the black tar splattered to the ground with a horrendous squelch. Lazarus was pushed a step or two towards the fire, but the shots had little effect otherwise.

Lazarus' eyes glazed over as the black ooze crawled over his face, covering his large beard so completely it looked as though it were dissolved. Those same eyes narrowed and a familiar smile grew across Lazarus' lips. The monster before Weston turned toward Charlie, a slow, plodding movement that started with a turn of the head and followed through with the rest of the body; the new black tendrils moved in unison with Lazarus' human legs. When it faced Charlie, it unhinged its jaw and screamed its blood-curdling cry once more. Charlie let his gun drop and put both hands on his head, tearing at what little hair was left. He mouthed "No, no, no, no..." but no sound escaped his throat.

Lazarus jittered towards Charlie in a slow, uncertain walk. As he moved off, Weston caught sight of Carlos and Virgil. The latter still grasped at his wounded stomach, blood now trickling from the corner of his mouth. Carlos remained kneeling over him, face pale and uncertain, and pistol now in hand.

Weston pawed at Dolarhyde beside him, his eyes unable to move from the scene that was unfolding in front of him. Charlie ripped at himself; slow, distracted scratches began to appear on his head and face. His mouth trembled and his watery eyes spilled over his cheeks, flowing through creases made by the pained expression of fear and despair. Still, he did not move. The creature moved toward him in its strange gait, tittering in an insect-like clicking.

Weston's hand landed on Dolarhyde's arm, and with a force of will, he tore his eyes from the horror before him, drew the scholar close, and ran into the surrounding forest of spruce trees.

4.

"Why didn't he run?" Weston growled as he pushed his way past trees and navigated over rocks. Dolarhyde stumbled along behind him, groaning when he could catch his breath.

"He could've run. Hell, he could've blasted away, could've killed the sucker," he panted as he ploughed through some low-hanging branches that whipped at his face. Weston knew the answer of course: Charlie was in shock. He'd seen it in the war; seen men go catatonic at they stared down cannon fire or the barrel of a gun. Though Charlie looked like a man who had seen his fair share of action in his lifetime, Weston was willing to bet that he had never faced a black, oozing creature that was once a travelling companion. Lazarus and his new spider-like appendages had blown through any and all of Charlie's mental defences. Tore them down and set them aflame.

A scream rolled over the silence of the night, a clap of thunder made of human pain. The scream was loud and long, it's ending so sudden that it made Weston's skin crawl. A laugh echoed after it.

He paused, halting Dolarhyde, and cocked his head to the side and waited, trying to hear a sound or sign in the expanding silence. The entire forest seemed as though it were holding its breath in anticipation of the unfolding night. He took some hesitant steps, careful not to disturb a fallen branch or twig; his coarse hand gripped the moss-laden trunk of a large spruce tree for balance. It was getting easier to see, the sky was brightening and the sun seemed to be on the rise, but Weston still had no idea where he was or how to escape. He hadn't thought to take note of any reference point or starting point when they ran out of the camp.

Weston caught glimpse of a path in the distance. It was little more than a groove in the otherwise thick with growth forest floor. Weston and Dolarhyde crossed on it and were forced to traverse it single file, as if an adult leading a child. The former scholar stumbled along, and Weston had to slow and guide him around large rocks or tree roots when they came upon them. Not for the first time did Weston toy with the idea of leaving Dolarhyde. The poor man probably wouldn't even notice, his mind as numbed as it was. It wasn't a farfetched idea to believe that Dolarhyde would never recover from the mental break; and what kind of life could a student and professor, or any man, live as a prisoner in his own skull? Still, the man had endeavoured to trust Weston, and as easy as it would make Weston's escape, he wouldn't abandon him, certainly not to the monstrosity that was once the bandit known as Lazarus.

They broke through a line of trees that surrounded the end of the path and stumbled into a small clearing. Patches of tall grass and large rocks or boulders jutted out of the ground haphazardly. It was brighter now that they had escaped from under the canopy of trees, and Weston wagered that dawn was well in progress. A rustle in the distance caused Weston to drop his hand to his pistol. He brought it to hip height, but nothing stood in front of him and his trigger finger wavered. There was movement on the other side of the plain, and his arm tensed. From behind a large rock, a horse trotted into sight, its head bobbing and shaking as it came, indulging in a meal of grass. He heard the rustling and snorting of others and left Dolarhyde as he ran to look beyond the rock. There were four horses, all saddled and ready, and a pack mule that had a look of neglect, tied to a stake pounded into the ground.

Weston grabbed the reigns of the first horse and began to lead him toward the opening of the clearing. Dolarhyde remained where he had left him, staring up at the sky with his mouth agape as one hand rubbed a stained white sleeve. Weston climbed into the saddle of the brown horse, leaned back and patted its muscular hindquarters. "Easy there, fella," he said and urged the horse into a steady walk towards Dolarhyde.

A sound of thunder and snapping branches accompanied the dark object that exploded from Weston's left. His keen eyes barely registered what was happening as his horse reared in surprise and black tendrils of tar were sinking deep into its throat, blood and ooze dripping to the ground together. Weston made a grab for his pistol, but the spider-like appendages buried in the horse pushed it backwards and he turned to prepare himself of the fall. Weston was able to manoeuvre his upper body so that it faced the ground, his lower half still tangled in the horse's stirrups. He managed to kick his left foot free before he landed and avoided the impact of the dying horse as it followed behind him.

The landing was still rough. Weston felt a sharp pain in his left wrist and the impact knocked the air out of his lungs. The horse landed on its back less than a foot from Weston before falling to its side. Its breathing was slow and laboured, and panic engulfed its large brown eyes.

Weston rolled to his knees and had his revolver out. Lazarus was moving away from him toward Dolarhyde; it moved quicker now on its strange gait. Weston levelled his gun at the monster and squeezed the trigger three times. Each shot was echoed by a thud and a jolt from Lazarus that told Weston he had hit home. Black ooze fell to the ground around the creature with each reverberation.

The roar followed.

Weston could see Dolarhyde in the distance: he had fallen to the ground, his eyes were wide and he began to moan. Dolarhyde scrambled backwards up the path. Good, Weston thought; get out of here.

Then the creature turned on him.

5.

Any remnants of the bandit Lazarus' countenance had retreated from the monster that stood before Weston. They had melted away into the thick ooze that made up the statue. The disjointed spider legs were steady and alternated lifting the man-like body up and down. The face continued to change, subtle changes from three-mouthed creature, to snarling wolf, to a cold man with an empty smirk.

Weston fell back, pain firing through his legs and back, and put both the horse and space between him and the creature. The monster moved toward him, slow and methodical, savouring the impending doom of its prey. Weston pulled the trigger again -- the creature's shoulder flinched, tar splattered, but it kept moving forward, a dry laugh wheezing on the wind. Weston shuffled back another two steps, braced himself on one knee, ignoring the pain, and took aim for the creature's head. He took a deep breath and squeezed the trigger slowly, the gun hauled back on his strong hands, and an instant later the monster's head snapped back and it stopped in its tracks. It was hurt, but not dead. Weston cursed and checked his bullet count. One. He cursed again, closed the chamber, and took aim once more.

The inhuman roar pierced his ears and Weston had no other choice but to clap his hands to the side of his head to deaden the sound. Black ooze poured from the centre of the creature's forehead, a shiny, black mask now matted over its revolving features. In each of those faces, Weston noticed, there was no smile.

Weston was prepared when it lunged at him with the unnatural speed carried by its alien limbs. He tried to time it right and jump clear of the charge, but the strange jittering movement threw him off and one of the creature's appendages struck him hard on the legs as it ran past him. He landed awkwardly, his legs pained, and he could feel something warm and wet soak his jeans covering his shins. Felt, but refused to look; he didn't need the distraction right now.

The creature growled and turned towards him. Three mouths stared down on him for a moment, each with its own teeth bared. It brought one of the oil-slicked, spider-like legs into its line of vision; a red liquid had joined the tar-like drop off. It made a clucking sound of disapproval and when it lowered its unnatural limb, all three mouths were grinning Lazarus' lazy, mirthless grin.

Weston propped himself up on his elbows and knees, slowly dragging himself to a wavering stance that shot courses of pain through him and made him queasy. He did his best to ignore the pain, but couldn't imagine his facial expression held anything but a look of anguish. He placed his gun in the front of his jeans, just behind his plain, silver belt buckle. He nodded at the creature, and mimed drawing his gun. A harsh laugh was his only answer.

The sun had begun to rise and the heat of the light fell on him. Weston had no plan: he doubted anything he did could kill the beast, let alone slow it down. The best he could hope for was to distract it long enough to keep Dolarhyde safe, if he was capable of escape. He knew where he was going to aim; it would be a difficult shot, but he imagined the pain would drive it back some if he managed it.

The beast locked its eyes on Weston, its face now more akin to a demonic hound than a person, bared its teeth in a lip-curled growl, and pounced. It darted at Weston, its awkward limbs still managing to carry it without hindrance. Weston gave it a moment, drew his gun and took as best aim he could while firing from the hip. The bullet hit home; again the creature's head snapped back and halted its forward motion. Black ooze dispersed from its right eye and the creature's human hands went to its face immediately as a growl followed by a high-pitched scream broke the air.

Weston tossed the gun to the ground, and prepared for the next charge. He would grapple if he needed, though he didn't have much hope for that course of action. Weston stood in the sun and allowed its warmth to absorb into his skin until he heard the shaky, unnatural movement of Lazarus back to life again.

For a moment Weston saw the face of Clancy's assassin, its features twisted with agony and fear, before it twisted again into a nightmare formed of tentacles, glowing yellow eyes, and hatred. Moving just as quickly as it changed faces, the creature used its jittering limbs to bring it forward and stab at Weston's face with one of those same spider-like appendages. Weston ducked and threw himself to the left, flailing under his own damaged legs. A sharp pain exploded from his right shoulder and then everything became a picture show.

He saw himself suspended in midair, an oozing black tendril piercing his right shoulder, flailing as it protruded from his back. Twin tar stains spread across the back and front of his shirt from around the unnatural appendage. He saw the beast grin through its flickering faces and oozing eye, straighten itself again, and lift him screaming off the ground. The picture show ended, the film cut to black, and he felt his throat constrict and his voice lift in agony.

He writhed. The tar dispersed around his wound began to crawl toward his face, though all sense would dictate that it drop to the ground. In his pain, Weston knew it was crawling to his face, and the recent image of Lazarus' own face dissolving under the black essence flashed in his mind. He tried to brush the tar off with both hands only to find his right paralyzed by the hideous appendage that still penetrated his shoulder. The tar continued to make its slow way towards Weston's terrified face.

The creature swung Weston from side to side, perpetrating the succession of pain he had been suffering all the more. In his anguish, flashes of images played in his head. He saw a giant stone temple surrounded by people with pale skin and white-blond hair who were bowing down in front of the black statue from Dolarhyde's box. He saw the tar from the idol shoot out rapidly to catch one of its worshippers, like a frog to an insect. The tar pierced the man's heart and he gasped. A hideous smile crossed his pained countenance. "I am chosen. I am the avatar of Slogutis," the man said before dying a gruesome death.

Pain, intense and burning, filled Weston's mind and drew him from the vision. When he snapped back to his senses, it wasn't his own screaming he heard. The creature had unhinged its jaw again and released its inhuman howl; its changing faces each expressed its own agony. Weston looked at his impaled shoulder where the appendage that held him in place seemed to be dissolving, melting like an icicle in spring, its tar-like substance no longer moving toward Weston's face, but dripping to the ground underneath his feet. The monster itself was doing just the same – dissipating, melting, and cringing. Despite his pain,

Weston watched the creature as its faces changed rapidly as if finding the right one would help it escape from whatever was happening to it. Even as Weston watched it, he could see the tar run off in rivulets making its alternating faces become thinner and lined, their noses sagging, and their yellow eyes becoming pouched and watery.

The beast was dying.

Weston fell to the ground where a wet sensation greeted him as he struck and something cold spread across his back. The sun's warmth eased his pain, but he covered his shoulder wound with his opposite hand; it came away drenched in black and red in equal measure. Weston struggled to his good elbow. The creature was still in front of him, but had fallen to its knees. The spider legs had melted into puddles of blackness that surrounded the beast on all sides. It had one human hand in front of its face, black tar falling so rapidly that it spilled over the cupped hand and fell to the ground below it.

Weston worked his way to his feet, fighting through the pain in his limbs; he cupped his wounded shoulder and left the creature to die. It moaned behind him, a whiny, unnatural noise that chilled Weston. He stumbled towards the path that had brought him to the plain, trailing gore behind him.

The path spilled into the plain with a tangle of branches from the tall spruce trees. As Weston approached, he heard a soft murmur, a drone that reminded him of running water. Weston pushed back the branches and saw Dolarhyde prostrate, lips moving rapidly, fingers twitching, and chest vibrating with quick, shallow breaths. Weston knelt next to the man, his eyes vacant and staring up to the sky.

"Nigel, are you all right?"

"Light defeats dark; morning uncloaks nightmare,"

the Englishman repeated through a croaking voice, saliva still gathered at the corners of his mouth.

"Wait here, Nigel," Weston groaned and staggered to the horses he hoped remained on the opposite side of the plain. As he moved away, Dolarhyde's strange message followed him.

In the centre of the field, amidst the jutting rocks and high grass, lay Lazarus' body surrounded by pools or black. Lazarus was himself once again, there was no black ooze covering him, the spider-like appendages were gone, and his face remained constant. His remains, though human once more, appeared to be partially digested. One side of his face was devoid of skin and muscle with only a bleached, polished skull in its place. One hideous green eye remained in the socket, and it seemed to follow Weston as he passed. He kept his distance from the body and he thought if he had a loaded gun, he would empty it into Lazarus just to be sure.

One horse remained at the hiding place behind the large rock. Weston eased his way over to the horse, spoke to it softly, and climbed into the saddle through the pain that wracked his body. He trotted it across the plain, keeping a fair distance from Lazarus, and approached the small path, already aware that the ride to Denver would be painful and long. There was no whispering as he approached the place where he had left Dolarhyde.

Weston dismounted and expected to have to track the delusional scholar through the forest. Despite the pain, he was comforted that the daylight would aid his search. Pushing aside the branches once more, he found Dolarhyde just where he left him. The man was motionless though his eyes were wide and his mouth agape: dead. Weston didn't need to approach any further to see it. The stress on his mind and body had won over its desire to live.

Weston made his way back to the horse that was grazing unperturbed at the foot of the path. Weston took a last look over the plain as he mounted and started off, the wind making the tall grass spill over in waves under the light of the rising sun, and a small black rock glinting there among the jutting rocks as he rode off to Denver.

Jeff Slade

A St. John's native currently residing in Salmon Cove, Slade is an avid reader who enjoys both making and hearing puns, playing the guitar, and cats.

Slade makes his publishing debut in *Chillers from the Rock*.

The Culling

I remember it like it was yesterday.

The three bodies lay spread out in a line before me, each on a wooden table equidistant from the next. They were covered in white sheets from the waist down, bare feet peeking out.

I stood in a small clearing in an unfamiliar wooded area. The only living things in sight were the snow-topped evergreen trees that hemmed the clearing in.

My guardian, Uncle Lachlan, brought me there with a man I didn't know. I only knew he was an invigilator for my final test in becoming a full-fledged member of the coven: the Culling. Anyone with potential in the Art has to go through it on their thirteenth birthday. Instead of blowing out candles on a cake, I was sorting corpses in the woods.

I'd never seen a dead body before that day. I've seen plenty since.

My uncle handed me three coloured stones before they exited the clearing: red, brown, and black for vampire, werewolf, and wight respectively. I ran my thumb across the coloured side of each one before sliding them into the pocket of my burgundy peacoat. The coat clashed with my red hair, but I didn't care; I was a stubborn child.

My task was to place each fist-sized stone -- fist-sized

for a thirteen-year-old girl at any rate -- on the foot of the correct table.

It reminded me of pin the tail on the donkey, only much more morbid.

The snow crunched under my feet as I slowly approached the leftmost table. My eyes were transfixed on the table and its previously living contents as I sidled around to the far side, keeping my back to the woods. I peered over the table and forced myself to take in the deceased's features.

Mercifully, the eyes were closed. The man's skin was pale, but not as ashen or gray as one would expect for a wight. His closely cropped black hair formed a widow's peak, pointing where I needed to look.

I cleared my throat, the sound amplified by the snowy silence around me, and stood on my tiptoes. Thankful to be wearing gloves, I placed my fingers on the man's chin and gently pulled downward. Pulling back his lips allowed me to see inside his mouth.

Fangs.

I let go and moved to the foot of the table, brushing off some snow before placing a red stone there.

Without looking back, I started toward the middle corpse. I didn't need to get close; its skin was far more gray and sallow than the previous one, and a quick glance at the third table confirmed its corpse too was lighter than the middle one.

I was anxious; was I about to finish the Culling? I pulled both remaining stones out of my pocket to pick the correct one, accidentally dropping them in the process. I wasn't quite sure what I expected, but I'd thought it'd be harder than that. I kneeled down and plucked the stones out of the snow, taking the black one in my right hand and dropping it onto the end of the middle table as I got to my feet.

When I turned to the empty last table, I froze.

A glance at the brown stone in my left hand reminded me it was the werewolf that had disappeared. Prior to that, I hadn't heard any noises other than my own and the occasional sliding snow off of boughs and branches; certainly nothing that caused any concern for my safety.

Before I could process anything further, I detected movement in my peripheral vision and whirled around. The first corpse, which I'd designated as the vampire, was sitting up and turning to face me, eyes wide open.

I had no weapons, aside from my wits. Those would have to do. I backed up instinctively until I bumped into the empty table, then felt around it in search of something I could use as a weapon. All I came up with was the stone in my hand, and I hurled it at the vampire's head with as much force as I could muster.

It bounced off its upper left temple where it landed, leaving a slight indentation but accomplishing nothing more than that. The vampire grinned and slid off of the table, calmly making its way toward me. It was in no rush.

All I could do was move behind the empty third table. Running through the woods would only slow me down; my clothing would almost certainly catch on the prickly shrubbery and softwood which surrounded me. An ensnarled target would be easy prey for my foe.

I had to think quickly, as the vampire was now standing on the opposite side of the table. I knew I had to attack before it did, so I struck out with the first thing that came to mind. Closing my eyes, I muttered under my breath, raised my fist high and then slammed it downward.

One of the largest nearby trees came smashing down between us as I manipulated the earth below, uprooting and felling it with swift, strong purpose. I closed my eyes at the sound, and when I opened them, I saw the vampire on the other side of the fallen fir.

"Missed," it growled.

Before it could do or say anything else, I leapt into action. The tree might have missed its mark, but it smashed the table between us into pieces. I picked up one of the shards as I ran over the tree branches. I aimed the jagged edge at the vampire's chest and threw all my weight behind it as I lunged forward.

I got back to my feet following the collision. The vampire didn't, a look of surprise permanently frozen on its twice-dead face.

As I brushed pine needles off my coat, a loud groan caught my attention. The wight was shuffling towards me, arms outstretched as it hobbled forward. It probably didn't want to give me a birthday hug.

Raising my arms, I felt my fingers tingle and buzz as I summoned forth a surge of electricity. Thin, powerful lattices of energy arced forward and found their target, stopping the wight in its tracks as it shimmied and shook, smoking in place.

After a few seconds, however, it started moving again. It turned out electricity was not very effective against the undead, shocking as that might sound.

I decided to try something different. Wiping the fresh sweat off my brow, I took a step backwards from the steaming corpse and concentrated once again. Calling upon my dwindling reserves, I flicked my left hand towards my enemy and a bolt of fire sizzled through the winter air towards it.

This attack proved much more effective. The wight fell to the snow-covered ground, flailing as the flames consumed its dead flesh. As it thrashed around, the fire spread from its arms to the fallen tree.

Smoke from the burning boughs quickly filled the small area, and my eyes started watering. I began coughing. Instinctively I ran for the opposite corner of the clearing until I remembered: there was still one foe remaining.

As if on cue, a large, dark figure flew through the smog. I was able to partly dodge out of the way, but the creature's claws still rendered three parallel gashes through the chest of my coat. I spun and fell onto my back. I wasn't sure if I was bleeding due to the dark burgundy colour of my clothing. I was sure that I would be bleeding imminently, however, if I didn't act fast.

The great lupine shadow that had sailed through the smoke mere seconds ago had turned and was now rounding on me. Its midnight-black fur and bright, sharp fangs, one in stark contrast against the other, became better illuminated by the fire. It paused long enough to snarl at me before it sprang into action, coming to tear out my throat.

I was nearly tapped out from my previous exertions. My hands reached around me, frantically in search of another piece of wood, something, anything to thrust between the animal and myself, but all I found was snow and ice.

Reaching down deep, I depleted the last of my energy and reshaped the surrounding ice with my remaining willpower. Just as the werewolf went airborne, an icy spear thrust out at the base of my feet. Too late to change its course, the beast impaled itself throat-first on the long, pointed shard of frost.

Its dying howl of anger and frustration slid into a warm gurgle, its breath warm and damp against my cheeks only inches away from my face. The werewolf went limp, and I pulled myself to my feet with a groan.

Exhausted, I surveyed the scene. The fire had died down on both the fir tree and the wight, though the latter was still faintly gasping and wriggling in place. With a sigh, I snapped off the end of the icicle, walked over, and plunged it down and through the wight's blackened forehead.

It stopped wriggling.

I sank to my knees, finally letting my guard down. I lowered my head and frowned at the drops of blood I saw in the snow. There were three drops, followed by a fourth, then a fifth, before I realized the blood was falling from my nose. I wiped it clean, then held my head as a newly discovered headache intensified.

The sound of boots crunching in the snow caught my attention, but I didn't turn around. All three of my enemies were down. If there were more, it didn't matter. I was spent.

"Less than ten minutes total. Impressive," said a male voice I recognized as my guardian's.

"It's impressive she's still alive," another man chimed in. The invigilator, a dim voice in the back of my head reminded me.

"Yes, yes, of course," replied my uncle. He knelt beside me and took a glove off his hand, feeling my forehead. "She'll be fine, she just needs to rest." Leaning in closer still, he whispered under his breath, "Good job, Ryan."

"It seems we have another elementalist on our hands." The other pair of boots scrunched once again as the invigilator examined the carnage. "My gods, Lachlan, can you imagine how powerful she'll be once she's older?"

"Of course," my uncle replied, squeezing my shoulder before returning to a standing position. "That's the plan."

Samuel Bauer

Samuel Bauer is a young local writer. A proud mathematician, Shad alumni, and part-time pathological storyteller, Sam enjoys writing, doing math, staying up way too late, and thinking about silly things way too much.

Sam is one of a handful of authors to be featured in all current *From the Rock* volumes.

Dark Peaks

I write this now for I know I am doomed. I shall never see home again, never experience the warmth of summer nor the heat of fire. If you are reading this, take it as a warning. Mortal men should not delve into those forbidding monoliths of the Himalayas. Only death and madness await those who seek the secrets that lie here.

I began planning this expedition at least a year ago with the intent of finding the fabled city of Shambala. I had heard it was a paradise, a place of verdant fields and ageless pleasure. There were six of us, intrepid explorers, fearlessly delving into the unknown. I was the leader, and I had brought three other experienced mountaineers, Scott, Thomas, and Jason from England with me. In Nepal, we had enlisted the help of two Sherpas, Kalden and Dote. Our expedition into the forbidden land of Tibet began about three weeks ago.

From the beginning, we should have known better than to seek what should not be known.

At every step of our journey, howling winds and biting cold besieged us. Rockfalls, blizzards, and the threat of avalanches were constant. It was as if the mountains themselves sought to kill us; twice they almost succeeded. The first time was only three days into our voyage: the ground beneath our feet fell away as we traversed an ice bridge. It was only dumb luck that saved us. Scott had driven a piton into the stone wall at the front, and James was having difficulty removing the spike at the back. The shattered ice left us dangling like the icicles on our beards above a gaping maw. As we dangled above it, several pounds of food fell in, lost to us forever. Scott successfully made it to solid ground, and his position allowed him to help us all to climb to safety one at a time. Foolishly undaunted, we continued.

The next brush with death, roughly a week after the first, was predicted by Kalden and Dote, who had felt we were being stalked. Late one night, they were proven right. We awoke to the sound of a gunshot, punctuated with a scream. Scrambling to dress ourselves to prevent frostbite from the punishing cold, we heard two more gunshots, and then silence. Finally emerging from our tent, we found Thomas and Kalden's tent had been ripped open, and Kalden sat shivering with one of the rifles in his hands. Thomas had a gaping wound in his left side, his left arm hanging uselessly. But all this I noticed later. My consciousness was filled with fear at the sight before us.

A great snow leopard lay bleeding on the snow. It was an imposing brute, seven feet long without including the massive tail. Its eyes shone with malice as it heaved great, pained breaths. One shot had pierced the beast's jaw and it hung from one side. The other two had hit the creature square in the chest, leaving it unable to move. We shot it twice more, in the head, and quickly got Thomas and Kalden inside the remaining tents.

The rest of that night passed silently. We decided to head back over the border, as Thomas and Kalden had gotten severe frostbite from the exposure to the brutal elements of the mountains. Thomas would not be able to use his left arm ever again; the muscles and tendons had been irreparably damaged.

We never got the chance to leave. Upon packing up the camp in the morning and making certain the foul beast was dead, we found our way blocked. More snow had come in the night and made the path back impassable. With dread in our hearts, we continued onwards, hoping we could foretell the dangers ahead.

We could not. After a week, the frostbite that afflicted Thomas and Kalden had grown worse. Three of Kalden's and two of Thomas' fingers had grown black and fallen off, and Thomas' arm had grown infected. The gangrenous stench killed our appetite. This was for the better, I suppose, as food was running low. Two days later, Thomas vanished from the camp, taking nothing with him save the clothes on his back. We never saw him alive again.

It was then that the most hideous part of this accursed expedition began. We began to hear whisperings, foul and unutterable by human tongues. They were impossible to locate, the source seeming to be between our own ears, though everyone could hear them. In the dread cacophony of these insidious whispers, we could only make out one thing:

Cala Null.

Cala Null.

I know not what these words mean, or even if I may call them words. But if you ever hear these syllables between your ears, know that you are better off dead. We discovered that for ourselves after another three days of travel, when we crested a ridge shortly after dawn. What we saw I tremble to describe.

A great labyrinthine city stretched out before us. The streets twisted upon themselves at strange angles with a horrid self-similarity. The huts were domed, tall, and twisted like the insides of a great monster too foul for the depths of hell. Then, the wind picked up, and forced us into the valley, towards that hideous city. As we approached, I soon began to wonder about the material used in the construction of these abhorrent structures. At the top of the ridge it had seemed to be mere granite, but as we walked through the streets with our hearts pounding, I could see it was not any natural stone. Inside the black marbled surface were thousands of minute cords, folding in on themselves as if braided. It seemed less like rock, and more like sculpted hair, hardened by the cold.

We were soon forced by the wind to take refuge in one of the huts. As soon as the door was closed, and Scott had lit his lantern, we saw that we had chosen the worst possible shelter. Leering down at us was a statue of a great ape, its ivory teeth glistening in the flickering light of the lantern.

As the wind howled outside, and the words--

Cala Null.

Cala Null.

--echoed in my mind, I inspected the statue as the others made ready for the night. The storm showed no signs of stopping. The statue was carved from the same material as the edifice that housed it. The statue was a full twenty or more feet tall. In its left hand, it held a lash with thirty-one tongues, each covered with colourful beads. In its right, held out straight, there was a gauntlet of some kind. It had ribbons of coppery metal issuing from it, and each ribbon twisted and turned, wrapping the arm of black stone in a bronze sleeve. But the most awful thing about the statue was its eyes. A vivid blue, they seemed to speak of ages past. But I found no solace in those eyes.

And then, the voice that had been whispering to us grew louder.

Cala Null.

Cala Null.

The door burst open, and a hunched figure pointed some hideous fetish at us, and darkness overcame me.

I awoke in a strange, frigid cavern. In the dim blue, all-encompassing light, I could see my breath on the air. My coat had been ripped and torn by some strange claw, and I wrapped the tattered rags closer around my shivering frame. The voices were much, much louder now, but all I could make out was that dread phrase.

Cala Null.
Cala Null.

I know not how long I was there, listening to the unnatural voice inside my own head, shivering in that frigid cave. But, after a time, I decided to explore my surroundings. I thought perhaps I would find some source of warmth. As I wandered in the cold stone environment, shivering and shuffling, trying desperately to cling to whatever little warmth my torn coat could provide, I soon saw that I should have never left. What I saw shall haunt me for the few hours I have left.

What I found can only be described as a cell. Behind the great bars of -- what seemed to be iron -- was Thomas. His body was preserved by the cold, shrivelled and slightly rotted. But, across his naked flesh, I could see movement.

And there were whispers.

Cala Null.
Cala Null.

As I peered closer, the whispers grew louder.

Cala Null.
Cala Null.

I approached even nearer, discovering the hints of

movement had become writhing, as if the muscles of the corpse wished to escape the confines of the skin. A great, hairy wormlike creature squirmed out of the body's gaping mouth. As it slid to the ground, I saw a glimpse of its dead eyes. It knew I was watching. It then turned on the bag of skin and bone and began to eat it.

This is when I noticed there was someone else in that wretched cell. Dote was there, stripped down to nothing. He sat with his back to the wall, and his legs stretched straight out in front of him, his arms serenely placed on his lap. But his eyes were wide and panicked. The creature finished devouring the body of Thomas, but Dote made no movement to escape from the hairy worm that had now turned its dead eyes to him.

The whisperings were louder now.

Cala Null.

Cala Null.

The worm slithered over to Dote, and ran over his legs. His eyes pleaded with me, but there was nothing I could do. I could not turn away. I was transfixed. The worm slid up his arm. His eyes were wide with terror. He no longer saw me, only the worm. The worm wrapped around his neck. It paused at his face, seeming to look him in the eyes. Then it slithered down his throat.

The only sign that Dote was not an agreeable host were his eyes. They closed in pain as the worm forced itself into his body. I forced myself to turn away. There was nothing I could do for him. I pulled the rags closer around me. The look in his eyes still haunts me.

After what felt like hours stumbling through that cave of unnatural blue light, I heard a noise other than my own ragged breathing and uneven steps.

It was a low chuffing sound, followed by a growl. I followed this echoing call to its source, a massive snow leopard. If the one that attacked us was large, this one was colossal. It was easily six feet tall at the shoulder, and twenty feet long, including the tail. It was eating something and took no notice of me. It tore at its meal, ripping flesh from the bone. As I crept from the cavern, hoping it would not see me; I must have made some small noise, because it raised its head, revealing just what it was eating. It was James.

I can only hope he was dead when the beast started tearing. It returned to its gruesome meal, and I, feeling panic grab hold of me, ran mindlessly through those cold caverns. I stumbled down one after another of the labyrinthine tunnels, hoping desperately to find a way out.

I found no other sign of my fellow explorers, namely Scott and Kalden and now I hope they are dead, not suffering a worse fate. A fate like mine.

Cala Null.

Cala Null.

As I rounded a corner, I was confronted by a massive room of ice. Thousands of dark figures covered in hair stared down at me from bleachers that lined the walls. They were built like large men, but where their heads should be there was nothing, instead their eyes glimmered from where their chest should be. The seats all faced a central altar, behind which stood a figure, glimmering with gold hidden beneath its long, matted hair. Past the altar was a massive exit, leading into a valley. Before I could recover from my shock, one of the figures leapt forwards, grabbing me roughly with seven-fingered claws. It dragged me to the altar, and as it shoved me down, I felt all control leave my body, save for my eyes. The whisperings were gone, replaced with what can only be described as a psychic chant.

Cala Null! Cala Null! Iao Lemura Cala Null! Alat-Venra Cala Null! Cala Null! Cala Null!

As they chanted, the one who glimmered with gold cast back its hair, revealing a serpentine head embedded in its chest amid scales of brown, black and coppery red. The arms and legs were jointed in three places ending in seven fingered hands and seven toed feet. These appendages tapered into viciously sharp talons. Its maw was lined with long, sharp, dagger-like teeth that had been filed and encrusted with gold. It looked at me as if I were no more than an object. The chant grew louder. I wanted desperately to clap my hands over my hapless ears. I could hear something arising behind me. I felt my body turn against my will. I could see it. I tried to shut my eyes, but even that small relief was stolen from me. One of the figures waved a metal stick at me. I felt control return. I was pushed towards the door. I ran.

Long strides carried me away from that dreaded place. Looking back, I could see it, that unholy beast, uttering those mad gibberings punctuated with screams of ecstasy. I stumbled down a slope. It followed. I squeezed through a crevice. It howled at my escape. I stumbled into a cave. All I can do now is wait. Capture by that dreaded beast is inevitable.

Cala Null.

Cala Null.

I can feel a presence in my body and mind. It writhes there like a maggot in rotten flesh. The beast, it grows nearer, I can hear its breath, I can...

Cala Null Iano.

Cala Null Iano.

The Dark God has found me. I know what I must do. For those who seek the secrets of the Himalayas, let this be a warning.

There is no Utopia here. No Shambala. Only death for the lesser beings.

CALA NULL! CALA NULL!

Nuckelavee

The moon hung over the rolling surf, the thin crescent an ivory broach in a moth-eaten cloak. Except for the tumbling, murmuring waves, all was still. No fish leapt, no winds howled, no crickets called, no owls hooted. Breathless and frigid, the spring night was corpselike.

And from that cold, heartless foam of the ocean, something emerged. Yellow veins pulsed with black blood, as the eyeless head took form. The vacancy of the eye sockets was contrasted deeply by the maw filled with jagged teeth the colour of sea-corroded bone. Next to emerge were the shoulders, narrow and bony. No skin covered the pale red of muscles and starched white of ligaments, as the inhumanly long arms continued to grow. The torso was just as emaciated as the shoulders, with the ribs jutting brokenly from muscles that stretched thinly over the gaunt cask of a chest. At the waist, the thing suddenly jutted outwards, outlining the back of a steed as malnourished as its parasitic rider. The legs of the steed had frills like gills along their outer edge; and it was here, at the hooves, where the arms finally ended. At the end were taloned, oversized hands. The steed's equine head rolled, and it opened its cyclopean eye. The red orb searched the hillside. Seeing no prey, it howled. The sound of drowning sailors, unwanted babes, and pure, undiluted fear issued forth. It began to run, the humanoid head, unnaturally large, lolling madly in a macabre comedy.

His heart was pounding as he ran through the dead, spring night. He could smell the beast, that stench that combined the sickly sweet of diseased wheat and the hot rot of putrid flesh.

The river. He had to get to the river.

Hooves thudded behind him. The wheezing breath of his pursuer pushed more and more of that stench into the air. He could feel the miasma start to take effect, start to weaken and sicken him. He kept running, adrenaline pumping through his veins, desperate to escape the beast.

He tripped.

The gangly long arms grabbed him roughly and pulled him up to face the eyeless, oversized humanoid head. He could feel that yellow veins pulsing with black blood and the smell started to become unbearable, and it was hot and cold and dry and wet and light and dark all at the same time-- and he screamed.

The scream echoed through the night, awakening her in her bed. The baby began to cry. Fear seized her heart, pushing it to her throat. She had thought it too early in the year. She grabbed her child who screamed and screamed. Wrapping them both in her cloak, she began to run.

The river. She had to get to the river.

The priest felt a chill come over him. Evil walked on the earth today. Rising from his knees, he grabbed his bible, carefully sealing the precious leather bound, Latin tome in its waterproof case. He rang the church bell as loudly and cacophonously as he could manage with his old and weak muscles. His charge, a young man, came quickly, face bloodless. The old priest pressed the case into his hands.

The river. He had to get to the river.

He took the case, and motioned for the priest to follow. The priest shook his head. Somebody had to ring the bell, to warn the town. The apprentice nodded, tears in his eyes. He locked his mentor in the stone church, and took off running.

The river. He had to get to the river.

The blacksmith didn't hear it over the sound of his clanging hammers, but his wife did. She rushed into the forge and grabbed him. He understood the moment that he saw her face. He rushed to the children's room, and gathered up his son, and roused his daughter. Carrying his sickly child, he led his family out into the dead, spring night.

The river. They had to get to the river.

The church bell clanged, its rhythmic sounds playing like a monstrous heartbeat in the night. The smell of rot and putrefaction of both flesh and plant was everywhere now. In the minds of all but the youngest, there was only one thought, ringing through their heads:

The river. I have to get to the river.

Bare feet ran over cold, almost frozen ground.

The first to reach the river was the apprentice. He slipped and slid over the mossy rocks, his feet already numb from the ground. Reaching a rock that jutted out of the river, he sat and waited and hoped; hoped he wouldn't return home to a dead body.

She could hear it behind her, hooves thudding. She ran faster and faster.

She hoped the scream hadn't been her husband.

The next to reach it was the elderly baker and his wife. The apprentice helped them into the river, and got them somewhere towards the shallows. He pulled off his cloak and gave it to the old woman. She needed it much more than him.

The priest heard a knocking on the door. His heart almost stopped.

He gritted his teeth, and kept ringing the bell.

The next to arrive were the blacksmith's family. The baker shuffled over and helped the apprentice take the sickly boy and carefully cradle him above the frigid water. The blacksmith picked up his daughter first, putting her on one of the boulders that had been rolled into the river generations ago for nights like these. She sat and hugged her toy close. Next he lifted his wife to the same spot, and she hugged their daughter even closer.

She couldn't hear it anymore, but that almost worried her more. She kept on running, faster and faster.

The river. She had to get to the river.

The church door started to buckle, but the priest kept ringing the bell. The door flew open, and the dreaded horseman stood, shadows playing across its grotesque form. With one hand on the bell cord, he scrabbled for his crucifix. He seized it and held it out, trying to ward off the beast. The gold began to heat in his hand. The pews began to smolder. He kept ringing the bell. His hand began to burn, smoke rising from it. He kept ringing the bell. The beast screamed, and the whole church caught on fire.

The bell went silent.

The apprentice wept, because he knew that he was apprentice no more.

She could see the river, and her heart began to slow. She could see almost all the village there, shivering in the cold air and water.

She tripped. She twisted her body, narrowly keeping herself from falling on her child. She could hear the hooves, coming nearer and nearer.

Her leg was broken, and the beast crested the hill, howling with malicious delight.

She looked to the villagers, pleading.

They were paralyzed with fear.

The beast neared.

The blacksmith rushed forwards, water cupped in his

hands. He splashed the beast with it. The beast reared up as the water touched its exposed muscles. The blacksmith grabbed the mother and child and rushed back into the river, almost falling.

The beast glared at the villagers with its one, blood red eye.

And, too late for many, it began to rain.

The beast howled as the fresh, pure water touched its unprotected flesh. It raced back to the sea, screaming in pain as it went, and dove in.

The silence afterwards rang out like a bell toll.

Shivering and cold, the townsfolk returned home. Hoping, and praying that those who didn't make it to the river had survived.

None did.

Nothing survives the Nucklavee unprotected.

Nothing.

Michelle Churchill

Michelle Churchill is a writer based in St. John's Newfoundland and Labrador. Her works include 4 short fairy tales published in *Kit Sora: The Artobiography* and short stories in the *From the Rock* series.

Michelle is a mother of two fantastic kids, an avid cosplayer, habitual volunteer, occasionally fosters kittens, and enjoys playing a bit of D&D with friends and family.

Leopold's ~~Cherubs~~ Princes

Wednesday Schedule
- *8:00 Wake Up and Breakfast*
- *8:30 Anton's First Feeding*
- *9:00 Lorenzo and Fred's Dentist Appointment.*
- *11:00 Video Call with Clement in Vancouver*
- *12:00 Lunch*
- *1:00 Free Time*
- *5:00 Supper*
- *6:00 Anton's Second Feeding*
- *7:00 Bed*

Julia sized up her newest partner as he buckled himself into the passenger seat. Fresh from cadet training, the young guard looked about twenty, and honestly that was pushing it. His hair had been styled with a bit of gel, dated but still passable as cool. She grinned, passing him the schedule for their shift. "The boys will like you."

"You think so?" He sounded hopeful as he glanced over the schedule, and snapped a photo of it on his phone so he wouldn't forget it.

Pulling out of the parking lot, Julia nodded. "John, you will be a breath of fresh air. You're what, two years in?"

"Four," John corrected quietly, fumbling with the gold ring that served as his badge of office.

"I've been asking the higher ups to send in younger

guards for years. Finally someone in the department is listening to me."

John smiled. "How long have you been looking after Leopold's cherubs?"

Julia's face grew dark, and she glanced over to her partner as she shook her head. "First tip of your shift, don't call them cherubs; they hate it, and I hate it," she said firmly. "I've looked after the three of them since they arrived in this country. I know the myths around them, Emperor Leopold's cherubs." She waved one hand around in mock terror. "Over two hundred years, and they still haven't shaken the horrid title. Leopold made them to show off his power, and when he was overthrown they were treated like monsters. Thankfully cooler heads prevailed and the few remaining are safe as wards of the empire."

"It's kind of like prison, don't you think? Poor kids," John sighed. "I don't think I could handle being under watch all the time."

Julia nodded sympathetically. "Things are changing for them, slowly but surely. The Senate finally plans to recognize Lorenzo as a prince. That's good for all of us. The boys will get a bit more freedom. They'll need a bigger piece of property, and our office will have enough work for some time."

Pulling into the dental clinic parking lot, John paused to marvel at the expensive sports cars parked in spaces reserved for employees. Julia grinned, empathizing with the tinge of envy on her young partner's face.

"Philip, who took the boys to their appointment for me, his mortal cousin owns this spot. Between the mortal daytime clients and vampires at night, I can't imagine the money they bring in. Something to consider if this gig doesn't work out." She winked.

Philip and two youths sat waiting in the lobby as Julia and John, still chuckling, arrived to greet them.

"Come along, boys, Julia is here. Time to go home." Philip rose, passing a quiet smile to Julia.

Lorenzo, a slight figure with neatly trimmed black hair stood first. He looked for all the world like a teen about to enter high school, right down to the shoulder bag with notebook and pencils. He packed away a heavy textbook, the bold print declaring in shining letters: *Public Speaking Tools for Communication*.

"Thank you for taking them to their appointment, Philip." Julia clapped her fellow guard on the shoulder.

"Never any trouble." Philip fondly ruffled Fred's straw-coloured mop of hair, urging him to get up. Fred looked only about ten, though his eyes were undoubtedly older. He was fixated on a spinning triangular disk in his hand. With a grin on his face, he flicked the disk, so that it spun faster and faster in a mesmerizing fashion.

"Fred, what on earth are you doing?" Julia asked, in a motherly tone.

"Dr. Emerson said Fred could have a prize if he behaved during his appointment," Philip said, pleased that the obnoxious trinket had encouraged good behaviour.

Julia rolled her eyes. "Remind me to thank Liz." She turned to Fred. "Come on, you can play with that thing in the car."

Fred stood slowly, still playing with his new toy. He paused only upon seeing John. Turning to Lorenzo, he rapidly spoke German in a low whisper.

"This is John. He's a new guard." Julia explained.

The small boy narrowed his eyes, speaking further in a mix of Italian and German.

Philip chortled. "Well, I'm back to the office." He whispered to John on his way out the door, "Good luck!"

Fred continued to mutter to himself until Julia placed a firm hand upon his shoulder. "Fredrich," she began, as she only did when she was cross with him. "You're not saying very kind things. It's also rude to converse in languages not everyone understands. I think you need to apologize to John right now."

"Sorry," Fred grumbled in English.

"Quite alright," John quipped back in Italian to the surprise of Julia and Fred.

The house was a one level unassuming bungalow on a quiet street. A single car was in the driveway when they arrived.

"Masha, we're back!" Julia called as they returned.

Fred pushed past the others, ditching his sneakers in the porch to run to the bedroom that the three of them shared.

Their bedroom was large enough for all of them to sleep during daylight hours. Lorenzo's single bed was made to near military precision. Fred's resembled more of a bird's nest than a bed. The last, a hospital bed, was framed by a monitor and a feeding pump. An armchair sat to the right of it.

"Anton, Anton!" Fred leapt to jump onto the hospital bed. He pointed excitedly to his teeth. "Look, I got new teeth. They wouldn't let me have fangs though. But look how shiny they are." He smiled wide. "Watch this!" He reached in his mouth, fumbling with the denture until it popped out. He revealed the gaping holes where fangs had once been, before returning the dentures again.

The small boy smiled, his own fangs visibly missing. He motioned for Fred to come closer, so that he could have a better look. He thumped a hand on the bed to get the attention of Masha, who was quietly knitting beside him. He made slow signs with his hands.

Understanding the signed words, Masha nodded in agreement. "Fred's teeth are lovely. He must have been brave to sit through all those fittings." Her voice hinted a melodic Russian accent.

Anton smiled and, seeing Lorenzo, signed some more. Masha glanced up from the scarf she was working on to wink at the eldest. "Yes, I think the new dentures make Lorenzo look most regal. The fangs are very dignified."

Lorenzo flushed, sitting down on the edge of Anton's bed beside Fred. "It's hard to talk. They're too big, I think." He struggled with his enunciation around the larger teeth.

Anton made a sign for laughter. His tiny hands reached out for Lorenzo's, moving them to mimic his own.

"Yes, Anton, I will need to start signing like you, I think." Lorenzo laughed.

The joyous mood in the room dimmed with the appearance of John in the hallway, typing away on his phone.

Anton grew agitated.

"That's just John," Fred whispered. "He's a new guard. Don't worry, Anton, he'll be truly dead if he bothers you."

"Fred…" Julia called out in warning from in the living room, having easily heard the remark.

The boy's eyes grew cold. "I'm not apologizing for that," he snapped.

Masha packed away her knitting, ushering John to follow her to the living room and leave the boys to catch up on their evenings.

"Masha visits us from the Health Department. She ensures that the boys are all fed their breakfasts, and checks in with Anton," Julia explained as they joined her.

"What's wrong with the little one?" John asked, tucking his phone in his pocket as he sat on the couch.

"There is little wrong with any of them, but there has been plenty of wrong done to them. Anton was discovered wounded, his throat especially, which is why he doesn't speak and must be fed with a gastric feeding tube. You saw their lack of fangs." She narrowed her eyes at both Julia and John. "That mutilation was on orders of your department."

Julia shifted in her seat uncomfortably, recalling the order with great distaste.

"He's still so tiny." John sighed.

Masha shrugged. "All vampires age slightly over the centuries. Child vampires don't follow typical patterns of development. Some grow up, some don't; only the centuries know what's in store." She returned to her knitting, as Lorenzo and Fred crept back into the living room, taking up seats beside her.

"Anton wanted to rest," Lorenzo explained. "He said he didn't mind if we called Clement without him. It's just about 10:00 now; can we use the tablet to call? Clement got a harpsichord this week. Maybe we could record him playing so Anton can listen to it whenever he wants." Lorenzo beamed hopefully.

Julia nodded. "Of course, for Anton. Not that you have been waiting for months for Clement to get that harpsichord, so you can hear him play."

Lorenzo squeezed his hands together, his eyes lighting up with obvious excitement. "Is that a yes?"

Fetching the tablet from the bookshelf, Julia propped it up on the coffee table, letting the boys make the video call. The signal rang and rang, finally beeping that there had been no answer.

"Did he forget what day it is again?" Fred complained from his spot on the couch.

"Just try again," Masha encouraged, sensing the boys' disappointment.

Again, there was no answer.

Julia checked her watch. "Maybe they're just busy with breakfast. I'll call the house." She dialled the number using the house phone, but the line led to the message manager.

Seeing the distress on both boys' faces, she hung up. "How about an early lunch?"

Masha caught on to Julia's attempts the cheer up the boys, quickly ushering them to the kitchen. The scent of fresh cattle blood hung heavy in the air as lunch was prepared.

A rapid banging at the door caused further disruption, and Julia rose to answer it. A bullish man stormed in. "Where is he?"

"Good evening yourself, Frank." Julia smiled cheerfully, ignoring his tone.

"Don't play games with me, Constable. Where is the wretch?" He stormed towards the kitchen. "Fred, get out here right now!"

Philip followed in behind, a look of exasperation upon his kind features.

Fred slunk out of the kitchen, his mug of blood in hand. Lorenzo trailed behind him, staying close. "Good evening, Sergeant," Fred spoke, making a point to slurp as loudly as he could.

Ignoring the impish rudeness, the guard took a hard grip on the smaller vampire's arm. "I warned you, Fred, that was your last chance." As Fred made to slurp again, he snatched the mug from him, setting it down on the bookshelf and hauling the boy to the door.

Philip interceded. "Hold up there, we don't know for sure it was him."

"Yeah!" Fred protested, wriggling in Frank's grip.

"What is going on?" Julia stepped between them. "Frank, you can't take Fred without informing us of what has happened."

Frank gritted his teeth in frustration. "Julia, we have two bodies' throats cut and drained of blood. Both less than two kilometers from here. What does that sound like to you?" He pulled on Fred's arm sharply.

"I didn't kill anyone," Fred pleaded his innocence. "I've been with Philip or Julia all night." He cried out like the child he appeared to be.

"As I told you," Philip murmured a quiet reminder, only to be met with the furious gaze of the Sargent.

"He's slipped away before," Frank hissed. "Don't pretend Fred hasn't. There are bodies that prove it."

"My brother is not without his faults," Lorenzo spoke clearly, to make his voice heard. He clenched his hands, fighting through his anxieties to speak as a prince might. "Fred has learned hard lessons; he does not take off any more."

Relenting, Frank released his grip, tossing Fred to the couch. "If I find out this was you, that's it. No more hiding behind your big brother; I'll petition the office to have you gone for good."

"Can we not threaten a child with execution?" Julia murmured.

"He is not a child." Frank sneered.

Masha crossed her arms, growing weary of this exchange. "You have the bodies, secured?" At Frank's nod, she continued, "Then we should investigate. No word from the house in Vancouver, and now bodies in our neighbourhood."

There was no further need for discussion. Both Julia and Frank departed, Frank waving to Masha to follow along.

Philip retrieved the mug of blood from the bookshelf, returning it to Fred. Settling down on the couch beside John, he shook his head. "Great start to a new job, huh?" he sighed sarcastically.

Two hours passed without any word.

Fred played with the now coagulating blood in his mug. Philip turned a page in his book, trying not to laugh at the mischievous vampire.

Lorenzo crouched in front of the coffee table, trying to use the tablet to get through to Clement, but without much luck. The device rang and beeped, but there was still no answer. Smacking the coffee table, he buried his face in his hand. "Clement, you survived all who betrayed us. You must survive this night, and all nights. You said music is the only light we have; don't snuff it out."

John glanced up from his phone, startled by Lorenzo's strange prayer-like babbling.

Philip dog-eared the page of his book, motioning to John not to be alarmed by the behaviour. Slipping to the floor, he wrapped a reassuring arm around Lorenzo. "You are safe this night and all nights. As is Clement," he spoke comfortingly.

That guarantee was lost to the ringing of the house phone. Philip rose slowly to answer; Julia's voice could be heard on the other end.

"Phil, suspect illegal vampire activity. House has to go into lockdown."

Without waiting for the order, Lorenzo and Fred wordlessly filed off to join Anton in the safety of their room.

"Illegal vampires? Here?" Concern crossed John's face.

Philip nodded. "Yeah, in a city this size we get a few little groups. Those leeches pretend every day is Hallowe'en, and they're foolish enough to think they're above any rules of the empire."

The phone rang a second time. Whatever colour had remained in Philip's face drained away as the guard in Vancouver reported the fire; Clement's music would play no more.

"We need to let the boys know," Philip said sadly.

John got up from where he sat. In a fluid motion, he drew out a knife and plunged it into Philip's heart.

Lorenzo and Fred sat on Anton's bed, each holding tightly to the small boy's hands, as the blood-soaked John entered their bedroom.

"Giovani," Lorenzo smiled brightly with his denture fangs, as he spoke John's real name. "We hardly recognized you. How you've grown. From a boy of twelve to a grown man, and it only took you about two hundred years." Lorenzo spoke slowly in their native Italian.

"I haven't come for small talk." Giovani closed the door behind him.

"No, you've come to kill us. That much is apparent." Lorenzo shook his head. "You want us all to go lie down in our beds? That's how you did it before, slaughtered our brothers as they slept."

"Don't," Giovani hissed.

"Don't what?" Fred laughed. "Tell the truth? Remind you of your betrayal, of your cowardice? How you came into the room when the littlest ones were still sleeping, and killed as many as you could? How you even got little Pascal to help you? The dagger you gave him was nearly the size of his arm. When he started to sob, you killed him too. You treacherous monster."

Giovani clenched his jaw, holding back from lashing out at their insults. He was determined to see this night to his desired ending.

"Joining the guard, and siding with leeches," Lorenzo jeered, taking a chance to break through the cold exterior. "Impressive; you really had us going. All this for what end? If you wanted to be Prince, you only needed to reveal your true self. You are the eldest among us." He opened his arms wide, inviting Giovani to take the title.

Giovani laughed at Lorenzo's efforts. "As if I want to be the empire's puppet, like you, Lorenzo. The night Leopold was overthrown, you think I took joy in ending the lives of our brothers. They couldn't run, so I saved them from falling into the hands of the empire."

Lorenzo clenched his false teeth angrily. "You could have helped them run!" he hissed.

Giovani looked to Anton, a sorrowful expression crossing his face. "I can see how well you've helped. Do you really think Anton's suffering is over because they let you play prince?"

Without further words, he freed his gun from its holster. The buckle hardly unsnapped when both boys dived to shield the smallest of them.

The bullet found its mark in the head of Lorenzo. The prince crumpled lifelessly to the floor. Anton and Fred watched dumbfounded. Giovani set with determination raised his weapon again, only to be caught off guard by Fred's slow applause.

The scrawny vampire jumped from his perch on the bed, prodding the fallen prince with his foot. "Clever distraction, wish I had thought of it myself."

Giovani brought up his gun, taking aim again.

Fred waved it off casually. "There is no need; I have

no quarrel with you now that he's gone." He bobbed his head towards his fallen brother. "The empire has done me no favours, but there is safety in numbers. Playing Lorenzo's game worked for the time being."

The phone in Giovani's pocket vibrated.

Fred grinned. "I couldn't help but notice, you have been fixated on your phone all night. Waiting to hear from someone?"

Giovani narrowed his eyes, to which Fred continued: "Two leeches, a bit grimy looking, both vampires less than a year." He smirked, watching Giovani's face absorb the realization. "I dealt with them already. I don't like that sort prowling around. Too dangerous for Anton."

"You killed them? How?" Giovani demanded, returning his gun to the holster, but leaving it unsecured.

"Slit their throats, bled them out; trivial really."

"But how?" Giovani puzzled.

Fred laughed. "The sun goes down by 6:30 this time of year. They don't get us up until 8:00. Julia is the best guard we've had, but her schedules make it all too easy. Hardest part was figuring out how to sneak out the window without setting off an alarm. But once I got that sorted, there's nothing to it. I've been getting my own breakfast for years; like they say, easy peasy."

"Obviously not." Giovani sniffed. "Frank seems to be on to you"

Waving a hand, Fred brushed the comment off. "Lorenzo wasn't as gifted at hiding bodies. Made me take him along, then made me take the fall for his mistakes. Couldn't risk the reputation he made for himself. That we're all poor innocent little twerps." He made a face of disgust.

Giovani paused, absorbing what he had heard. Anton fidgeted in the bed nervously. Keeping a casual manner about him, Fred crossed to Giovani's side, clapping him heartily on the back before throwing his arms in the air and turning his elder so they embraced tightly.

"Let me join you, I have no love for this empire. I'm quick, and small, and I'll be far more use to you than some rotten leeches," he whispered, drawing back slowly to sit on the edge of Anton's bed. "There is just one more thing you need to know," he added, ducking his head. With shaking hands, Anton held the gun that had secretly been lifted from Giovani's holster and tossed with the casual throw of Fred's hand. Without hesitation, the smallest vampire fired two shots. The first wounded, and the other struck Giovani between the eyes.

"No one harms my brothers, and lives!" Fred spat.

Anton was still shaking as the weapon tumbled onto the bed. With terrified hands, he signed frantically to Fred.

"Yes, I know I said mean things about Lorenzo. I didn't mean it, Anton. I had to lie so Giovani thought I was on his side, do you understand that?"

Anton nodded, his face streaked with tears of blood. Fred hugged him tightly. "They will be back soon. You need to be brave tonight, Anton. You can do that."

The tiny vampire nodded again, blood still flowing from his eyes.

Slowly, Fred knelt beside the body of Lorenzo. He kissed his brother's cheek. "You deserved better than this, you were the greatest of all of us. Rest well, brother."

Heaving a heavy sigh, Fred retrieved the knife Giovani had used on Philip. The scene was only partly set. He grumbled at the task that lay before him. "Anton, when they arrive, remember Lorenzo was the hero: he distracted Giovani so I could throw you the gun. Make sure they know Lorenzo was brave." Fred's eyes welled up with heavy tears; he fought hard to keep them in. "Do not forget our brother was a hero. You make sure they know that."

Anton still shook as he signed, and his eyes begged Fred to tell the guards the truth.

"You have to do it, Anton, it has to be you. You heard Frank; I'm one slip up away from my head in a basket. He's just itching for any excuse to be rid of me. They find me standing here with two dead guards and a dead prince, and I'm gone for good. Frank won't care that John was Giovani, or that he was working with leeches to undermine the empire. He'll just be happy to be rid of me. He just thinks I'm trouble, that I'm no better than those leeches he rounds up on a nightly basis. If I'm not around to protect you, who will." Fred clenched his jaw, fighting to show courage in front of his little brother.

The small vampire let out a soundless cry, watching as Fred wiped his prints from the knife with Giovani's sleeve. Taking a quick breath Fred wrapped Giovani's hand around the knife handle, then plunged it into his side, drawing it abruptly downward to his hip. He quickly took up position, crumpling beside his treacherous brother. The smell of his own blood letting out to the floor overwhelmed him as he drifted out of consciousness.

It was nearly sunrise. The scent of blood was everywhere, blood of humans, vampires, even the wretched cattle blood. Opening his eyes slowly, Fred realized that he was in his own bed. Julia and Masha were fussing over him. Frank was on his cell phone rapidly talking to the head office. There were other vampires, guards he did not yet know.

"He's with us again." Julia smiled, as she pressed a

warmed cup of blood into his cold hand.

Fred shuddered, the cup slipped from his grasp, shattering into a thousand pieces on the floor. He glanced up at Julia, wrapping his small arms tightly around her, hiding his face in her blouse. Only once he was shielded from the other guards did he grieve, a great wailing cry the likes of which none had heard before. Frank ended his call, stepping forward, his pen clicking with agitation.

Julia shook her head. "Let him be; he is only a child."

Bronwynn Erskine

Bronwynn Erskine is an Ontario native currently re-siding in Newfoundland. Erskine is an avid steampunk enthusiast and acrylic landscape painter.

Erskine made their publishing debut in 2018's *Chillers from the Rock* with their chilling tale: "Scarlett Ribbons," returned in 2019's *Flights from the Rock* with "Feather and Bone," with "The Lindwyrm's Bride" in *Mythology from the Rock*, and was featured with three stories in *Acceptance: Stories at the Centre of Us*.

In 2023 they released their debut novel, *By Reservation Only*.

Scarlet Ribbons

"He doesn't love you."

The voice strokes down Claudette's spine like an icy hand. She shivers and draws the red silk dressing gown closer around her thin shoulders, and tries to pretend it's only the wind whispering in the leaves below the balcony.

"You know he doesn't. You saw the way he was looking at that waitress over supper."

She grinds the end of her cigarette out in the ashtray on the balcony's marble railing and lights another. The tip flares red as she inhales, and she stares at its glowing coal instead of the moon rising full and silver on the horizon. Instead of the man sleeping in an indolent sprawl across her bed.

"Do you think he was imagining her while he touched you tonight? Is that why he closed his eyes? The better to pretend it was another woman in his arms?"

The man in her bed stirs and murmurs, but doesn't wake. His face is turned towards the half open balcony door and bathed in soft moonlight. It smooths out the contours of his face and makes him look terribly young.

"He's pretty when he sleeps. Such sweet red lips, and those shoulders. Like a young Adonis, isn't he? It made you willing to overlook his flaws when you first met him."

"Shut up," Claudette whispers, eyes squeezed shut and fingers trembling. Hot ash spills from her cigarette and ghosts across her knuckles.

"You were so sure this time would be different. That he'd be different from all the others you've taken home. And he did seem different for a little while. The first few days were amazing. The first week was good. But that's over now. It's become unavoidably obvious that he's just like all the others. He doesn't love you."

She takes another draw and finds her gaze drawn, completely unwilling, back towards the bed. He is nice to look at, asleep or otherwise. She still finds her stomach aflutter at the sight of all that lean, graceful muscle. It's much the same thing she felt the first night she brought him home, but the lust is tinged with something else now.

"That's right. You know you want to."

With a shudder, she wrenches her gaze away. Growls, "Stop it. I'm not playing your games anymore." But there's a tremor in her voice that she can't quite still. The cigarette smoke has lost some of its savour.

"You always overthink this part."

The voice purrs like a satisfied cat. Like everything is going just the way it wants. She hates herself for the shiver of pleasure the tone chases across her skin.

"You don't want to be alone. That's why you always try to convince yourself this isn't what you want. That if you just wait a little longer, he'll love you as much as he keeps saying he does. You remember how well that worked out."

The reminder draws a different kind of shudder from her, and her free hand moves like it's got a will of its own. Her fingers brush the ugly, puckered scar just below her left breast through the light material of her robe.

"That's right. That's what happens when you give them a second chance. The white ash wood burned like a frozen sun

there, a breath away from your heart. You were lucky his aim wasn't very good."

She looks away, though the voice is everywhere and nowhere, and thus impossible to look away from. She wants to argue, to deny, to make excuses. But on cold nights like tonight, as the year falls away toward winter, she can still feel the awful, icy burning of it. The scar has never quite stopped aching.

"Of course you remember. And this one's had his chance already. There's no need to draw things out any longer. It's the indecision that always makes it harder for you."

"I don't want to be alone." She says it softly, echoing the voice's earlier words and testing them on her tongue. They taste true. Bitter and smoky and true.

"Of course you don't. But it'll be better when he's gone. You can find someone new, someone who means the things he whispers in your ear at night when his hands are on your skin. Someone who's not like all the others."

She stares out at the moon, fully risen now and casting the world in stark edged argent shadows, and tries to remember how many there have been before him. She's lost count, she realises with a vague sense of shame. She used to keep such careful track, and now she can't remember.

"It doesn't matter how many. None of them are really worth remembering beyond the brief pleasures they gave you. None of them loved you. And this one's no exception."

"He doesn't love me," she says with a sigh. This, too, has the taste of bitter truth upon it, and she allows herself another gusty sigh full of smoke and regret.

"No, he doesn't. So you may as well go back inside and get on with it. The waiting and agonising only make it worse. Only make you suffer the doubt longer than necessary. Every time it comes to this point, you fuss and fret. You second-guess yourself. But you know that once you get started everything will be

fine. The doubt never lasts beyond first blood."

With another delicate shiver that has nothing to do with the cold she scarcely feels, she stubs out the second cigarette and straightens up away from the railing. She stares hard at the man in her bed and bites her lip.

"As soon as the skin parts and the blood runs slick and hot over your lips, all that indecision will be gone."

She can taste blood already, but her own watery blood from her bitten lip offers no satisfaction. He stirs again, restless, like he can feel the intensity of her gaze upon him. It makes her tremble with anticipation.

"He's still asleep. He won't put up a fight when you open a vein. He'll wake up after that, of course, but isn't that half the fun? That's right, go back inside now."

She's at the door before she realises she's moving. It's a surprise to find her fingers pressed against the sliding door, the glass cold and solid beneath her skin. It grounds her, makes her hesitate a moment.

"Remember how warm you feel when he puts his arms around you."

She does remember. He feels like a furnace against her cool skin. She tries to hold onto the thought of how warm and alive he is, but the voice has other thoughts.

"Just think how much warmer you'll feel when his blood is running down between your breasts. Matting in your hair. Imagine how that heat will feel sliding down your throat and coursing through your veins."

And oh, how she can imagine. She takes a hesitant step forward, slipping in through the half open door, and already she can feel his warmth. The silk sheets caress her thigh as she reaches the bedside. She wants to crawl back into bed and curl up next to him.

"Yes, that's right. Can you smell the blood under his skin?"

It smells sweeter than any dessert she can imagine. She trails her fingers lightly over the curve of his shoulder up to the back of his neck.

"That's right, right there. The skin's thin there. It'll part easily under your teeth, and let all that lovely warmth out for you to play with. You want that, don't you? It'll be easy. You know that by now. Just start with a kiss, just a chaste little brush of lips. Like he gave you the first night."

His skin is hot and soft beneath her lips as she kisses the curve of his throat. She can feel the light scratch of stubble against her cheek, and the slow movements of his breathing. Her fingers curl into the sheets as she fights the urge to dig them into his skin. To gouge deep scarlet ribbons out of his smooth flesh. She gives his throat a teasing little lick, and feels him begin to respond in his sleep.

"Doesn't he taste good? He's so soft, so warm. You know you want that. And all it takes is a little bite to get things started. Yes, that's right. Just like that."

Anastacia Hopkins

Anastacia is an actor, director, and producer for both film and theatre. She is a lover of Newfoundland supernatural folklore, graphic novels, and lazy days at the beach reading.

Anastacia makes her publishing debut in *Chillers from the Rock*.

The Cache

It was the type of night where you wanted to be indoors. Fog thicker than forgotten gruel choked the entire island making visibility impossible and sounds inaudible. It was like being caught in a vacuum and Neil wished more than once that he had heeded his old man's warnings and just stayed home.

Looking at the ground, he took three steps before the persistent fog swallowed it up too. Cursing, he tried not to think about why he was in the woods (or at least he *hoped* he was still in the woods) instead of playing video games and drinking beer with the b'ys. Grunting, he shifted the weight of the burden on his back and continued to trudge on.

"Has to be close by now..." he muttered to himself and started when something wet and prickly hit his face. Taking a shaky breath, he let out a string of curses. "Damn-tree!" he finished with, and had cause for another string as he stumbled on an exposed tree root and fell to his knees.

Getting back up, he had a fleeting thought about the stories he had heard concerning these very woods growing up... of the Hag and other evil creatures just waiting to grab anyone who dared to enter their woods at night without the proper protection of bread or turned inside out garments... "Bull!" he said; however it was said in that overzealous way one uses when trying to convince one's self otherwise.

So, on he went, moving slower as he grew weary and the weight on his shoulders became even greater. "Can't be far now..." he repeated like a mantra in between curses as he was hit by unseen branches that dropped cold rivulets of water down his shirt and face. Every now and then he would stop to rest or listen as a noise of rustling leaves surrounded him like canon fire before just as suddenly disappearing into the dense fog, leaving him with the overwhelming sensation of losing his hearing in its wake.

Heart pounding and the eerie silence settling upon him, he finally felt the rough surface of rock against his shoulder and knew that the first part of his journey was over. A burning lump formed in his throat and he tried to swallow it down. All he had to do was drop... *it*... and he could be on his way.

The cave was the perfect spot to hide something no one wanted to be found and Neil definitely did not want this burden found. The fear of the woods would only help him to keep it a secret... and even if *it* was found, he would be long gone... No one would even know he was guilty. It wasn't his fault anyways... If only she hadn't -- Best not to think about it.

No longer able to carry *it*, he dropped *it* to the ground and began to drag *it*; moving backward in shuffling steps, he found the mouth and hauled *it* inside. Panting, he kept going, wanting to get as far into the cave as he could to make sure it was would be a long while before *it* could be discovered by people or animals. If he hadn't panicked, he would have thought to bury it instead of foolishly going into the woods.

A groan emanated within the dark maw and he nearly fainted from fright. Just as he realized that it wasn't coming from anything human, the floor gave way and he was falling... falling… falling…

Landing with a thud that knocked the wind out of his lungs, Neil rolled over. There were crunching sounds and something sharp poked him in the ribs, causing blood to trickle into the fabric of his shirt. As he reached for his lighter, he could feel something smooth and cold against his skin. Resisting the urge to jerk his hand away, he pulled the lighter out and lit it.

The hiss of the Zippo as it produced the precious glow gave him comfort. It was a comfort instantly forgotten, as in its small sphere of light he saw a yellow dome with two gaping holes and a knowing smile. Hand shaking, he moved the little light about, and everywhere it landed a more gruesome sight was revealed. Countless bodies in various stages of decomposition were littered everywhere and as the light moved, it came upon his Sarah and her empty brown eyes that were only hours before filled with laughter.

Terrified, he scrambled up the crumbling dirt wall and out into the foggy night. He ran senselessly, driven by the need for safety. The woods were closing in around him, but he thought he might make it through.

Then he heard his name.

"Neil," it called.

He came to a halt.

No one knew where he was.

"Neil," it called again.

No one at all...

He ran with the conviction that his life depended on his escape from the woods. Some of the bodies from the cave had been clothed from the old days... The stories were true! ...And now he was in one.

He tried to take his coat off, but something tripped

him. For the third time that night, he fell. This time he couldn't stop himself from falling forward. Arms pinned in his coat sleeves, he stuck a rock as he went down. The world spun, swirling the fog surrounding him, then righted itself just as quickly.

Blinking against the searing pain in his head and the stinging tears that were falling down his face, he tried to get up only to fall back down. Whispers surrounded him as branches shook in a sudden breeze and then all went still. All he could hear was his heart beating in triple time and the sound of his heavy breathing. Then came the laughter; high in pitch, it flew at him from all sides.

Prayers he hadn't uttered since childhood flew from his lips. The laughter increased and he squeezed his eyes shut against it. A great gust of wind blasted him. Screwing up the last of his courage, he shook his coat off and scrambled to his feet. Not daring to look at anything but the ground in front of him, he ran as fast as he could.

"Neil! Neil, stay! We want to play!" sang a thousand voices. All of them were a mix of taunts and pleas as they raced alongside him. Some even seemed to whisper right in his ear. "Neil! We know what you did!"

The last came as an accusation accompanied with nails raking along his neck, cheek, and chest, drawing blood in their wake. He screamed. Invisible hands pulled his hair, ripped his clothes and slapped him, leaving burning welts along his exposed flesh.

"You killed her, Neil!" they screamed at him.

"I'm sorry!" he cried. "It was an accident!"

"Liar!" They knocked him to the ground.

"I swear! I never meant to...Please, you have to believe me!" he begged.

"You killed her! You killed Sarah, Neil!" they said in disgust. "Did it feel good? Did it, Neil? Did it feel good to knock her around?" they asked.

"It was her fault!" he shouted.

"What did she do?" they asked.

"She knows what I get like when I'm mad!" he explained. "She never should have laughed at me..." He waited. Nothing happened.

Relief flooded over him and he moved swiftly through the trees. If he didn't have to keep Sarah's body a secret, he would have one hell of a tale to share at Mike's bar. He'd be the man who went into Doucette's woods and came out alive.

Just ahead, he could see a faint orange glow from the streetlight; the fog was starting to dissipate and he'd have a clear drive home. A twig snapped behind him and he paused. Then he laughed. The fairies had let him go! He had nothing to worry about! Hell, they thought it was Sarah's fault too. She knew better; he had warned her time and time again...

A smell filled the air... a horrible putrid scent of decay that made bile rise up into his throat. Gagging on it, he stumbled forward trying to get away from the pungent odour. Something suddenly moved to his right. Glancing down and over, he saw a pair of dark eyes looking up at him. A shiver ran down his spine. "Sarah?" he asked in disbelief.

The fog lifted and the moon shone down upon him and the upturned face of the dead girl.

"Hello, Neil," the corpse said, a twisted smile crossing her face before abruptly yanking him down into the earth. His screams mingled with the laughter of a thousand voices and the whispering trees as the fog closed in on the glen, swallowing everything up and returning the woods to silence.

Ali House

A native Newfoundlander, Alison is a graduate of the Fine Arts program at Sir Wilfred Grenfell College (MUN), and past recipient of the Golden Crescent Wrench Award. She is the author of *The Six Elemental*, and has had short stories published in *Sci-Fi From the Rock*, *Fantasy from the Rock*, *Unexpected Stories* and *Bluenose Paradox*.

She currently resides in Halifax, Nova Scotia, where she works in arts administration and spends more time than a person should in and around theaters.

The Deal

Claire had been prepared to make a sacrifice. She had heard many stories about people who sought out the witch for a favour and never returned, but those stories also claimed that every favour asked for was granted. One man wanted help for his poor family, and although he never returned home, his family became very wealthy the next day. One woman went to seek revenge on a man who had deceived her, and though she was never seen or heard from again, the man was trampled to death by horses a few days later.

When her sister fell ill, Claire tried desperately to bring her back to health, but as her sister grew weaker and weaker, she knew that there was only one option left. She had been prepared to give her life in exchange, so when the witch offered to cure her sister in return for one month's servitude, Claire was more than happy to accept. Perhaps the witch had taken pity on her, she wondered, and given her an easy task.

The terms were that Claire had to keep house for the witch, performing any possible task that was given to her, and that she would not leave the witch's forest until after the thirty-first sunrise. Claire shook the witch's small, bony hand in agreement. The witch grinned and declared that Claire's sister would be in full health by the morning.

The work was harder than Claire had expected. She had to cook, clean, maintain the grounds and the garden, and do any other task the witch came up with. Some days she would spend hours putting things in order only to find a mess the next day. The witch only gave her a few minutes to eat or rest, keeping her constantly moving. Some days Claire thought about running away, but then she remembered her promise to the witch. Claire thought of her sister and how wonderful it would be to return home once her time had been served.

The only time the witch took pity on her was when she slept. After working twelve gruelling hours, Claire would go back to her small room within the witch's house. There she would mark a line on the wall, to count down the days that had passed, before falling asleep, exhausted, while the sun was still in the sky.

The witch's forest was quite different from the forest that surrounded her village. The trees were all a sickly grey colour and had no leaves or pine, just bare gnarled branches. She didn't like when a task took her into the forest, and tried to spend as little time in there as possible. The wind made it seem as though the trees were whispering to her, mocking her. The grass was brown and dry, making the green of the gardens seem unnatural.

She saw no other living thing, except for the witch. There weren't even any animals or bugs. Any questionable creatures or objects in the house were already dead. Claire had wondered if she would see any of the other people who had come to ask favours, but there was nobody but her, the witch, and the trees.

Finally her thirtieth day came and Claire arose to a bright morning. The sun filtered through the branches much the same as it had any other day, but today it seemed brighter. She couldn't help smiling as she walked out to the kitchen, receiving her duties from the witch. Only one more day and she would finally be home, back where she belonged. The task had been difficult, but it would be worth it to see her sister's healthy, smiling face.

After finishing her chores, Claire was exhausted, but decided to stay awake all night and watch the sunrise. She made herself a cup of strong tea and sat outside, watching the sky. She thought about all the wonderful things that she would do once she was back home, the people she missed, the places she would visit, and the food she would eat.

Suddenly she noticed that the sun hadn't set. She had been sitting outside for a long time, but the sky was just as bright. A terrible idea started to form in her mind, but she ignored it and went into the house, checking on the small clock the witch kept in the kitchen. The clock proclaimed that it was almost midnight, and yet the sun was high in the sky.

"Problem?" the witch asked.

Claire turned around, startled by her sudden appearance. "The clock says that it is midnight, but the sun is still up."

The witch smiled. "That clock goes by village time, dear."

"Village time?" She shook her head, confused. "But there is only one time."

"Is there?"

Claire felt the terrible idea start to form again, but she shook it off. "I have been here for thirty days, and in the morning, I will go home."

"Our agreement was that you would leave when the sun rose for the thirty-first time. How can a sun rise if it does not set?"

Dread washed over her. "You cannot..."

The witch smiled wickedly. "If I recall correctly, the

sun has not set since your arrival. Hence, you cannot leave."

Claire raced outside and looked at the sky. The sun was still shining through the branches, showing no signs of wanting to set. She tried to think of a time when she had noticed darkness in the forest, but there was only sunlight.

"Don't worry, dear," the witch's voice was suddenly behind her. "The sun will set after another hundred hours or so, and then the night will come. You'll learn the timing soon enough."

Claire thought back to the past thirty days she had spent toiling in the witch's house and how it had not even measured up to one sunrise. This could not be. How could the sun not set or rise here? How could one day last almost a thousand hours? Did the witch have control over the sun or was this some kind of illusion meant to keep her here until the end of time?

Who knew how long the nights would last or if the sun would even rise again? If this were the case, she would die of old age before she could leave.

"No," she said aloud. "A day is made up of twenty-four hours. I have worked my thirty days, and in the morning I will leave."

"If that is what you think, dear." The witch laughed to herself and went back into the house.

Claire stared at the sunlight filtering in through the trees. She spent hours waiting for the sky to change, but it didn't. Finally she went back into the house and checked the clock. It was eight am, well past sunrise in the actual world.

"Has the sun finally risen?" The witch's words came out of nowhere.

Claire turned around, but the witch was nowhere to be seen. As she looked around the room, the witch began to laugh. Her laughter grew louder and more terrifying, and soon it filled the entire house. Claire put her hands over her ears, but the sound couldn't be shut out. She ran from the house, into the ever-present daylight and raced through the trees.

The trees seemed to have grown extra branches, blocking every path she chose. Branches scraped at her skin, cutting her as if they were blades. The whispering of the wind grew louder until it sounded like soft voices telling her to give up – that there was no escape.

Finally she could see the clearing that led to the village and her home. In her heart she knew that she was right – that she had served her time and should be allowed to leave – and she raced forward.

With each step the ground seemed to grow softer, and her feet sank deeper the further she ran. Her right foot sank into the ground and refused to come free, no matter how hard she pulled. The clearing was less than twenty feet away, and she grabbed her foot, trying to pull it free. It was then that she noticed the skin on her arms had turned a sickly grey colour. Panic rose inside her as she tried to pull her foot from the ground, but the ground was growing around her foot, encasing her leg. She reached for a tree to help pull herself forward, but her arms and fingers began to grow longer and she couldn't grab anything.

Frantically, Claire looked around for help, but all she could see were the grey trees. As tears filled her eyes, she began to see that there were souls trapped inside the trees – the souls of humans who had dared to seek out the witch and ask for a favour – staring at her with pain and regret in their eyes. She tried to yell that she had served her time and that she was free to go, but her mouth wouldn't open.

The other trees watched silently as the transformation finished, and the woods fell silent again.

The Taste of Copper

When I was three years old, my mother showed me how to place a copper penny on my tongue and hold it still for one minute. It was something the two of us shared – a ritual we did every single night before bed. She told me that it kept the bad dreams away, and I have to admit that I can't remember ever having a bad dream as a child.

As I grew older, I learned that the other children in the city didn't have the same night-time ritual. When I asked my mother why nobody else did this, she simply said that our family was different. At first she was reluctant to tell the whole story, but I pushed until she gave in.

After hearing it, I wished that I had never asked.

Long ago, when my grandmother was a young child, she lived in a small village on the coast. The village has since been abandoned due to resettlement, but if you decided to go there now you would see the remnants of houses and graveyards, silent and waiting.

One winter's evening, when my grandmother was very young, word spread from a nearby town that there was a strange woman in the area. It was odd for a person to be wandering at night, especially in winter, and the townsfolk wondered if the woman might be a witch or a demon. They hid themselves in their homes, locking the doors and turning off the lights, hoping that the stranger would think the town was abandoned and pass by.

Eventually they heard a hacking cough making its way into the town. Those that chanced a look saw an old woman dressed in dark rags, using a tall branch as a walking stick. Every so often her body would be wracked with that terrible cough, doubling her over in pain. She slowly shuffled through the town, taking in the dark houses.

It was the snow that gave them away, showing the footsteps of earlier journeys throughout the town, stopping at buildings that seemed abandoned but were too nice and well kept. The woman began knocking on doors and windows, begging with her rasping voice for food and shelter, but the townspeople stayed quiet. They knew how evil spirits pretended to be helpless, to make unsuspecting people invite them in. They would not risk such things.

The woman knocked on every door, shouting that she knew they were inside, but the townsfolk were paralyzed with fear and prayed that she would leave them in peace. Eventually she left the town, but not before laying her curse:

You people have no mercy, but you will not forget me so easily. If you love your pennies so dearly, keep them. But rest assured that one day you will all know what it is to feel an emptiness in your stomach and coldness in your bones. One day you will all know how it feels to be helpless.

And then she disappeared into the night.

The townspeople wondered if they had done the right thing, if maybe she had been nothing more than an old woman after all, but they all agreed that letting her into the village would have brought disease and sickness. They had done the right thing.

A few days later, a group of men who were out hunting found her body. They were unsure whether she had died of starvation, the elements, or her illness. They buried her in a shallow, unmarked grave and tried to forget about all the unpleasantness the woman's visit had brought.

Everything returned to normal, but after a while the townspeople noticed that something was wrong with their food. No matter what they ate, everything tasted bitter and rotten. Even food that was fresh or brought in from other towns had the same taste. Some whispered that it was the curse, come to torment them for turning the strange woman away. Others were sceptical, but there was no logical explanation for what was happening.

Every man, woman, and child in the town began to starve, unable to keep food in their stomachs. As they wasted away, a chill crept through their bodies, the likes of which they had never felt before, not even on the coldest nights of the year.

Thankfully a solution was found before too many perished. Remembering the stranger's words about keeping their pennies to themselves, a woman decided to put a penny in her mouth. After a minute she found that the rotten taste had given way to the copper of the coin, and she was able to eat again. She spread the word to everyone and the village was saved.

My mother explained that this curse did not stop with those who had lived in the village, but travelled to their offspring as well. She and her brothers and sisters were affected by the curse, while my father, who was from another town, was not. So every night I had to place a copper penny under my tongue to keep the curse away.

I was young enough to trust her implicitly. I believed every word and followed every instruction. But then I grew up, and I began to question her story.

Why would someone curse an entire town for not helping? Did she curse any other towns or was this one special? Were curses even real? And if they were, why would it affect me – someone who was born decades after this had happened? Would it pass on to my kids, if I had any? Were pennies made of copper anymore?

Doubts filled my mind. I was a rational, educated person, and this story went against everything I believed. So one night I decided that I would not do my nightly ritual. I was haunted by bad dreams, but I had expected as much. With the story of the curse foremost in my mind, it was bound to manifest as nightmares. The next day I was able to eat just fine, so again I did not put a penny under my tongue. Nothing bad happened. The curse was no more – if it had even existed in the first place.

Eight days later it started. No matter what I tried to eat, everything had a stale, unpleasant taste to it, as if it had been left sitting in the elements for years. Every drink, even water, tasted rotten and bitter. I knew that I needed food to live, but the thought of eating repulsed me. Whenever I tried to keep anything in my stomach, I would have to fight to stop it from coming back up – a fight that I would often lose. Days passed and I noticed how thin my arms and legs were getting, and how hollow my face looked. My energy was waning, and I could feel a chill inside of me that I had never felt before. It felt as if someone had replaced my blood and bones with ice, and no matter how many sweaters I worse, I couldn't make the chill go away.

I refused to believe that this was the curse. There had to be a realistic explanation, like a dormant illness. I went to a doctor, but he could find no reason why this was happening and suggested that I go a psychiatrist, as it was probably all in my mind. I never went. If this was my mind playing tricks, then it would have happened right after I stopped using the penny, not days after. No, this was something more – something inexplicable.

I still don't know if I truly believe in the curse, but I can think of no other explanation. Perhaps it is too late, perhaps I have left it too long, but it is the only hope I have left. So I will take this penny and place it on my tongue, and I will keep it there until the curse has broken. I don't know how long this will take, or if the curse will break my spirit before I break it, but I can only hope that I will survive long enough to once more know the taste of copper.

Eryn Heidel

A native of North Battleford, Saskatchewan who currently resides in St. John's, Heidel makes her publishing debut in *Chillers from the Rock* with her chilling tale: *The Pursuit*.

Heidel graduated from Memorial University with a Master's in English in 2017. Now she spends most of her spare time solving the mysteries of the universe and keeping the answers to herself. She is a freelance editor who has taken helm on the *Coral Beach Casefiles* series.

The Pursuit

My only intention in detailing this account is to come to grips with what I saw, and to warn you not to follow in my footsteps.

It was the beginning of spring when it happened, which meant it was cold, damp, and foggy. At around 8:30, I found myself burdened by heavily wandering thoughts as I bent over my desk and my studies. Instead of progressing in my assignments, I was wondering. I was thinking about the hike my grandfather had taken me on, up Signal Hill. It's a beacon, a glimmering reminder of the proud history of telecommunications progress, and home to a bounty of tactical buildings, cannons, guns, and the implied spectres of military casualties. There is another hill on Signal Hill – an afterthought, like a less attractive sibling. It crouches near a small body of water called Deadman's Pond, and that small peak is called Gibbet Hill.

"Do you know why it's called Gibbet Hill?" my grandfather asked me as we neared the top.

I hazarded a guess: "Is it named after someone?"

"It's not who it's named after, it's what it's named after," he said. "There's a reason this is called Gibbet Hill, and there's a reason that's called Deadman's Pond."

We had reached the top of Gibbet Hill by that point, with the road winding up Signal Hill just behind us, and below us the pond, still as a mirror, not a breath of wind that day. The pond was a stone's throw straight down. Rolling distance, you could say.

"Gibbet*ing*," my grandfather began, with emphasis on the action, "is when you dip the body of an executed prisoner in hot tar and hang them up for months 'til they rot."

"Oh."

"Then, when the bodies are good and decayed, they roll the bodies down the hill and into the pond. Dead-man's Pond."

"*Oh*."

"And now you know."

"And now I know.

It's easy to treat history as fiction. So, the night I went off in the cold and the fog, hardly able to see beyond the point of my own nose—yet brimming with morbid curiosity—I wasn't expecting anything totally out of the ordinary. A few thrills, maybe; a notion of supernatural possibility, perhaps. But it may have been that setting off despite hanged men, skeletons, and common sense, doomed me from the very start.

As I approached the hill from below, I had every intention of walking up the road, only to find out that the street I wanted to take was closed due to construction. In the hazy mist, I could see dormant equipment resting beside torn up pavement and sidewalk. Excavator heads lolled near precipitous gravel pits. Chunks of rock were strewn about the street. I decided against that route, and descended into the Battery instead.

The Battery, like all things at the edge of St. John's it seems, has its own little miseries to contend with. The small neighbourhood at the edge of the Narrows appears like an innocent, serene spot to live, but true enough it's dealt with deadly avalanches and rockfalls that have swept homes and people out to rest efficaciously and indiscriminately. It's a place of contradiction, home to impossibly narrow, winding roads that branch off in directions I never knew were possible. There is one rule to remember when navigating through the labyrinthine streets of the Battery. It's easy enough to remember, even if it is counterintuitive: you have to go down to go up.

At almost every fork in the road, in order to get to North Head trail, I took the road that took me down. Downward, downward until I was so near the harbour that I could feel the spray of salt on my cheeks. The waves that night moved in jerking, restless motions, retreating en masse, gathering, roiling together, until some invisible force regurgitated the bulky bundle of water back onto the rocks once more. The erratic motion made me seasick watching it, so I pressed on, downward, until finally the road swung up once again and I was on my way up the incline of the Battery and onto North Head Trail.

On a clear night, St. John's acts as a sort of nightlight, illuminating the trail that hugs the cliff from behind. But that night, the fog was so thick that it trapped all the city's lights within its veil. As I shouldered my way onto North Head Trail, wary of the drop into the gurgling waves below, I noticed at last that there was nothing to light my way. I was alone.

Not to be deterred, however, I was content to be foolish. I pressed on, past the squat buildings with barred doors, once belonging to an infantry that fought in battles too numerous to name or recount. I bristled as I walked past those doorways; even with doors shut, the thought of something openable was enough to raise my hackles. Little did I know that by continuing along my way, I was opening a door that should never have been opened.

The beginning of the North Head Trail, the lowest point of the walk, is also the narrowest. At one point, the trail embraces the cliffside so closely there is not so much of a patch of grass or rocky outcrop beneath you to catch your fall if you should slip or twist an ankle. A long chain has been anchored to the rock to provide a macabre sort of handhold. I gripped it loosely enough to shimmy along the trail, my back pressed against the rocks. I glanced back once again, blinked in the thick of night to see any hint of light coming from the city, but saw nothing.

I did hear the low drone of the foghorn, which sounded every twenty seconds. A warning. A guide. When the faculties of vision are inadequate, the foghorn sounds to remind you that you are not alone. For sailors, the foghorn warns them to be wary of rocks. For me, the foghorn was a reminder that despite what I couldn't see, I hadn't strayed that far from familiarity.

As I got farther away from the city, farther east near the rocky edge of the trail, I began to hear less and less. In the silent moments between the blasts of the foghorn, I was stunned by just how quiet it could be. I listened intently for even the ocean, and found that I couldn't distinguish the rush of the waves from the static buzz of silence in my ears. I only heard my own breaths, and the faithful foghorn. But I was so far out, and now I had ascended high enough, that I couldn't see the city and I couldn't see the ocean. If it weren't for the familiar gravel trail and the numbered wooden stairways that guaranteed my direction, I would have been hopelessly lost. But as I surveyed what little I could (not much more than shadowy, shrouded rocks and trees a few feet in any direction), I decided that I had gone too far to turn back around; I pressed on.

I navigated the rough terrain with my squinted eyes focused on the ground immediately ahead of me. I hopped from stone to stone, avoiding any patches of wet gravel glistening mud that threatened to take my feet from under me, all the while trying not to think about the oppressive fog pressing on my shoulders. In the distance, the fog-horn blew once more, and I released a shuddering sigh of anxiety as my ribcage tightened around my lungs. I came across two boulders that I either had to squeeze between or clamber over, and I could not remember having done that before. At one point the gravel trail became muddy and stuck with irregular rocks. The well-worn trail had been consumed by the chaotic, erratic sludge. It must have been hit by a mudslide, but there was no indication that anyone had marked off this section of the trail as a danger. I decided at that point that I needed more than my limited night vision in order to traverse the trail safely.

I fished my phone out of my pocket and wiped the moisture off the screen. I squinted in the heavy fog and lifted the device closer to my eyes. When I left the house earlier that evening, my phone had been at a healthy-enough 65% battery. When I pulled it out of my pocket, it had drained to a measly 20%. I hesitated on the lock screen, lingering between two decisions: use the flashlight on air-plane mode in order to see where I was going, or maintain a cellular anchor to the real world. I swallowed and wiped my damp fingers (hands clammy from the moisture in the air or the anxiety I felt in my gut, it's hard to say) on my pants in order to enter the passcode. I flicked on airplane mode and turned on the flashlight, and for the first time all night I was truly alone.

The foghorn sounded. The flashlight was powerful enough to illuminate the path immediately in front of me, but if I tried to shine light on any shadows huddling in the dense fog, I was greeted only with the reflected light in millions of miniscule water droplets. At the most eastern point of the North Head Trail, the fog rolled in in thick waves, cutting off my view at times of my own hands.

I had successfully circumnavigated Signal Hill, and if my sense of direction was correct, I would be standing on a rocky outcrop about half a kilometer down and east from Cabot Tower. I searched the fog for any indication of the spotlights that I knew should light up the building, but found nothing. I couldn't even see the shadowy outline of the top of the hill itself.

As I continued upward, I lifted my gaze from my foot placement for a moment to once again take stock of my surroundings and paused, nearly dropping my phone in the process. Up until that point, I had encountered amorphous shadows that were obviously rocks, and tall, gangly-limbed figures that were obviously pine trees, but there was something odd about the shape ahead. I blinked, and rubbed my eyes. A shroud of mist passed between us and I lost view of it for a second. I took a step forward, and the figure moved.

At first, it appeared to be roughly human size, but then the thing grew until it was about ten feet tall. It raised its arms—if it even had arms—and it appeared to be wearing a cloak. I took a startled step backwards, and another. I realized that this thing, whatever it was, was not a shadowy figure at all. It was more like a black hole, sucking in the minimal light around it. Even in that darkness, it was darker than dark. It was a void. Smoky tendrils of pure blackness snaked out from beneath its hood and penetrated the grey fog. These tendrils dissipated into the air, but they were targeting me. The wind changed, either by chance or by the intention of this hulking hooded figure, and brought with it an unearthly chill that wasn't like any cold that I had ever felt in my entire life. The cold seemed to come from inside me, gripping my heart, and penetrating out from there. I was wearing a sweater and a thick coat, and any heat that I had trapped within those layers was instantly lost.

The cloaked figure slowly lowered its arms and began to approach. It had no gait like any living creature, instead it seemed to sweep from left to right, the edges of its cloak flapping back and forth and sending those little tendrils out wherever the hem lifted high enough to let its dark essence out into the world.

I backpedalled, gripping my phone tightly in my hand. I briefly considered turning the flashlight off, but I decided that it would only handicap me in the long run. *Whatever that thing is*, I thought, *it can probably see in the dark*.

I turned around and began to run in the opposite direction. I left what remained of the washed-out trail and instead climbed over the rock nearer the cliff's edge. I could finally hear the ocean again. The foghorn sounded. I turned my back on the water and watched as the figure swept over the trail, following my route. Every few sweeps it would stop to pivot, look straight at me (at least, I assume it was looking—I never did see any eyes), and extend its arms and release more of those black tendrils into the night air.

I considered my next move, my heart pounding in my chest. My fingers were stiff with cold, and trembled uncontrollably. I gripped onto my phone until my knuckles were white. I had two directions I could go: left to go back down the way I had already come, or right to the stairs that would take me up the final stretch of the hill and into the Cabot Tower parking lot. The figure was taking its time, very slowly approaching at the pace of a leisurely stroll. I was certain I could outrun it. But I was also more inclined to take the shorter route back to the safety of civilization.

I turned to the right and sprinted back over the rock to the gravel trail. I found a set of stairs. They were narrow and set steep into the rock. They went down. For a moment, I despaired: I thought I was much closer to the final stairs that would take me up the hill. But then I remembered: I had to go down to go up.

I quickly glanced over my shoulder. The figure was standing where I had just been, at the edge of the cliff. It turned to look at me, extended its arms, and began to sweep toward me once more. Instead of taking the shortest route to get to me, it appeared to be taking my exact steps.

I turned back to the stairs, both hands on my phone and directed the light at the stairs. The stairs were marked with numbers, letting any hikers know how many staircases were left to go up or down. These ones were marked with the number four. Good. I was close.

I carefully and quickly tiptoed down these stairs. In the dim light and the fog, it was hard to distinguish the end of one stair and the beginning of another, and the last thing I needed was to slip and fall. I made it down those stairs, and navigated a series of irregular rocks, vaulting over dips and lithely stepping over cracks until I came to staircase three, which thankfully took me upward.

I took these stairs two at a time, grunting with the effort. There must only have been twenty or thirty steps, but my quad muscles burned from the strain. At the top, I jogged a few paces and slowed to a fast walk, keeping a close eye out for the final two staircases that would take me to the top of the hill. They were the longest staircases, if I remembered correctly, and there were at least two hundred steps to go.

The stretch between staircase three and staircase two

was a lot longer than I remembered, and a lot steeper. I found myself bending, leveraging my steps with my hands and tucking my phone under my arms as I pulled myself over tall rocks that I don't remember ever encountering before. Finally, I came across the next staircase.

It went down.

That wasn't right. It couldn't be. The last two staircases went *up*. I distinctly remembered it. It was a certainty of the North Head Trail: the last two staircases were hellishly steep, and hellishly long.

I pointed my phone at the plaque that showed which number this staircase was. It was the number 4.

It wasn't possible. It couldn't be. I felt suddenly light-headed and grabbed the rail for support. My eyes darted back and forth as I attempted to register what was happening, but then I felt the shuddering of my bones as a colder-than-cold breeze wafted up from below me.

There, at the top of what was supposed to be staircase three was the figure. It paused, watching me. I stared right back at it, and it didn't move. It seemed to be mocking me.

I checked the number on the staircase again and swallowed hard. It was still staircase four. When I looked back, the figure was slowly approaching once again, so I descended. Then I sprinted across the divide between staircase four and three, hoping to gain some distance between myself and the thing, and hurried up the final stairs of staircase three. I clamoured over all of the steep and terrible rocks, coming upon another staircase. And it went down. It was staircase four again.

I groaned in frustration. This time I was getting used to the lay of the land, and I was able to navigate it expertly. I jumped down the stairs two, three, four at a time. I leapt from point to point between staircases. This time I took the stairs going up staircase two or three at a time: as many as I could manage in a single bound.

At the top of staircase three I paused to catch by breath, coughing and wheezing. I wiped my mouth with the back of my hand and directed my flashlight in the direction of the figure. It was in the valley between staircases. I began to step backward, and spun around on my heels to find the staircase again. And I don't know why I noticed it right then, but I realized I hadn't heard the foghorn in a long while. I paused, and counted in my head as long as I was brave enough to do so. Twenty seconds. No foghorn.

A niggling panic began to set in, biting at the edge of my lungs which threatened to compress into hysterics. I pushed the blind panic into the corners of my brain, focusing on the task at hand. I began reciting a mantra: you have to go down to go up. You have to go down to go up.

I completed the circuit again in record time. Then, when I reached the top of staircase four again, and just as I was about to plant my right hand on the railing to leap down as many steps as I could at once, my phone battery died. The light went out.

I swore under my breath, blinking in the sudden darkness. In relying on my phone, I had lost most of my night vision. I was paralyzed at the top of the stairs, my heart hammering at my ribs and my breath coming in short spurts. I couldn't hold it in anymore, I shut my eyes and the panic gripped my lungs; a high-pitched scream tore out of my mouth. My brain was blanketed by terror, my knees—which were already shaking—buckled beneath me, and I collapsed. The hand holding my phone slammed into the gravel, the sharp rocks scraping my skin. I weakly grasped the railing above me with my right hand.

I took three long breaths through my nose, and out

through my mouth. I opened my eyes, and found that I could see, barely, but enough to get through this obstacle course that I was already growing used to. I pulled myself up, and turned to face the figure that I was sure was closer than ever.

It couldn't have been more than ten feet away, close enough for the thinnest of the black tendrils to reach my ankles and wrap around them. They felt like tiny static shocks as they were absorbed through my pant legs and into my skin. It wasn't painful; it was nothing at all. My whole foot went numb and a wave of anaesthetic peace washed over me. As the figure approached, I felt calm. I felt ready. I just wasn't sure what for.

In a final, desperate burst of adrenaline-fueled rationality, I gripped the phone in my hand, raised it high above my head, and threw it at the figure with as much force as I could muster. I watched my white phone fly through the air and go right through the figure's chest. There was nothing solid to it at all: not cloth, not body. I listened for the tell-tale crunch of my phone hitting rock, but heard nothing. It went into the figure, but it didn't come out.

Without another thought, I planted my hand on the railing and fled down the stairs. I ran so fast I had no control over how quickly I was going. The momentum flung me down those stairs, my weight shifted, and I felt myself toppling forward. I could see the end of the staircase approaching. I threw my hands in front of my face and fell forward, palms outstretched, and tumbled. I rolled, landing on my back, and when I opened my eyes, I saw stars. Not stars in the night sky, but rather bright flashing fireworks that exploded in my vision while I tried to make sense of an unhinged, spinning universe.

My lungs were frozen. I gasped, and gulped, like a

fish out of water, desperately clawing at my throat while my paralyzed torso jerked for air. I finally sucked in a deep breath. I lay there, dazed, and I opened my eyes as a thousand tiny pins and needles pricked at my arms and legs and peace rushed over me like a heavy winter duvet. Black tendrils cascaded down the staircase and sunk into my limbs while I stared up at an empty sky blanketed by fog. I turned my head and saw the thing sweeping down the steps.

I dragged myself into a crawling position, shivering, feeling out my fingers and toes. Everything was accounted for. I began to crawl faster, dragging my shins over jagged rocks and dirt, which tore through the fabric of my hiking pants and skinned my knees raw. I finally pushed myself onto my feet and stumbled over rocks and reached out for where I knew the next railing would be. At the very least I would be able to pull myself up the stairs if my legs couldn't carry me.

I reached, reached, and my fingers slipped through the air. I fell forward, jarring both my wrists as they impacted the cold, hard ground. I winced, choking back tears as my eyes searched the ground for the beginning of the next staircase. It wasn't there.

I pushed myself up and turned around, looking in all directions where the rocky ground seemed to fall away, and I realized I was standing on a plateau. I was surrounded by an impenetrable fog that could conceal any depth; I had no way of knowing how high up I suddenly was. The staircase that I had fallen down had disappeared, and there was no sign of the shadow thing, at least for the moment. Tears gathered at the corners of my eyelids, and I kept turning around and around until I grew dizzy.

I stopped spinning and placed my hands on my knees to catch my breath. I shut my eyes tight and took a step backwards as I considered my options. If I was at the top of a hill, then I must be able to climb down somewhere. All I needed to do was start.

I straightened up, rounding my shoulders out, and breathing out through my nose. When I opened my eyes, the thing was there, as close as it had ever been. It towered over me, black smoke billowing out and swallowing everything in that foggy blackness. It seemed to grow into the hill, becoming part of the rocks. The ground I was standing on began to darken and soften. My bright yellow sneakers sunk into it; it was sticky, like mud, and as I struggled to move my feet, it seemed to suck me down further.

The thing stood there, looming, faceless. It was confident it had me. But I was not about to give up.

I mustered up what was left of my strength and hauled my feet through the black muck to the edge of the plateau. I gazed warily into the fog, and my eyes met only with a paradoxical whiteness that shone through the darkness of the night. Somewhere out there, there was light. There had to be.

I had sunk down nearly to my knees. What I had learned was that this thing, whatever it was, was relentless but slow. It could be outrun for a time, but its only strategy was exhausting its prey. If I stopped moving, I was dead. The waves of peace that washed over me were designed to make me stop being afraid, and to accept my fate. It was working. I wasn't afraid.

In a final burst of strength, I threw my weight forward, over the precipice, and gravity did its work. At first, I only slumped forward, my feet still hopelessly stuck in the mire, but then I gradually descended as my body weight was pulled down and down. My feet came unstuck with a sucking slurp and I plummeted into the murky fog.

I heard a screech from above as I fell. Without much thought, I covered my head with my arms and braced for impact. My shoulder came into contact with a grassy outcrop, I rolled down, and a stray bump lobbed me into the empty fog. My limbs splayed and an electric pain stabbed through my left arm. I thought for sure the next impact would come and I would die.

Instead, I plunged into a dark body of freshwater. The sudden sound of dull crashing and bubbles filled my ears with a deafening immediacy. Startled, I let out all of my air and the bubbles rushed past me towards the surface, but it was impossible to tell which way was up. I began swimming, my left arm uselessly dragging behind me, and eventually I found my way to the surface of a pond. I gasped, spluttered, and coughed, helplessly pawing at the surface of the water in an attempt to remain above it, but my clothes and my heavy jacket kept dragging me beneath the surface.

Somehow, my flailing caused me to drift close enough to the shore than I could touch the bottom of the lack with my toes. I let myself sink, and I pushed off the bottom of the pond until I washed up on the rocky shoreline like a dead jellyfish. I felt like one: my left arm was on fire with pain, my right arm was completely numb from the cold. My lungs were both constricted and my throat was raw. I managed to shrug my jacket, laden with water, off my shoulders and I dragged myself away from the water. As I did so, I head a familiar sound: the foghorn.

I cried with relief. I stood up, leaving my jacket on the ground behind me as I stumbled away from the pond. I knew where I was: I was on the edge of Deadman's Pond near the road. The fog had lifted somewhat, and I could see signs. I could see buildings. I could see the top of Signal Hill and Cabot Tower as shadowy outlines above. I could see car headlights through the thinning fog.

I staggered towards the road when I felt it again, the familiar sensation of static and peace. I spun around, and there the thing was floating just inches above the surface of the pond. This time, it glided towards me at a startling pace. I stumbled backwards, tripped, and fell onto the pavement.

"Leave me alone!" I screeched, shutting my eyes and curling into myself.

Just as it was about to envelope me in its shadowy cloak, a pair of headlights rolled toward us, and the shadowy thing dissipated into the darkness. The driver slammed the breaks and honked the horn, putting the car into park.

"Jesus, are you ok?"

Soaking wet, sobbing, and with a cracked shoulder blade, I was a mess. The driver drove me to the hospital where I was fixed up as well as could be expected. I had escaped.

But every now and then, when it's dark and the fog rolls in, I lock my door and I close my blinds. I go to bed early, read a book, and sleep through it. I try not to think about it too much, and I try not to panic when, just as I'm drifting off, I feel a wave of peace and the staticky tingling of nothing slowly creep up on me.

Peter J. Foote

Born and raised in the Annapolis Valley of Nova Scotia, and the son of an apple farmer, Peter studied archaeology in university. He is employed as a boiler and refrigeration operator, is an active Freemason, and runs a used bookstore (Fictionfirst Used Books) out of his basement in his spare time.

Believing that an author should write what he knows, many of Peter's stories are a reflection of his personal life.

Peter holds the distinction of being one of only a handful of authors to be featured in all the modern *From the Rock* collections to date.

A Friend In Shadow

Rattle, thud, rattle: the gloved hand tries to open the heavy steel and glass door. Finding it securely locked, Harold presses his face against the cold glass, pushing the bill of his hat backward and unconsciously mimicking his hairline. Warm breath fogs the glass as he turns on his flashlight and peers inside the building.

Shadows jump and shift as the powerful beam of the light pans over the lobby of KRS Research Corp. Chairs morph into ten-foot tall robots on spindly legs, like props from a 1950's H.G. Wells movie, and the red light of the security camera becomes the glowing eye of an evil cyclops ready to unleash havoc upon the world. Shaking his head and dismissing the foolish fantasies, Harold turns off his flashlight, and the lobby instantly retreats into mundane darkness.

Flashlight returned to the holster on his belt, Harold turns away from the exterior doors and meanders across the parking lot. Doing his best to skirt the numerous puddles and clumps of snow that the spring rains haven't yet melted, Harold comes to the edge of the parking lot, peers down the slope of the hill, and contemplates the town and wider world below.

Like a statue at the shore's edge, Harold lets the lights and sounds roll up the hill and wash over him. While most of the town has rolled up its sidewalks and gone to bed, the old Apple Barrel Tavern is still going strong.

The house band is doing a Metallica cover, and the strong beat of the drums causes Harold's heart rate to quicken while his toe taps the asphalt in time with the music. Through tree branches naked of leaves, the bright neon sign highlights a group of people his own age stumbling out of the tavern, laughing and hanging off of each other as they head for the parking lot. Car doors slam, hoots toot, and cars peel out to form a serpentine convoy out of town heading in the direction of "Lovers Lane."

Harold waits until last taillight is lost behind curve of the road before he sighs and mutters, "Maybe Mom is right, I should finish filling out that application and go back to school. Maybe then I could have a life and a future."

Finished staring down at a world that seems to be going along just fine without him, Harold averts his eyes, turns away, and with shoulders slumped, continues his patrol around the building.

As he nears the loading dock at the back of the research complex, a small grin creases Harold's face to replace the frown there minutes ago. Stepping into the range of the flood lamp above the loading dock doors, Harold quickens his step, splashing through puddles as his shadow lengthens out behind him. The elongated shadow of the security guard quickly catches up, and zooms ahead of him in an arc as he thinks, *I can't seem to ever beat you, my friend.* Leaving the radius of the flood lamp, Harold's shadow starts to dissolve back into the darkness of the night which spawned it; but before it is completely gone, Harold waves, sees it mirrored and says, "I'll catch you next time, friend!"

His only companion now behind him until his next set of rounds, Harold's shoulders once again droop, and he starts dejectedly kicking a hunk of ice that the plow missed across the asphalt in front of him. As such, he doesn't see the clouds roll in. Blocking out the meager starlight, the low heavy clouds blanket the area and soon it starts drizzling. The warm raindrops beat a gentle pattern against his overcoat, and a thin trickle of water meanders its way between his shoulder blades. Grunting resignedly, Harold turns up his collar, and burrows into his coat.

Withdrawn into his own thoughts, Harold doesn't notice that when the warm rain meets the partly frozen ground, a thin band of fog is created, lifting itself from the ground. It contracts and pulses with a faint white light like a vein pumping blood, and soon tiny ribbons of fog snake out from the host body and hesitantly explore the world around them. Some delicate cords tunnel through a forgotten pile of dead leaves, others weave themselves through the wrought iron of a bench, and still others flow over the concrete curb in front of Harold.

Kicking the hunk of ice off centre, it skips sideways, hits the concrete curb and shatters. His distraction gone, Harold finally notices that the warm drizzle hitting the cold ground has created a fog around him and little tendrils, suffused with a pale white light, probe outward. "It's probably nothing more than a byproduct of the street lights diffusing through the fog or a trick of my tired eyes. Mom always said I had too much imagination."

Watching the slim tendrils of fog creep out in front of him, Harold imagines that they are tentacles from a Lovecraftian horror reaching out to grab him and pull him to a gaping mouth. Smiling, he's reminded of the movie he watched with his nephew last weekend while on his monthly visit to his sister's house.

Removing his flashlight from his belt once again, Harold widens his stance, holds the flashlight two-handed, and when the narrow beam of light stabs skyward says, "Come at me, Sarlacc, I don't fear you!" With that, he starts swinging his flashlight as if it were a sword made of light.

Giggling like a child on the playground, Harold slashes at the nearest tendril of fog, causing its tip to vanish almost as if by magic. Caught within his mental drama, Harold dismisses it as a trick of the light or a result of his movements, but the remaining tendrils start to pull away from the flashlight. Sensing that he has the "enemy" on the run, Harold splashes through puddles as he hacks and slashes all the narrow ribbons of fog within reach of the powerful beam of light, until a honking car horn in the distance brings him to his senses.

Harold hurriedly fumbles off his flashlight and with burning cheeks returns to his security rounds around the research building. Unnoticed by the retreating form of the guard, the decapitated tendrils of fog start twisting together like jungle vines and become a single composite. The once pure white light mutates into a sickly yellow and the pulsing tentacle of fog oozes after the human, gathering its wounded brethren as it goes.

Rounding the last corner of the complex, consumed by thoughts of hot coffee and the new Sam Bauer novel sitting on the desk in his security hut, Harold doesn't notice the broken and twisted tendrils of yellow fog that rise from the cracks in the pavement around him. Swaying back and forth like a blind worms, the tendrils reach and probe at the world around them, and one of twisted tentacles brushes the heel of Harold's boot as he walks past.

Shivering at the sudden chill that races through his body, Harold jams his hands deeper into his overcoat pockets as he unknowingly outpaces these first disfigured tendrils of the fog. Such is the nature of luck, it rarely holds, and in seconds, the tiny broken tendrils of fog combine into a coiled limb and race after Harold.

Like a runner from a bean plant in a child's fairy tale, the tendril of fog quickly catches Harold, and in a quick snap, wraps itself around his right ankle. Harold cries out in pain as a lightening bolt of icy cold robs his leg of all strength causing him to collapse onto the wet asphalt.

His first thought is that he has stepped into a pothole and has twisted his ankle, but a single look robs him of that belief. His pain-addled mind struggles to comprehend what he is seeing: sickly yellow worms of fog are creeping up his leg, each touch blistering cold.

Harold realizes that he is under attack.

A massive slug-like creature suffused with a diseased light has grown up from the pavement and wrapped itself around his right leg. Squeezing him tightly, Harold can only watch in dumb fascination as the fog throbs in time with his racing heart. The unhealthy yellow light that emits with each pulse gets stronger as his leg gets colder and weaker.

Harold frantically tries to pull his numbing leg from the grip of the creature, but can't even crawl from his prone position, hands scrambling on the asphalt that tears his leather gloves. Crying out in panic, his frantic voice echoes off the empty buildings around him as Harold stabs his hand at the creature, but it's like trying to strike mud; it merely reforms once his hand passes through. Desperately, Harold claws at the slug-like creature, bile rising in his throat as he touches the cold flesh, but to no avail. Caught firmly in its grip, Harold's fingers cramp with cold as they slide through the thickening body of the fog creature.

Seeing tiny worms of fog inch their way up his leg, Harold flails at them wildly and, with tears running down his cheeks, he cries for help, only to have the fog swallow his words.

Like tree roots through sandy soil, the spikes of cold travel into Harold's groin, and from there put out feelers throughout the rest of his body. Robbing him of warmth and life, Harold instinctively knows that if the fog finds its way to his heart, he will die.

With strength born of mortal danger, Harold fights to crawl away from the body of the fog creature that has encircled him. Harold forces himself forward an inch, then two, then six, before collapsing a foot away from where he fell, his gloves lost and fingertips a bloody ruin, and his body still firmly within the grasp of the creature.

Harold only crawled a foot, but it was enough to put his outstretched and bloody hand within the cone of light emanating from the window of his little security hut, causing a shadow of his outstretched hand to form.

The shadow of his outstretched hand moves...

The shadow hand starts rotating and thickening before Harold's eyes. The hand expands into an arm, then fills out and becomes three-dimensional. With shadow fingers laced between his own, Harold is pulled to his feet with supernatural strength, and as he is lifted from the asphalt, his shadow arm bellows out like a sheet on a clothesline into a fully formed mirrored copy of himself.

Supported by the iron grip of his living shadow, Harold can't help but stare into the inky black features of the face and see the faint traces of a smile stare back at him.

His shadow-self speaks in a ragged whisper: "Scorch-Bite, give me Scorch-Bite".

"Wait... What's happening, what are... Augh!" Anything else that Harold might have said is lost in another cry of pain as the fog-creature redoubles its attack, clawing further up his body, wrapping itself around his waist, squeezing and draining warmth from Harold's trembling body.

His Shadow releases its hold upon Harold and thrusts its own black hand into the fog, encircling his waist and clawing at his belt. Without the Shadow to support him, Harold's numb legs give way again, and he drops to his knees as the fog rising higher.

"Scorch-Bite, we need Scorch-Bite to fight," his Shadow repeats, and Harold realizes that the Shadow doesn't seem to be affected by the fog creature. The inky black arm of the Shadow can dimly be seen snaking through the sickly yellow body of the fog creature, and he can feel the Shadows touch as it paws at his thigh.

Harold's mind races like a slug through molasses, struggling to find meaning in his Shadow's words. "The flashlight!" Harold mumbles weakly as the cold invading his body causes his breath to fog in front of his eyes.

"Yes, Scorch-Bite. We need it. Help me!" his Shadow replies as it tries to pull the secured flashlight from his belt.

Gritting his teeth until his jaw cramps, Harold thrusts his trembling hand into the body of the fog creature. Gasping in pain, his fingers cramping and losing dexterity by the second, Harold is barely able to fumble open the clip holding the heavy flashlight to his belt. Using the last of his strength, Harold slowly pulls the flashlight out of its leather case, but just as it clears the case, the cold robs his arm of what energy it had left and he drops it...

Only to see that his Shadow makes a deft catch before it hits the ground and could roll away.

Kneeling upon the hard asphalt, his lower body co-cooned by the coils of the fog creature, cradling his now blue and frozen arm, Harold can only watch as his Shadow turns on the flashlight.

The cry of pain Harold made earlier when he was first attacked by the fog is a dim echo of what now issues from the mouth of his Shadow as it turns on the light. The soul-shattering scream from the Shadow beats upon Harold's ears like wings from a massive midnight bird.

As if struck by lightening, his Shadow-self stiffens with its arms and legs outstretched, the light emitted from the flashlight putting the scene into stark relief.

Instead of disappearing from the light source, the features of the Shadow become clearer to Harold's; his own face and features are there, but as if roughly sculpt-ed from stone. The Shadow's face twists in pain, its eyes narrow and jaw clenches. The surface of its skin twitches and jumps, and Harold is reminded of that time his uncle tricked him into grabbing the electric fence that kept the cattle contained, and how his muscles spasmed in pain for hours afterward.

Reaching down with the hand not holding the flash-light, the Shadow grabs Harold's arm and tries to pull him away from the grip of the fog creature. Helping as much as his weakened body will allow, Harold can't help but notice that the 'skin' of the Shadow is slowly cracking and splitting like sheets of paper in a fire, and a white glow can be seen where the 'skin' seems thinnest.

Even with its inhuman strength, the Shadow can do no more than pull Harold three feet away from the main body of the fog creature, the pulsing tendril still connect-ed to the security guardand holding fast.

The invading cold now weaving itself into his chest, the desire to close his eyes and sleep is almost overpowering. With half-lidden eyes, Harold watches as his Shadow-self slices into the fog tendril using the beam of the flashlight like a weapon.

Like a broken rubber band, the tendril snaps back into the main body of the creature and the piece that was coiled around him dissolves into nothingness before his eyes. No longer supported by the tendril and with no feeling in his legs, Harold falls upon his side but is able to turn his head enough to watch the battle unfold.

Harold is unable to explain why, but it looks as if the Shadow is more solid than it was mere seconds ago, but also more fragile in a way, like fine china. The splits and cracks in its skin now run through its body like rivers, and its movements are becoming wooden. It's clear that the act of holding the flashlight is causing the Shadow untold damage and suffering, but nevertheless it's standing firm between Harold and the fog creature.

Warmth and strength flood into Harold's legs as normal blood flow returns, along with the pins and needles causing him to gasp. Harold fights to rise upon shaky legs, the effort causing sweat to bead upon his brow, and watches as his Shadow gives up its life for his own.

The fog creature strikes at the Shadow, fresh fog tendrils rising out from cracks in the pavement and darting out at the Shadow. Tentacles of sickly yellow fog lash out at the Shadow only to be slashed by the beam of the flashlight and dissipate into nothingness. As fast as it hacks and slashes, the Shadow can't stop them all, and for every strike that connects, a part of the Shadow crumbles away like embers from a burning log.

Risking a glance backwards, the injured Shadow turns to Harold and says, "Run inside to light." But this brief moment of inattention costs the Shadow dearly. A partially severed tentacle whips out and connects, the air snapping from the blow, cleaving the left arm of the Shadow which crumbles into a pile of ash as it hits the ground.

With fear giving him strength for a first, then a second stronger step, Harold is able to get his weak and trembling legs moving. Much like a newborn calf, he starts hobbling towards the safety of the security hut, but looks over his shoulder to watch his Shadow-self's final sacrifice.

Missing its arm, and the rest of its body crumbling away, so that a pile of ash encircles the ground around it, the Shadow nevertheless continues the battle. The fog creature also appears to be nearing the end: many of its tentacles lay listlessly upon the ground and its body has started to dissolve into nothingness. However, neither combatants seem willing to yield nor give quarter as weakened tentacles still strike the Shadow, and the flashlight burns the fog creature and its limbs.

Perhaps sensing that Harold's eyes are upon it, the Shadow turns to him again with its right cheek and jaw having crumbled away. Black eyes pierce Harold's own, and a voice touches his mind: "Goodbye, friend."

Knowing that its fate is sealed, Harold can only give a tiny wave and say, "Goodbye, my friend in shadow," as he limps off to the safety of his security hut and the coming dawn.

Shannon K Green

A gifted author with a talent for the strange, Green has been recognized in both the genre community and the contemporary literary community for his pursuits. In the past, he has been shortlisted for the 1996 Arts and Letters Award, and well as won the 2015 Audience Choice Steampunk Newfoundland Showcase.

Green made a splash last year with "Lower Antarras" in *Fantasy From The Rock*.

The Wine Dark Sea

He stared into the grey wall outside the window, as if he could force the fog away with the intensity of his gaze. Instead, the bank of mist thickened, further obscuring the barely visible prow of the vessel.

"Glaring at it won't get us home any faster, Romney. The crew are making what headway they can, but even with the nav-sats and GPS, they need to be able to see where they're going," a voice said behind him.

Seeing the ghostly reflection of Graham over his shoulder, Romney turned to face him. "No, it won't, but it makes me feel like I'm doing something to help get us back to shore faster. We're already a week late and..."

Graham cut him off. "And with your baby expected next week, you just want to be home, I know. Let's do something to take your mind off it. I'll set up the crib board; you get some coffee from the galley. After that, you grab something from the ship library and turn in. When the sun comes up, and the fog lightens, things will look better."

"I'm just worried about Lydia. It's our first baby and I want to be home for the birth," Romney said as he strode toward one of the tables in the lounge. "And, I might as well admit it, I'm a little homesick too. I'm not used to being away from home this long without her."

Graham retrieved a deck of cards and one of the cribbage boards from a cabinet along the port wall of the lounge. "It's always a big adjustment when you've been out of the field for a while, and losing the sat-phones definitely hasn't helped with the re-adjustment. The captain says we should be ashore in three days. Yeah, it's almost two weeks behind schedule, but we both knew that was a possibility when we signed on. Just like we knew it was possible we'd come back with something like we've got in the hold." He looked back to Romney with a gleam in his eyes. "Our names will live forever now, not just passed down through our kids. We may be late getting home, but it will be worth it once our find makes the news."

Romney sighed. "I'll get the coffee, you get the board ready." Making his way down the corridor, he glanced through a porthole and noticed that some of the crew-members were in the smoking section they affectionately called the dog's walk, staring intently to the east, or at least what he assumed was the east. He'd never been that good with direction, especially not at sea. Stepping through the nearest bulkhead, he followed their gaze. There was nothing to see, save the fog, which coiled like a cat preparing to sleep.

He begged a light from one of the deck hands and watched the fog roll and coil in the distance. Certain things, he reflected, like staring at the waves on a beach, sitting before a fire, or the wind in the leaves of a grove of trees, triggered a primal portion of the human brain. The same portion of his mind he felt responding to the heavy fog that hung around him now.

Throwing the end of his cigarette overboard, something he did in protest of the captain's constant badgering not to, he continued to the galley. Grabbing one of the serving trays, he loaded it with a coffee carafe, two mugs, a small bottle of milk, and several packets of sugar. Romney was just searching for a snack to go with the coffee, when he saw the night cook staring out the window.

"Soren, anything fresh from the oven? Maybe some of those amazing brownies you make?" Romney asked.

The man did not reply; his eyes were fixed on something outside the window.

Romney tried again, tapping the man on the shoulder as he said, "Soren? Anything fresh for a hungry man who should already be in bed?"

The portly man jerked his gaze from the porthole. "Rom, I didn't see you there." His accent always made Romney think of a Jamaican who had lived in outport Newfoundland long enough to take on some of their inflections, despite the man being from Sweden.

"Sorry to interrupt, but Graham and I were killing some time and I was hoping for two things. First, that you had some tasty treat we could munch; and second, that you'd join us for a game if you get a break."

Soren looked at his watch before saying, "I've got blondies coming out of the oven in five minutes. Sorry I can't do more of the brownies you like so much, but the cocoa ran out. I will bring us a few of them and sit in for a hand or two before I have to start the boys cooking breakfast, cool man? Us stranded fathers-to-be got to stick together."

"If for no other reason than that we'd drive everyone else crazy with our worries," Romney responded, adding a third cup to his tray.

"Have you noticed anything strange in this fog? I keep thinking that it's making shapes like my wife," Soren said, before adding in a quieter voice, "Well, like she was when we met ten years ago, and was still the most beautiful woman I'd ever laid eyes on, instead of the person I love now." Shaking his head, Romney took up the tray and left the galley as Soren's gaze returned to the porthole.

As he made his way back to the lounge, he noticed that the group clustered on the smoking deck had grown in number, all staring in the same direction. Sure, there was only one direction that wasn't the ship, but it was odd that all eyes seemed fixed on the same distant point when the world beyond three feet was effectively a wall of grey.

In the lounge, Romney saw that Graham had seated himself at one of the tables on the starboard side and was staring out the large window while absently shuffling a deck of cards. Setting the tray down on a nearby table, he poured coffee for the two of them and joined Graham.

"It's beautiful in its way, isn't it?" Graham said. "How it coils and twists about itself, like yarn when a kitten plays with it." Placing the cards on the crib board, he said, "You deal first, because you got the coffee."

Taking the deck, Romney shuffled and dealt the first hand. "What's got you all philosophical and generous?"

"You know what we've got in the hold. You know what we found in that cave. Proof that there was either a landmass that sank or that there were people who lived at what is now more than six thousand meters below the surface of the ocean! When we tell the world about this…"

"We'll be a laughing stock for thinking a few baubles in a sub-sea cave prove either of those. For all we know, what we found was thrown off some ship a few weeks ago."

"Not covered with that much algae and sediment. Not when people see the sonar scans that show the cobblestone roads leading to the cave. But when people see the foundation stones along that road. We found ruins at six thousand meters! In international waters. Never mind what we can make from such a discovery through le-

gitimate means, we can declare it a nation of our own!"
Graham stood staring out the window as if seeing visions
of himself as king of this underwater realm. Slowly, he
removed his glasses and polished them with the tail of a
handkerchief from the breast pocket of his jacket. "What
the...? Do you see...? Romney, come look out this window please."

Coffee in hand, Romney rose from his seat and followed Graham's gaze. "I see fog, lots of blasted fog that
is slowing this ship down despite possessing the technol-
ogy to find the exact GPS coordinates of any stone on the
seafloor." Sipping his coffee, he continued, "Sure, it's a
fog that behaves weirdly; I mean, I've never seen a fog
that seems to coil itself up like that. Or one that played
quite so with my eyes. It's acting more like a fire than a
fog, to be honest, showing you images of dancers and....
Is that a woman dancing on the waves?"

"By my count, I believe it to be thirty women dancing on the surface of the white crests of the wine dark
sea. Wind swept hair held in check with the stars of the
sea and each singing with the voice of an angelic choir,"
Graham responded as if quoting something. "I think we
may need something stronger than this coffee to get us
through the night, or maybe we may need to go on deck
to clear our heads."

As Graham polished his glasses again and peered
near-sightedly out the window, Romney watched the figures dance. There was no other word for the fluidity of
their movement. The women matched their rhythm to the
waves as they marched like the ballerinas he had seen in
the ballet his mother had dragged him to every month as
a child. Wave crest to wave crest they danced. Occasionally one would turn; pirouette, he supposed, was the better term.

Opening the window, Romney thought he could hear a chanted cadence. "Soldiers on the march," he said quietly. "Soldiers on the march, shielded by their worth of self. Armed with indignation and righteousness. They sing their ridicule and prance ..." He could hear himself speaking the words, but could not understand them. He knew the poem, but did not know where it had come from. He looked to Graham and saw the same bewildered look he knew he would see on his reflection.

"They come to take their right. They come to show their might. They come tonight," the pair finished the verse as the dancers on the waves advanced on the vessel. A blinding light appeared in the fog, causing the watching pair to jump before they realized it was merely the ship's spotlight being shone on the oncoming cohort. The choir became deep silhouettes in the silver wall the light made of the fog.

Graham coughed. "Shielded by worth of self indeed; I believe they're all jay-bird naked. I will repeat myself, we need something stronger than coffee if this is what we're seeing and we're reciting some poem neither of us seems to know."

Silently, Romney drank off the last of his coffee and retrieved his backpack from the corner of the lounge. From somewhere in the bag he produced a bottle of rum and poured a generous tot into his now empty mug. He passed the mug to Graham and took a very long pull straight from the bottle. "It was meant to be my celebratory drink if Lydia had the baby before we made it back to shore. I think thirty women marching across the waves to our ship means we won't make it home before she does."

Graham swallowed his rum and presented the mug for a refill. "Shall we move to a less defensible position to meet the onslaught, or at least attempt to clear our heads of whatever fugue it is that now befuddles us?"

In response, Romney started toward the deck where he found Soren transfixed by the gathering on the waves.

Outside the vessel the singing grew louder. Romney thought it a dead language he had learned to read, distorted by years of living in the S.O.F.A.R. channel. As if whales had learned to slow down Latin into syllables that could travel several kilometers before being reassembled into words. The sailor in him thought, 'These ladies speak slower than farmers'.

The singers came to the ship in a ragged line. One stepped forward and spoke in a deep melodic voice, "You have taken from our lands. Something important to our people. Return it to us and we shall let you wander our skies. Refuse, and we shall take you to your punishment."

Romney stepped onto the deck. "We thought the items abandoned, lost artifacts of a dead people. Our apologies. I will have your belongings brought out and returned to you. I will make the arrangements now."

"Hurry, Sky-travellers. There is some need for urgency," the singer said. "The relics are required this eve." The choir behind the soloist resumed their chanting. The fog about them seemed to swirl in time to the spoken words.

"Romney, there is no way the captain will let you throw that stuff back into the sea. There is no way I will let you," Graham said quietly. "If it was so important to them, then they should have had some sort of guards on it. Besides, do you really mean to throw away this chance?"

Romney looked at his friend in shock. "We discover a new people, a new civilization, perhaps even a new species; and your response is to steal from them?! No, we must do this peacefully. We will still get you your fame and fortune and book tours, but not by stealing a few baubles. Soren, send somebody below decks to retrieve the cases please."

The chanting had grown subdued during this exchange when the soloist spoke again: "Please, Sky-people. Time grows short. You must return what you have taken."

Soren pointed at the choir, who maintained their dancing and singing. "I've sent men below, but I fear they have as well. Are we going to take it on faith that they won't simply cut through our ship when they have what they want?"

Romney stared out at the group. Their numbers had dwindled and the fog had grown thicker. The chanting wasn't diminishing, the chanters were. Glancing about the open deck, he saw that the fog had thickened fore and aft, swallowing the other watchers aboard the ship. "I headed the survey; what was found there is in my care. The captain looks to the safety of the ship; and Graham, you were the junior partner on this venture, along for the excitement. We agreed to that at the beginning and we will stick to that now. Now where in blazes are the crew with those pelican cases? It can't take that long to..."

He stopped abruptly as he saw one of the dancers enveloped by the fog which momentarily turned red in the glare of the ship's light. Turning to Graham in disbelief he caught the same thing happening on deck; one of the crew, the crane operator he thought, disappeared in a swirl of fog which turned red as it thickened.

"Please, Sky-people!" the soloist shouted. "We must have the remnants to appease Krasi Skoteini Thalassa. Otherwise she will feast on our land and yours. You will never outpace her; your land will never be free of her." As she spoke, more of the choir disappeared until there remained a bare handful of voices in the now ragged chant.

Romney sprinted below decks, stepping over puddles of pinkish seawater at every porthole. The two-deck journey felt longer than the marathons he had watched his wife run. Panting as he reached his destination, he grabbed the first two cases and turned to return to the dog's walk.

"Throw them in the moonpool, it's closer," Graham said. "I'll throw in the other two."

Resuming his sprint to the dog's walk, he shouted over his shoulder, "You throw in those two, I'll take these up and throw them to the choir and tell them where to find the other two." Panting, he did his best to push his speed beyond what he knew he was capable of. Sides throbbing, each breath a storm of fire through his throat that did little to inflate his overworked lungs, he reached the deck he sought and raced towards the bulkhead.

Fog poured through the open bulkhead, swirling to take the form of a woman several months pregnant. Before his eyes, the fog turned the colour of red wine as he felt the cases drop from his hands. And felt no more.

Paul Carberry

Paul Carberry is a huge proponent of the horror genre and its place in literature. He has two children, daughter Dana and son Rick, with his wife Leah.

Paul has published seven novels with Engen Books: the four-novel *Zombies on the Rock series, Carcharodon, The Last of the Dragons* and *The Cottage Across the Lake*.

He has also had numerous short stories featured in publication in anthologies such as From the Rock and Terror Nova, including The Light of Cabot Tower, Into the Forest, and Halloween Mummers.

Into the Forest

A sliver of silver moonlight splashed into the room, its watery metallic glow bathing the room just enough to ignite the impassioned colours on the walls. The warmth of the day had seeped away, and a cold breeze blew in through the open window into Adam's room. The wintery air was so chilled it hurt to breathe. The fire Adam had lit before he went to bed had been extinguished, with only the low glow of embers remaining in the hearth. The darkness in the room felt like a thick liquid suffocating Adam, slowly swallowing his soul. Swinging his legs out of bed, he placed his bare feet on the rough wooden floorboards. The stench of smoke and mould were heavy in the room; it had been four months since his wife had gone missing. Adam spent the majority of time searching for clues to her disappearance, neglecting to keep their home tidy. The floors were stained with dirt, tears, and rotting food.

There were rumours throughout the village that his beloved wife, Kathy, had left him for another man, but he refused to believe that she would betray his trust like that. He had been a noble knight of the king's court and provided her with everything they could ever want, and she had given him his precious daughter, Bailey. He had given up his life as a knight seventeen years ago when she was borne, but continued to advise the king, allowing him to provide a humble life for his family. Making matters worse for Adam was his daughter's strange behaviour since Kathy's disappearance.

At first he could tolerate Bailey's tantrums. She would cry and scream all hours of the night, blaming him for her mother's vanishing. Bailey heard the rumours about her mother leaving them for another man and blamed Adam for pushing her away. Then the screeching turned to outbursts of kicking and biting; she would flail her limbs in violent, chaotic strikes. She had become a ticking time bomb, demolishing the furniture and dishes in fits of rage. With every provocation, she would lash out at him until she was red in the face, then she would try to run away into the nearby woods.

Adam was at his wit's end with Bailey, but she was all he had left in this world. She was the only reason now for his existence; without her he would have given up on life entirely and ended this aimless search for Kathy.

Adam lit the torch in his room and headed down the hallway towards Bailey's room. The boards creaked underneath his feet, and the flickering pale yellow light sent his shadow dancing all around him. He slowly eased the door open, allowing the torchlight to seep into the room. The light crept lethargically over the empty bed while a stiff breeze nearly doused the torch. The drapes fluttered with the drafts of chilled air flowing in from the open window.

"Bailey?" Adam felt his heart flutter inside his chest. He feared for his daughter alone with the unknown dangers that prowled in the woods.

Adam raced back to his room and pulled on his armour which still shone brilliantly despite him ignoring its usual polishing over the last few months. The orange torch flame danced warmly over the cold steel of his sword, the light getting lost in the scrapes and dents of the worn blade.

Adam grabbed the sword and rushed outside, but even the frigid air couldn't stop the sweat from rolling down his face. Adam's heart was throbbing with fear; he could hear the sound of his own pulse thumping inside his ears. Dread pierced his stomach like a knife slowly twisting in his gut. Adam's breaths had become erratic.

Adam raced around his house to his daughter's window and looked down at the mud, trying to trace his daughter's footprints. The torch cast a dull yellow hue over the soil, but the ground had grown hard from the frost and hid the direction she had gone. Adam looked upwards at the full moon which hung in the sky like a great luminous pearl. The orb of radiating white light was unfettered by any clouds, whilesparkling silver stars were scattered across the night sky like the scattered embers of a dying fire.

Adam hurried towards the dark woods, praying that he would find his daughter there. Stepping into the forest, the trees stretched for eternity and their canopy of branches and leaves above him robbed Adam of any moonlight. Black knotted tree trunks created a narrow path that led deep into the perpetual darkness, disorienting his senses. The earth was covered in decomposing leaves while the path was made uneven by roots that erupted from the ground. The pale torchlight revealed footprints in the rotting leafs, drawing Adam further down the path. Branches that spiked off into every direction made it difficult to navigate through the dense blackness. With every step deeper into the forest, Adam could feel the darkness drawing closer, pressing down on him. The densely packed trees remained still despite the icy cold breeze that howled all around him. Adam looked down at the ground. The prints had grown larger, sinking deeper into the earth now. The foreboding isolation and darkness was playing tricks on his mind; the tracks started to look like giant paws.

Adam was drawn further into the forest. He thought he could hear a choked cry for help over the screaming wind. Adam's heart thrashed around in his chest, but he pushed forward down the ominous path. A thick root tripped him up,and the torch went hurtling through the air before the flame vanished into the bushes.

Darkness enclosed over him, silvery light dribbling through the tree branches above. A rustling sound reverberated from somewhere behind him. Adam scampered over to the bushes and swept his hands over the wet earth, desperately searching for the torch. His fingers stumbled across the coarse wooden shaft of his torch -- the cloth was damp, but there was still a subtle glow emanating from the torch. Adam ripped the cloth from the sleeve of his shirt and gently wrapped it around the dying flame; the dry white fabric erupted in a blaze.

Adam let out a terrified, shuddering breath as he gazed upon the giant beast inching towards him through the tree branches. The creature snarled its lips back revealing yellow jagged fangs stained by blood. The gnarled smile frothed with spit as it closed the gap between them. The fur was mostly black with silver streaks peppering the sleek coat, its coat matted to its body by fresh blood.

Adam tried to back away, but tumbled backwards over the same root and crashed hard into the ground, his sword flying out of his hand. The wolf lunged on top of Adam, the massive creature pinning him to the ground. A loud growl erupted from its mouth before the wolf's razor sharp claws tore into Adam's cheek.

Tears streamed down Adam's face to join the blood pouring down his check. He wasn't crying from the pain, but from the startling realization that his search was over. Despite everything, there was a certain amount of peace instaring into Kathy's blue eyes one last time before his life was over.

Halloween Mummers

Jessie snuggled her head into Alex's chest, covering her legs with a blanket. Alex sat in the corner of couch and Jessie made herself comfortable on the rest of the couch. They were watching a movie on a TV that hung above the fireplace. The curling flames swayed and flickered, casting long shadows across the hardwood floor. The wood fire sent its warmth and light throughout the living room while two mugs of coffee sat on the coffee table in front of the mantle. Outside the wind howled, making the seams of the house creek as the rain pattered off the windows. A dull orange glow from the hanging pumpkin lights in the window caught Jessie's platinum blonde hair. Alex stared at the television intently, paying close attention to the horror movie he was watching. Jessie didn't like scary movies, but the slow stream of trick or treaters had stopped hours ago.

"What an awful night for trick or treating." Jessie tried to start a conversation so she wouldn't have to listen to the dreadful noises on the TV. After a few awkward moment of silence, Jessie looked at Alex's scruffy face. His black rimmed glasses rested on his crooked nose which had been broken in a fight outside of the bar last night. The skin around one of his eyes had turned black and was nearly swollen shut, but he managed to keep track of everything that was happening in his movie.

"I said it's an awful night." Jessie's voice had shown her frustration more then she had meant it to.

Alex turned his head to look at the bowl of treats next to the door. "Depends."

"Depends on what, Alex?"

"Depends on how you look at things, I guess." Alex turned his head back to continue watching his movie.

Jessie knew he was headed somewhere with that vague statement. If she wasn't so bored, she would have left it alone, but having nothing better to do, she decided to play along. "Well, it's wet and cold out. I mean, that to me seems like a terrible night to be outside going door to door looking for candy."

"Exactly."

"Exactly? Are you agreeing with me or did you have a point to make?" Jessie made no effort to hide her frustration now.

"Well, look at the bowl and tell me what you see?" A smirk on his face made a wave of wrinkles under his eyes.

"A bowl full of candies and chocolate bars." Jessie wondered where he was going with this.

"Exactly."

"Exactly what?" Jessie groaned.

"Think about it. If every kids' parents bought treats to hand out like we did, then the kid got to stay home tonight, watch a scary movie, and eat those treats without having to put in any of the work." Alex stretched out for his coffee, but couldn't reach it with Jessie resting on him. Jessie propped herself up enough to get Alex his coffee. "Since you're already up, you mind grabbing me some of those candy bars?" Alex laughed.

Jessie gave Alex a playful punch in the stomach. "You

jerk." Jessie pushed the blanket aside and put her feet on the hardwood floor. The fire hadn't been burning long enough yet to warm the floorboards and a chill ran up her backside. She made her way over to the bowl and looked down at all the treats. "What do you want?"

"Just bring it all over, I'm sure we aren't getting anyone else," Alex called out from the couch.

Jessie looked over to find he had pulled the blanket over himself. She grabbed the bowl and just as she turned to walk back, a loud knock on the door startled her. "Looks like you will have to share," Jessie teased.

Jessie opened the door and was startled by a gust of wind that pushed the door all the way open. Three people stood on the porch dressed up like mummers from Christmas time. The first one was a rather tall man wearing a flowered dress with a pair of polka dotted men's boxers pulled on over the dress. His hairy legs ran into a pair of yellow rubber boots. A white sheet with triangle eyeholes and a frown drawn with red lipstick covered the face and was tucked into his dress. The second person was much shorter and wore a black and blue plaid jacket over jean coveralls with the pant legs tucked into green rubber boots. They wore a pillowcase with ragged eyeholes and a frown drawn in black marker to cover their face. The last mummer stood in the back wearing a lacy red nightgown over a black sweater with a white hood covering their face as well. Large black circles were painted around the eyeholes and an innocent smile was painted in red where the face should have been. "Any mummers 'loud in?" one of them said.

Jessie laughed. "Wrong holiday, guys, but I love the costumes." None of the mummers had bags for trick or treating. "Maybe you should take those bags off your head so you can collect some candy." Jessie held out the candy dish.

"No one will let us in?" one of the mummers piped up. "You'll regret that."

"What did you say?" Jessie couldn't believe what she heard. "Alex, come over here."

"Let's see if the neighbours are any nicer." The mummers turned to leave just as Alex got to the door.

"What's wrong, dear?" Alex said. "What are they wearing?" he said as he noticed their strange attire.

"One of them said, you'll regret that." Jessie could feel her hand trembling.

"Regret what?" Alex reached out and took the bowl of candy from Jessie's hand.

"Don't be a jerk, Alex; what if they had tried to force their way inside?" Jessie was glad they were gone, but she still felt crept out by the whole encounter.

Alex didn't say anything; he just shrugged his shoulders.

"Thanks, dear, I feel so much safer." Jessie pushed her way past Alex and headed back to the couch. Alex unplugged the pumpkin lights in the window and drew the curtains closed before sitting back down next to Jessie. "I can't watch this, I'm changing the channel."

Alex started to object, but must have seen the frightened look in Jessie's eye and just nodded in agreement. Jessie knew she wasn't going to be able to get to sleep anytime soon without one of her sleeping pills. "Could you please get me one of my bedtime pills?"

"Sure." Alex headed upstairs while Jessie surfed the channels for anything that wasn't related to Halloween. Everything had a Halloween theme tonight, so she settled for one of the comedy shows airing their kooky holiday special. Alex returned with a pill and he sat back down on the couch. Jessie tilted her head back and threw the pill down her throat; she couldn't wait to fall asleep and get this night over with. She put her head back on Alex's chest and after a few minutes drifted off into a restless sleep.

A loud knock on the door startled Jessie out of her sleep and she nearly jumped to her feet. "What was that?"

"It's probably the neighbours coming to apologize for the loud screaming." Alex pushed his way off the couch and headed towards the door. Jessie's head was muddled and she felt groggy from her pill. The door creaked open. "Can I help you?"

"I'm looking for my friend, have you seen him?" An eerie voice came from outside.

"It's a little late to be trick or treating, even for someone your age," Alex barked back.

"Who is it, Alex?"

"I'm sorry, we didn't let you're friends in earlier and I'm not letting you in either." Alex closed the door and locked it.

"Who is it?" Jessie could feel her nerves fraying, sending erratic impulses throughout her body. She wanted to run to the phone, but she couldn't move or control her body from shaking.

"One of those people dressed up like a mummer." Alex's voice was filled with anger. Rage was surfacing in him once again, the same temper that had gotten him the black eye at the bar. Alex stormed over to the window and opened the curtains. "What the hell is she doing?" Alex raced over to the door and put his shoes on.

"Alex, don't leave me here alone," Jessie pleaded, feeling the dread grow deep inside.

Alex didn't listen to her pleas, throwing the door open. "Call the cops." Alex slammed the door shut behind him.

Jessie jumped up and ran over to lock the door. She walked into the kitchen to get the phone, but it wasn't on the charger. Jessie cursed Alex; he probably left it lying around somewhere. She scoured the kitchen table and counter tops for the phone, but it was nowhere in sight. Jessie headed back into the living room to get her cell phone.

"Where did I leave it?" Jessie couldn't think straight, the effects of the drugs still clouding her thoughts. She looked over the coffee table and the bookcase to no avail; her phone wasn't in plain view. Jessie could hear Alex cursing at someone outside.

Fear gripped her heart and made her want to hide under the blanket, but she needed to see what Alex was screaming at. She put her hand on curtains and started to pull them back slowly, terror hindering her motor skills. Outside was nearly pitch black except for the dull yellow glow of the streetlights. The doorknob jingled as someone tried to turn it, then a loud knock threatened to break the door down.

"Alex." Jessie ran over to the door to let Alex in. She threw the door open and nearly toppled over backwards.

"Have you seen my friend yet?" The mummer with the smile stood on the porch.

"Get out of here!" Jessie screamed franticly, unable to summon the courage to move. Only a few feet separated the two.

"Are you sure you haven't seen him? He said he would meet me here." The mysterious voice made Jessie's skin crawl. The mummer started to move towards Jessie methodically, her hands by her side. Jessie noticed dark red specks over the mummer's neck and nightgown. The mummer inched closer now, slowing raising her hands towards Jessie. The intruder was close enough now that

Jessie could see her green eyes staring back at her.

"Get out of here." Alex grabbed the prowler by the shoulders and hurtled her off the porch and onto the wet lawn. He slammed the door shut behind. "Have you called the cops?"

"I can't find the phone." Jessie was nearly in tears. Alex raced into the kitchen and she could hear him rummaging through magazines on the kitchen table and cursing under his breath. "What's going on?" Alex rushed back into the living room and headed straight for the couch with a panicked look on his face. He started ripping the cushions off the couch and looking underneath it as well. "Alex?"

"My cell phone's dead, where's yours?" Alex flipped over the last cushion.

"I don't know?" Jessie shuddered, her heart palpitating.

Alex darted upstairs to look the phone. In the silence, Jessie could hear something tapping against the window. She just turned away from the window, praying that the sound would go away. She stared into the fire and her heart jumped into her throat; she could see her phone melting on top of the burning ashes in the fireplace.

A pair of hands grabbed Jessie from behind and spun her around.

"Why is the bedroom window left open?" Alex shook Jessie back and forth, trying to bring her back to her senses, but all that escaped her lips were silent gasps. Alex turned to look towards the deliberate tapping at the window. He headed straight for the curtains; Jessie reached out to try and stop him, but her legs wouldn't budge. Alex tossed open the curtains revealing the mummer with the smile standing there, tapping a pair of keys against the glass.

"Get out of here!" Alex yelled furiously.

The mummer stopped tapping the glass and pointed

her finger at Jessie. Alex craned his neck and followed the aim of her finger. "Jessie!"

Jessie spun around and jumped back as the mummer with the red lipstick frown stood in the kitchen. Alex pushed his way past her and met the assailant head on. Alex didn't see the kitchen knife in his hand, but Jessie could see the end of the blade sticking out through Alex's back. A stream of blood slowly flowed down his stomach and started to pool on the floor.

Alex turned his head towards Jessie. "Run." Blood gurgled in his throat as he fell to the ground.

Jessie's instincts finally took over and she rushed towards the front door, but the knob was turning. She could hear the lock opening so she changed directions and dashed up the stairs. She looked behind her as the front door opened and just as she reached the top, she felt a strong blow to the side of the face, sending her tumbling down the stairs. The world spun around as she toppled head over heals, a barrage of pain shooting from every nerve ending as she descended the stairwell. Jessie crashed into the feet of the smiling mummer, who reached down and pinned her to the floor. Jessie thrashed around, trying to break her assailant's grasp, but she couldn't. Her ankle had been broken during her fall, the bone jutting through the skin. The stairs creaked as the other intruder made his way down, dragging a sledgehammer behind him. The heavy metal head banged loudly off each step.

"Why are you doing this?" Jessie pleaded to the three mummers. The mummer with the black frown pulled off his hood; she had no idea who he was or what he wanted. He just smiled at her for a moment. "Please let me go?" The hoodless mummer raised the sledgehammer above his head and held it there, staring down at her. "What do you want?"

"You should have just let us in."

Matthew LeDrew

Matthew LeDrew holds an Honours Degree in English from the Memorial University of Newfoundland with a minor in Anthropology, and studied Journalism at College of the North Atlantic in Stephenville, Newfoundland. He has also worked with both Transcontinental Publishing and the student-youth magazine *The Troubadour*.

He has written eighteen novels for Engen Books: the ten book *Coral Beach Casefiles* series, *The Long Road, Cinders, Sinister Intent, Faith, Jacobi Street, Infinity, The Tourniquet Reprisal, and Exodus of Angels* the latter three with co-author Ellen Curtis.

He lives in St. Johns, Newfoundland.

Flickers in the Night

The first time he'd come at her she had been nineteen years old and he'd been in his mid-twenties. She didn't know exactly how old he'd been because when, much later, she'd filed a police report she discovered that he'd lied about his age. In the grand scheme of things, it had been by far the least of the things he had lied about.

They had been arguing all afternoon. It was not their first argument by any means, nor would it be their last. It had been a year since they'd met and each of those fifty-two weeks had been punctuated by at least one argument. There were arguments about money and arguments about other men, arguments about other women and people she knew at work and people he knew at work. There was an argument for every flickering star in the night sky, it seemed sometimes, but that argument when she was nineteen had lasted all day.

It had started when they'd gone out for breakfast. They had chosen some fast food establishment that held the promise of endless pancakes and when he had pulled their car – a rusted beater from an age when rustproofing came included – he pulled in too close to the Chevy next to them and nicked it. "Careful," she said, through clenched teeth, wincing as she heard the metal touch metal. He had turned to her, surprised, and the fight had begun. There had been something in her tone that had hurt him, that had insulted the way he thought of himself or had given voice to his deepest insecurities, and so he responded in kind. And as soon as Ryan Valler had lashed out at Lisa Rowdan, Lisa Rowdan lashed right back – equally hurt by his anger, his frustration, and his ability to swing into moods where she felt she couldn't speak.

The argument went through breakfast and into dinner, through dinner and then stopped while they went to a movie. After the movie she had attempted to apologize, and something in her tone had irked him again, and the fight had resumed into the evening. In its tenth hour she had left the room he was in and closed the door to take a breath, and something about the way she had closed the door had set him off. He had stormed after her, flung the door open, put a finger in her face, and yelled. She cursed at him, and he responded by placing both hands against the nape of her neck and shoving her back against the wall.

It had been months since she had finally been rid of him for the last time, but every so often Lisa would still feel him near her... The spicy fish stench of a man left unwashed for several days would come too close to her on the subway and remind her of that state of him at the end, and it would be like he was there with her. Or someone would touch her arm a certain way to get past her in a crowded market and she would turn and expect him to be there, her hand usually on the bottle in her purse by the time she turned and realized it wasn't.

She'd first caught a glimpse of him in The Market on Tuesday. The Market was a massive collection of strip malls and restaurants that may as well have been its own tiny, self contained city. Concrete streets ran between businesses separated into perfectly equal square lots of glass and brick, each with their own separate address and power. Dozens of patrons walked back and forth, these streets as busy (or sometimes busier) than those on the outside. There were no vehicles; all traffic was strictly by foot. Still, there were collisions as people scuttled about, paying no attention to what they were doing or where they were going. They just kept texting or dialling or web-surfing their way right into another human being's face.

Lisa had manoeuvred between patrons seamlessly. It was a hot day – the type of hot that got people out of their homes – and the streets had been lined with tables to expand The Market beyond its concrete walls. Rickety, water-stained folding tables lined the parking lot stacked high with goods, both displays from venues inside The Market to exhibitors that had paid for a day-use of the space. There was practically everything at The Market and no rhyme or reason to the way it was presented: fried rabbit was next to Pokémon cards which were next to discount paperback novels which were next to a table selling custom buttons and cheap tattoos.

She had seen him while stuck behind a confluence of people plugging the way in front of her, staring at a man at the clam-shucking booth two tables over. It had been brief – so brief that Crowley had later tried to tell her it was nerves – but he had been there. He had been staring at her from four rows of people back, his height allowing them to see past them all and straight at her. She'd turned incidentally and they'd locked eyes, and in that moment she knew who he was and why he was here. Tightness weighed down between her breasts instantly then, and she felt her stomach cramp as digestion ceased, sending that blood and energy to her limbs and preparing them for flight.

But he was gone by the time she looked again. But he had been there.

There are studies that say the human brain can find

one angry face out of a sea of smiley faces 99% of the time, even when they flash by at only a millisecond. Evolutionary advantages left over from when being able to spot a threat in a fraction of a second was as necessary for survival now as it had been one-hundred-thousand years ago. Was that true of faces that were recognized to be menacing even if they weren't scowling or frowning, she wondered? She thought it was, and the growing tension in her gut confirmed it.

They had met at a club she hadn't been old enough to get into that served cocktails long past the legal hour. There had been lights and a smoke machine that was improperly named – it spewed dust, not smoke, shooting it into the air and letting it hang there with its putrid dry smell. The lights were purple and blue and red and yellow that flashed and flickered in the night, the strobe light pulsating to the beat of the house music and making their movements staccato and crisp, like polaroid pictures flipped to try and make a film. That same smell of sweat had been in the air that night but it had been intoxicating, mingled with spilled drinks, second-hand smoke, and perfume to make a smell that neither of them would ever be able to pin down, but that somehow kept them dancing when they filled their lungs with it.

They had started dancing, neither of them sure how. Each of their pairs had left for drinks and when the house music played and the lights went up, the rhythm took you and you had to dance. His hands were on her hips and she moved with him, him behind her, and with the same instinctual lack of understanding about how they had started, they were kissing.

She'd seen him the second time on Friday, while having coffee with Xander at a cafe on Larchmont Boulevard. It was a small place with spread-out seating – the kind she liked – and a wall of flavours and accoutrements. The entirety of the east-facing wall was made up of one sectioned window that let in all the light from the early morning Los Angeles sunrise.

There was a building across the street that Xander was keeping his eye on while sipping his coffee and acting as a sounding board for Lisa – she found that he was often able to multitask in conversation only while listening, not while talking, and was fine with that. She was sipping an impeccably made cafe ole and eating a piping-hot helping of Romesco Grilled Cheese. She had been in the middle of a story when she turned to look out the window and saw him.

He was sitting at a restaurant across the street, eating a sandwich.

Lisa had stopped in mid-sentence.

He was sitting on a bench with his legs splayed out in a dubious example of man-spreading, taking up as much room as physically possible. He was wearing shorts and his knees were scabbed and dirty in a way she'd never seen before, to the point of being almost black. If she had seen anyone else across the road out of her peripheral vision, she may have been able to convince herself that those were knee pads, but Ryan Valler had never been never been the type to even wear a seatbelt, let alone knee or shoulder pads.

He was wearing a solid red shirt that demanded attention. Against the stainless steel of the city it screamed, *look at me, I'm right here* in bright, primary colours. And he was staring at her. He hadn't been at first, but it was if he'd known when her eyes had fell upon him and reacted in kind, shifting his gaze and locking it on hers.

"What is it?" Xander said after waiting for her to complete her thought.

Lisa turned back to him reluctantly. "My ex is across the street," she said, her hushed tone imparting the gravity of that statement without having to vocalize it. She stared ahead at nothing and pretended to drink her coffee as Xander turned.

"Where?" he asked.

"On the bench."

"There's no one on the bench."

She turned back and found that Xander was right; the bench had become vacant. It was quickly reoccupied by other commuters – it was, after all, Los Angeles – but Ryan was nowhere in sight, falling back into the crowds he'd come from.

She'd seen him act in violence that first night, not forty minutes after their lips had touched for the first time. There had been more drinks and two trips outside to smoke and at least one shot and the house music had revved up again, and as one of her crew was vomiting the others had dragged her back onto the dance floor. The room was packed far past fire regulations – they did not care for age or alcohol restrictions, why would they care about fire codes? – and was more of a mosh pit than a dance floor. Two hundred people were crammed into a space designed to fit forty, each of them moving and swaying drunkenly more one minute than the last. It was less of a dance with one person and more of a dance with everyone in general.

Sweat poured from Lisa and she smiled perpetually, her hands above her, catching trails of light. Someone kissed her neck and she thought it was Ryan again in the dark, and she led him off the floor before she realized it was someone else. She tried to move away and he made one step toward her to ask her to stay, whomever he was, and suddenly Ryan Valler had been there: the strobe making him appear suddenly, eyes fire-red with fury.

The man had been a foot taller and twenty pounds heavier than Ryan, but within moments the fight had been over, and he was kissing her with hands whose knuckles were rendered loose flesh.

It only occurred to her years later, once it was ending: how had he even known she had wanted to get away from the man? The answer was simple: he hadn't, because that hadn't been why he'd done it. She learned then the simplest truth, far too late for it to have mattered: Men capable of violence were men capable of violence. Period.

Although the street was empty, she knew she wasn't alone, the same way she'd known on the street before that and the street before that. Her anxiety had flared within her three streets prior, tightening into a small metal ball in her chest before stretching out, its tentacles reaching her biceps and triceps and calves, making each ache as they flexed and pulsed with speed still in reserve. She walked fast, but didn't do more than that, her fear never letting her do more or less than that -- if she went slower, he would catch her, it said, but if you go faster, he will chase you.

Lisa felt trapped on a city street that was as wide open as a street could be: wide empty roads giving way to side-streets and parks that provided ample space to run and dozens of places to hide. Yet her anxiety trapped her into fight or flight mentalities, and feeling unable to do the former, all it would allow her to do was the latter. Any attempt to think of a solution other than that was muddled and hazy, impossible to take form. She couldn't think anything, couldn't do anything, couldn't plan anything: all she could do was move forward towards home, her legs pressing her forward like pistons, moving at the same steady, tense pace that would cause them to cramp but unable to stop.

Now the streetlight that had been surrounding her flickered. It sputtered once, then again, then died completely, leaving its frosted fixture with the ephemeral glow where light had once been. She could still see the street in front of her – light pollution was rampant in the city, so much that pure dark was almost a figment of the imagination – but a shiver still ran through her as she looked from one end of the street to the other, searching for some sign of life. Los Angeles had not been designed to be seen without its people: street and storefronts looked like dried carcasses when divorced from the life that typically teemed through them.

She continued forward down the street towards her home near Station Z2. As soon as she stepped past the sidewalk square she shared with the malfunctioning streetlight, the next began to flicker. She stopped and it stopped, continuing the tell-tale electric buzz made by dirty power and neon lights.

There hadn't been anyone on the bench when she and Xander had gone over to it, but there had been a single blackened line that went all the way from the topmost board to the board that cupped the arch of one's knee. It was warm to the touch when she had touched it, and she'd pulled back, and Xander had said he'd smelled, "ozone."

She hadn't known what ozone was supposed to smell like but she smelled it now: the burnt tang on the air that reminded her of citrus. It was a sour taste in her nostrils and the more she tried to parse how little sense that made, the more confused it made her, and so she pushed it aside. Whatever the smell was it was all around her now, and the soft hairs on her arm were standing erect. The hair on her head was rising too, ever so slightly. She could feel it like a charge on the air, the charge that comes before the dry lightning that proved the bane of this dry city time and time again.

She missed New York. There was no such thing as 'dry lightning' in New York... no such thing as dry any-thing that she could remember. New York was perpetual-ly damp and clammy to the touch, which made it alive to the touch. Los Angeles was warmer – even in the depth of the night as it was now – but it was dryer by far... Nothing could live in Los Angeles had the city not been there, she thought sometimes while parched by the summer heat.

The streetlight in front of her went out and so did the one beyond it, and her breath caught in her throat as she was wrestled back to reality. All the lights across the street went at once, as though they'd been caught in some localized brownout. She felt gooseflesh course over her again, every part of her standing on edge as she scanned the street for any sign of life that might have helped her. There was a liquor store, a gun store, another gun store, a shopper's deli, and a small door that looked to be the back entrance to a club... but no sign of life, not even a rat or a pigeon. She couldn't blame anyone; she didn't want to be on the street either.

She scanned her surroundings over and over again as she pressed forward, making her way toward home one step at a time. Liquor store, gun store, gun store, shop-per's deli, club. Liquor store, gun store, gun store, shop-per's deli, club. Liquor store, gun store, gun store, Ryan.

She stopped.

He was leaning against the bulletproof glass of the gun store's display with his arms folded in front of his chest. He had appeared as if from nowhere, his bright red shirt materializing from the cosmos itself between her third and fourth sweeps of the street. He was smiling, she could see from here. She knew that face and knew it well, the way his right cheek bumped up and impeded his vision when he smirked.

He locked eyes with her and she realized her breath was caught in her throat. She forced herself, with great effort, to breathe normally.

Ryan straightened, rising from the balls of his feet onto their flats and coming forward from the glass. The harsh, Algerian font of the word GUN stood apart and aside from him, making a tableau of his presence.

Lisa hadn't used the word 'tableau' since college and didn't in her mind now. She didn't think consciously or artistically of anything in the scene, only of Ryan's piercing blue eyes and the way they were locked onto hers. The word was peripheral, igniting something in the deep recesses of her mind: Weapon. Run.

Run.

She edged forward on the sidewalk, making her way to the next square and then the one after, all the while keeping her eyes trained on him.

When she had made it about five feet and her stride was beginning to hasten, the light of the illuminated gun store began to flicker and flit. The strobe effect of the failing light cast dark shadows against Ryan's face, heightening the deep turrets that ran down from his nostrils, defining his cheeks like plucked cherries. The smile he'd been watching her with broadened, and the deep shadows made his teeth appear black and vacant.

The light highlighting the word GUN shorted out, plunging his entire side of the street into pitched darkness. It didn't even retain the glow of light that bulbs usually did.

On the street behind her, one of the doused streetlamps jolted to life, shining a circle of light down on the sidewalk underneath it.

Ryan was standing in its center, his smile wide and those blue eyes of his burning bright.

Lisa made a high-pitched sound that caught in her throat, yet still pierced the air like a blade. She turned and almost slipped on her flats and did the thing she'd sworn she'd never do again, the thing her brain had been yelling at her to do with every instinct bred by two hundred thousand years of evolution.

Run.

She kept him in her peripheral vision as she ran, starting with small quick strides before graduating to longer sprints. He remained under the same streetlight, smiling from ear to ear. The light above him had started to flicker as she turned away, bolting quickly toward the corner that would merge her onto her street.

When she turned the corner, he was there and she almost slammed into him. He was caught in a beam from the spotlights that lit up the train station. The light surrounded him and was him. It seemed to shine into the back of his head and light up his eyes like a jack-o-lantern's. She gasped and skidded to a stop, her flats catching on the sidewalk's debris, and fell back onto her tailbone. The impact rocketed up through her, providing brief shimmering clarity to the pain but mulling everything else.

He was standing above her, the way she'd promised herself her never would again, with that same nascent smirk that promised that whatever happened, no matter what he said after the fact, part of him would enjoy what was to come.

She pushed back against the concrete with the heels of her feet, kicking as though she were on a bicycle, as though she were trying to spin the world's orbit, and

Ryan, away from her. She retreated a spare inch at a time until he crouched down to be on a level eye with her and she stopped, frozen in place by those sky blue orbits.

"Hello, Lisa," he cooed, with the same James Dean swagger she remembered, if not a tiny bit raspier.

She swore at him under her breath, wishing she could think of something more biting or poignant to say, but unable to think past her left brain screaming at her to flee and her right brain yelling at her about the pain in her back.

He reached out and grabbed her ankle, the closest thing to him, and pulled her toward him. His touch was hot and dry and shot a static shock up through her powerful enough to hurt and make the thin hair on her arms stand up.

The light behind him went dark and then returned with him gone, now across the street under a street lamp again at the base of station Z2.

Lisa blinked, unable to process what had just happened and still feeling the ghost of his touch around her slender ankle. He was watching her from across the street again, his arms folded in front of him, his mouth curled up in a smile.

She pulled herself to her feet and hurried down the street, watching her shadow flicker as behind her the lights blinked on and off.

The second – and last – time he had laid his hands on her it had been during a fight over her job. She remembered because he had thought she was spending too much time there to 'only be working the job.' The fight had again been a long one, lasting well into the evening. Plates had been thrown at walls and the neighbours had called the police – twice – something that, when

it happened in The City, you knew things were going bad.

The flesh on the back of his knuckles was already burnt and peeling. When she insisted for the fifth time that there was nothing happening at work and he put his hand through the drywall, it shot searing, electric spasms of pain up his arm — so white hot that he ground his teeth and popped a molar in the back. He turned away from the wall and brought the same fist against her, hitting her in the collarbone with the same hammer-fist motion he'd used to knock her dance partner unconscious on the night they'd met.

She'd fallen to the floor and had hated herself for falling to the floor. By the time she got up, he had stormed out. By the time he had come back, she had quickly packed a bag and was gone. She didn't know it, but he had destroyed the apartment they'd shared in his rage at her for leaving, even the oven and fridge. At 4am the police had been called again, and this time he'd been brought in for the night. When he'd come back the next afternoon, the landlord had pasted an eviction notice on their front door and changed the locks.

She'd known she had been pregnant for a week and a half, and at the time had made the decision to quietly remove it from their lives without his knowing. That night had shifted the plan: there had never been a time when it was ever going to be the three of them, but that night she knew that he was the one that had to be aborted. She got on a random bus out of town, chosen by asking a stranger to pick a number between one and ten, and had started her trek west.

"Crowley!" Lisa yelled as she entered the apartment, ducking her head out into the street behind her. She couldn't see him, but she knew he was there. He'd been there the entire way home, never more than a block away and always accompanied by those same flickering lights.

"Xander!"

Neither of them came rushing from their bedrooms or in from the living room.

She screamed an obscenity with a hoarse voice sick from exhaustion. As if on cue, the bulb in the kitchen began to flicker on and off.

She stared at it, unable to pull her eyes from the dancing, jolting husk of glass.

When it had been following her on the street it had been one thing, but somehow this was another. Its invasion into her homestead made it different: more real, somehow, than it had been. It wasn't some abstraction in a city chock full of abstractions; it was in her home and in her kitchen and there was nothing she could do about it.

She backed up, keeping her eyes on the arcing electricity in the bulb. It jumped from one prong of the bulb to the other in curving arcs, sometimes above and sometimes below, so quickly that it formed an almost shape. It was an eye staring down at her, like the eye of Sauron looking down at her from Mount Doom, but she wasn't wearing the ring. She hadn't worn his ring since her last day in New York, when she'd slipped it from her finger and thrown it -- not into boiling lava, but into the frigid waters of the Hudson.

She backed up until she was in the null space between the kitchen and the living room, nudging a chair with her hip as she backed up. Crowley's room was on the wall to her right, slowly coming into her peripheral vision, and Xander's was still out of view but on her left. Neither had a lock and both had bulbs in place in the ceiling, too high up for her to reach without aid.

Her pace hastened as much as she dared backing up, and she found her back against the door to their bathroom. She fumbled for the knob – unable to find it on her first try even though its placement was so familiar to her – staring at the light as the arc of its electricity grew.

The bright blue sparking lines grew outward, sparking down to the floor even though there was no point there to attract it.

Her hand found the knob and she twisted it, falling back through the bathroom and bringing herself up solid against the sink. She kicked the door shut and lunged forward against the vengeful protestations of her back muscles and locked it, then stood in her small bathroom, wringing her fingers through her hair.

"Hnnn," she said involuntarily, her nails scraping her scalp as she looked from one corner of the tiny room to the other.

The light above the sink started to fade, then returned brighter than it ever had been before.

"Dammit," she cursed. She reached for it, and the moment her fingers extended, a shock sparked from the bulb to her middle finger. She yelped and pulled back, watching as the light came in and out, flashing with the same pattern and pace as his horrid laughter always had.

The lock turned.

She backed up and tripped on the edge of the tub, falling back into its basin.

The brass doorknob began to shimmer and glow as it turned, finally letting the latch come loose and swinging open. He was there. Ryan Valler was in the one place she'd sworn he'd never be again: in her house and in her personal space. He was smiling that smile that in any other circumstance, on any other face, might have been boyish. On him it was sinister, a symptom of malcontent without consequence that was charming in youth but became ever more dangerous with age.

He looked at her, cowering in a tub that could barely

fit her in a room with no exits save the one he stood in front of, and his smile grew. "You never were the brightest bulb," he sneered, leaning in towards her.

She stared at him, unable to turn away from those electric blue eyes. Her breath had caught in her throat and lodged there like a stone.

He leaned forward, not yet touching her, both hands arched and ready, as if savouring the moment before contact.

"Not the brightest bulb?" she repeated under her breath. "You're one to talk."

She pushed the release for the faucet and freezing cold water shot out of the showerhead, cascading down instantly.

As soon as it hit him, the room erupted in bright blue and he screamed without opening his mouth, the sound of him filling the entire house. The bulb above the sink blew in a spectacular firework as Ryan pulled back, and she heard the other bulbs in the house do the same. Suddenly the entire house was dark, and he was the only thing made of light. He shone bright neon blue in jolting flashes, banishing the dark like a strobe light.

Caught in the strobe effect she didn't know or care the origin of, his face alight with blue and purple hues and the stench of sweat and burning dust, he looked like he had on the night they met, on the dance-floor of an underground club she should have known better than to go to.

"Get out!" she screamed at him, loud enough to be heard above the crackle of energy. "Get out of my life!"

His teeth began to glow black behind electric blue gums, and suddenly the resemblance to what he had been on that night, lifetimes ago, seemed like a gift. A chance to put to bed the wrong of that night, to see him for what he was and say no – not in my life, none of that. I will not have that in my life. She pushed forward into the neon and the spicy sweat just as she had that night entering the club, but instead of drawing into him, she pushed him away, laying both hands flat against his chest despite the sparks and the jolts that rang through her system, shoving him hard against the back of the shower.

His eyes burned bright – they always had – and his mouth moved but no sound came.

He had no voice.

"Out!" she yelled, so loud she closed her eyes.

Suddenly there was only darkness. For a time that was all there was, until finally the blue light of the moon and the orange glow of the city began to filter in through the window, outlining the still form of Ryan Valler on the floor of her bathroom.

"So there was this car there," Xander said, entering through his kitchen window and holding it open for Crowley to step through. "And I get in it and I start it and I yell at him, 'Reap the whirlwind'!"

"You didn't say that?" Crowley chuckled.

"I did. Unfortunately."

They stopped. Lisa was standing with her back leaned against the half wall that divided the kitchen from the living room, facing the door to the bathroom like a sentry.

The hair on Xander's arms stood on end and he noticed for the first time the stench of ozone in the air. "What's wrong?" he asked, stepping forward.

Lisa's frown deepened. She'd poured herself a coffee but had not drunk any, letting the steam waft up around her like a blanket. "Ryan's here," she said simply, nodding her head toward the bathroom door.

Xander turned, his eyes narrowing. Lisa wasn't sure if

it was her imagination in the dim dark of the apartment, but his pupils seemed to expand, as if to take in more of the meager light.

He stepped forward to the base of the door, took a deep breath, then pushed it open.

There was nothing in the bathroom but a pool of water and the stench of burnt ozone on the air. The window was open, and there were scuff marks along the wall leading up to it, making the situation clear.

The whole of Xander clenched as he turned back to Lisa. "He can't have gotten too far. I'll find him."

Lisa smiled slowly. "No... I think I made my point."

The Lakehouse

The memories of my childhood are viewed through a deep fog not easily penetrated.

I grew up in a small town near the easternmost tip of Newfoundland, in a place known for deep mists and heavy rain that hit with maniacal, unfettered fury.

The houses that were built near the sea were functional, though not made to last because they couldn't last -- not against the constant onslaught of the salt and the sea. They were saltbox houses, and were either kept in constant care or allowed to quickly deteriorate, like kidneys in the wake of rampant alcoholism.

It is a strange thing to watch a community crumble. The western mind is not adept at processing such things – we're used to buildings and monuments that last for generations, not ten years. We erect memorials to these lost homes in our minds, remembering every time we pass by a vacant lot or a skeleton of a foundation: "That's where Phanny Gilbert's son used to live."

The homes inland – the ones that lasted – held special reverence for me. They were like the cathedrals of my town, standing for generations even as the landscape changed around them, the Stonehenge of out-port life. Inland homes were where the upper class lived, and were the main source of envy for a young man who never had enough money for a cola from the school vending machine. The people who lived in the inland homes did not go to work in the fish plant at fourteen; they owned the fish plant at twenty-five. Inland homeowners existed in a special sort of limbo – nowhere near wealthy enough to matter anywhere outside the community, but so wealthy that their existence caused great shifts within the community.

From the time I was old enough to walk to school on my own, the crown jewel of those inland homes was The Lakehouse.

The Lakehouse was a building in the very centre of town, the sun around which everything else orbited. It was large and white with pale blue storm-shutters that were never replaced and always looked new. The Lakehouse was not just an inland home; it was protected on all sides by trees from the saltwater air that corroded everything it touched, remaining pristine and untouched in all the years I passed by it.

While the rest of the community crumbled and rotted, The Lakehouse remained strong and proud, towering above the sea-level shanties like a reaper as death came upon them, rotting the town from the inside out. I bought it in my thirtieth year, almost on a whim, for only five thousand dollars. Property values had plummeted in the years since my generation – the last generation to prosper there – had left for more urban developments.

In all the years I had walked past it and even all through the real estate process, it never once occurred to me to wonder why it was called The Lakehouse when it was nowhere near any lake, nor any other body of water in town.

I never met the realtor. The deal had been made online on lunch hours and after the nine-to-five grind of Town

Life had ended each day. When I arrived at The Lake-house, looking as tall and as sacred as it ever had, the key had been waiting for me under the front mat along with the deed, folded neatly into a zip-lock bag to keep out the moisture.

I had been in the market for a home for some time, but the market was not with me despite its sellers constantly claiming it was. The oil boom that had caused mortgage prices to skyrocket had ended, but realtors refused to lower the prices on their homes, not wanting to lose on their investment, so homes stayed on the market for years at a time with no-or-miniscule changes in price. It was a bubble that was soon to burst, but that didn't help me find a home now.

In my desperation I had expanded my search wider and wider, increasing the sphere surrounding St. John's for which I was willing to part with my hard-earned money, until finally the sphere had enveloped the town in which I'd grown up. I hadn't even realized it when it had happened... I had left in that time in youth when map reference was less important than relative space, and I hadn't noticed when the blue circle on the real estate website had devoured my tiny harbour.

The Lakehouse had appeared as available for purchase, the symbol for opulence and affluence from my youth, for only seven thousand dollars total, less than what I had saved for a down payment for a home in the city. As reckless as it may have been, my impulse led me to contact the realtor who wasted no time making me deals – he had had the home on the market for the better part of a decade with no offers.

The deal had been processed in less than a week. Any time my lawyer or I had an issue or concern, the realtor acquiesced by lowering the price immediately. By the time the deal closed, I had bought the building that in my youth had been the Tower of London and the Taj Mahal rolled up into one for a dollar less than five thousand dollars, cash. No mortgage, no down payment, no fuss, no muss. In seven days I had gone from immense frustration to a homeowner, and with the same amount of will as used to buy a pack of Skittles at the checkout counter at Sobeys.

My town had crumbled, a ghost of what it had been.

A black, tar-like moss had caked its way onto the side of every building that faced the sea. It looked the same consistency of thick black mold, toxic mold, and it stank like confervoid: the stench of rotten shellfish and salt that had a way of barrelling past all olfactory defenses and embedding itself between one's eyes for hours.

The houses closest to the sea looked like they were rotting from it, gaps in their structure giving way to the tattered remains of living rooms: couches and family photos and paintings still adorning the walls. The resettlement and destruction of my community had happened slowly over time, but people had left their belongings as though they had left on the run from some unforeseen natural disaster... or as if they thought they were coming back, and never did.

Despite that, The Lakehouse remained untouched.

The rest of the town seemed small, somehow, in the same way that returning to any place after a long absence did. Our minds distort the size of the things we see in our youth, but The Lakehouse was as large as ever, as though it had grown with me. It towered into the trees with twelve windows on the front end alone, and at least six on every other side.

There was no back door.

Inside the living room, like all the decaying living

rooms I had seen on my drive, was fully decorated in the dated style that was old when I was young, plastic coverings over it to make sure no human ever enjoyed the feeling of its surface. It occurred to me when I ran my hand over the embroidered knit flowers of it that, to my knowledge, no one had lived in The Lakehouse in my lifetime.

The kitchen was completely new. The realtor had tried to update it several times over the years of trying to sell, investing more and more until he realized it was a sunk cost in a declining area and stopped, too late. I spent thirty minutes looking over the appliances – most with the stickers still on them – and realized that I could likely sell it all and make my five thousand dollars back immediately.

The bedrooms – nine of them – smelled of musk, and the bathrooms had been recently cleaned. The wallpaper was miraculously intact, and one of the bedrooms sported racially insensitive designs that were put on the walls of boy's rooms years before I was born, cartoon blackface caricatures and original peoples depicted with exaggerated features and stereotypical dress. Racism in Newfoundland was an odd thing, permeating a culture which had little-to-no contact with the cultures they maligned. The blackface caricatures were endemic of this, looking not-quite-right when compared with the figures that appeared in the Censored Eleven or *Gone with the Wind*.

I made the choice very early on that, historical significance or not, those papers would be taken down and the rooms repainted.

There was no hall on the first floor, each of the eight rooms led into the next and one had to step through them all to reach the last. This was strange to me – not just as an architectural curiosity, but because I had pictured the interior of The Lakehouse so many times in my mind's eye, and it was nothing like that. The main foyer led into the living room, which gave way to the reading room (currently packed with more hardcover books than I could read in a lifetime), then the kitchen, the dining room, the pantry, the laundry, and finally the back room.

The back room was an oddity, taller than the rest of the rooms on the floor. It was where the breakers were, and I deduced quickly that it had been built as an addendum to retrofit electricity onto the home, the ceiling built high to hide the wires travelling up to provide power to the upper floor. The room was tall but thin, with only enough space to open the door. There were two windows that looked out upon the back yard and a storm door that had been boarded up with several pieces of two-by-four and plank board. The boards had been poorly secured in place, the nails sticking out a half inch from the board like rusted hooks, waiting to slice unexpected flesh during a power outage.

I looked out that back window at the trees that bled into the forest that eventually became the wilderness that surrounded my hometown for the first time since I was a boy, and was filled with equal parts nostalgia and dread as the branches moved among their deep shadows conspiratorially.

The loudness of the quiet was unsettling that night. It settled over you like a sheet of plastic, slowly suffocating you by the time you realized it. One got accustomed to the city – the noise quickly became white noise, the sirens and horns and yelling facing into the background of existence. Without it the silence became deafening and distracting, the ears constantly reaching out to find purchase on something, searching to discover what was wrong – where had everyone gone?

I went to bed early that night, and with all the lights

of The Lakehouse shut off, my ears finally picked up the soft, rhythmic sounds of the water, and they drifted me off to sleep.

I might have left well enough alone at that, if I'd known what would happen next.

It was on the third night, just as I was drifting off to sleep to the sound of the waves that had lulled me to sleep as a child, that it occurred to me suddenly and I sat up straight in bed: we were too far inland to hear the waves.

I told myself I was wrong, that reality was currently proving me wrong, as I continued to hear the soft crashing of calm water over and over again... that the sound would go further than it had in my youth because there were less people and devices to drown it out... But somehow I knew I was wrong; in that second of realization I knew.

I laid awake until three am and then went downstairs, through the reading room and the living room and the foyer, all the while hearing the crashing of the waves, until I stepped out onto my front stoop... where there was nothing. Nothing but the soft rustle of the evergreen trees, whose branches made shifting motions despite there being no wind, sending me back inside with gooseflesh on my arms.

The moment I was back inside I heard the waves again.

I spent almost an hour going from room to room, convinced there was some device making the sound: a Bluetooth speaker or some such thing, programmed to make soothing night time sounds that would lull the buyer into a false sense of calm, installed by the realtor in desperation. I found no such device, but the sound got louder when I went from the living room to the reading room, louder again when I went into the kitchen, the dining room, the pantry, the laundry, and was almost deafening when I entered the small back room.

The sound, I realized, was coming from beyond the boarded door.

When morning light came, the sound stopped.

I walked around my lakehouse to the backend, just as I had on my first day there, and confirmed there was no door on the backside. I went back in through the front door, through the foyer and living room, reading room, kitchen, dining room, pantry, laundry, and into the back room. I looked out the windows on either side of the barred door and saw my backyard, where I had been standing moments before.

I went to my car and got my crowbar.

I came back and pressed the hook of the bar into the wedge of space between the two-by-four and the door, sunk it in as far as it would go, and then pushed with all the leverage I could muster.

It came so easily I fell on my feet. It came as though it had *wanted* to come, as though I were not so much pulling it free as I was giving it permission to do what it had been anxiously waiting to do for eons. The board came loose not at the ends, but where the bar had been wedged, snapping in half with even my minimal force and falling to the floor.

The board cracked again when it hit the tiled floor, separating into two pieces. The back of it was covered in a thick, mossy blackness that looked very much like the black moss that had been around the decaying remains of the homes near the sea. It slithered and seemed to move in the uneven light of the back room, like snakeskin. The inside of the board had been corrupted as well and it oozed out of it with the consistency of Jell-O pudding, slowly spreading and forming a puddle at my feet.

The place where the board had been nailed to the wall hung limply now, each edge dribbling thick black ooze down the doorframe, tainting their white with streaks of black.

The second and third boards came just the same, and the fourth and final was so full of rot that it splashed into my eyes and mouth when I took my crowbar to it. I screamed and cursed when it happened and made my way to the washroom. For a moment when the tap was running, I would have sworn it was running the same blackness, but when I dried my eyes and looked again it was clear well-water, straight from my own pump.

By the time I made it back down to the back room, the liquid black rot covered the floor of back room fully three feet around the door. I avoided stepping in it as best I could, reached out, and against all sense, I opened the door.

The door opened onto a calm lake, roughly half a kilometer across and shaped like a kidney. There was a small stone beach all the way around it, and then thick, dense forest that the eye could not penetrate. The forest wasn't made of evergreen trees though; the trees had palm leaves. The sky was a bright clear blue even though I saw no sun in it, and the water on the lake matched it in kind: so calm that from the doorway I could see past the surface to the stone below in some areas around the shore.

There was a small island in the centre of the lake, no larger than what could allow a man to sit, made of nothing but stone.

I stared at this sight out my back door for quite some time, before I leaned back and looked through one window, then the other, seeing my backyard. I closed the door and walked around to the backyard of my lakehouse and found nothing but grass, *dry* grass at that. I got an orange pylon from my trunk and placed it in the center of the yard, directly in front of the area between the two windows, and walked back through the foyer and living room, reading room, kitchen, dining room, pantry, laundry, and into the back room. I craned my head through both windows and saw the pylon there, then opened the door and saw no sign on of it, only the lake.

There was a back stoop and stairs that led from my door to the beachside, in the exact style and color as my front deck. I swallowed, and despite all reasonable expectation of sanity, I stepped through the impossible door in my back room out into the lakeside.

The back of my house looked the same, although the trees grew tight to it. The palm leaf trees were not palm trees, but tall trees with wide trucks that sprouted a fresh crop of palm leaves every few feet of its shape. They grew so dense as to be a natural fence surrounding my home, a wall blocking me from venturing around to the front and seeing what was different there. Would my car be there if I could have circled around, or would something different have been in its place? If I had moved my car, would the thing have moved too? I have no way of knowing.

A thin layer of the black slime that covered my childhood home was spread over the back of this version of my lakehouse, still thin enough as to be translucent. It shifted and moved in the sunless sunlight, as though it were wriggling its way further up the architecture of the house over time.

The windows of my upper floor were boarded shut with plywood, a soft red light emanating from around their cracks. It was not the light of a fire; it was the light of neon, of the signs that buzzed at night in the city that would have lulled me to sleep and avoided this entire mess had they really been there.

I walked around the lake slowly, taking in the stillness of the air. There was a quiet and a calm that was familiar, but that I had trouble pinning down until I was about halfway across the circumference of it, crawling over a particularly large rock to avoid touching the water. I don't know why, but I knew I shouldn't touch the lake water... It was mostly clear, but there was a deep black cloud in its centre around the island that discouraged experimentation.

It was when sliding down the opposite side of that stone that the feeling was pinpointed in me: it was the calm of home. The calm that had been eroded away by years of neglect and decay and tumor was here, sitting placidly in the air of the lake, waiting to be breathed in. And I did breathe it in; I closed my eyes and took several deep, full breaths, filling my lungs in through my nose and out through my mouth and felt calmer than I had in years.

There was a rustle in the palm leaves behind me and I turned, too quickly on the rocks. My foot twisted and I fell onto my thirty-year-old back onto the uneven stone and felt bruises form that would cause me trouble for some time, my elbow penetrating the surface of the lake.

I removed myself from it quickly, ignoring the fierce pain of the movement. When I looked, the black cloud seemed to have moved, stretching from its place around the island for me. I backed up, kicking rocks as I went, until I was away from the water's edge and closer to the upper edge of the beach, where the line of palms started.

There was a slithering hiss over my shoulder, and when I looked behind me there were a pair of pallid yellow eyes staring back at me from between two palm fawns. I screamed and it came out of the wood after me, planting its – his – feet down on the stone. He was small

– toddler sized – with bright yellow eyes and no mouth or ears. He was the shape of a toddler's shadow, but completely black, dripping the same swirling, living ooze that was trying to make its way over my lakehouse.

It was nude, that was the only way I knew its gender, and despite its humanoid shape and size I knew instinctively that it was full-grown.

It hissed at me through its eyes, the pupils shaking and shimmering with the sound like a rattlesnake's tail, and I turned and ran from it – I ran from a thing the size of a toddler, because I knew in my heart that if it touched me, it would morph its way over me and eat me like rot ate meat.

I ran over the stone I had slid down and along the uneven stone of the beach back toward my lakehouse, panting from fear and exhaustion. I looked over my shoulder three times to see if I was being followed: each time the swirling black mass boy was still there, waiting atop the stone... and each time there were more of him, coming out of the patchwork of trees as though they were the living shadows, standing at the water's edge and glaring at me with hissing eyes. Every time I looked, that black circle around the island was stretched toward me, an optical illusion that made it always aim at your eye.

My feet hit the stairs the led up to my back door and I looked up and froze in my tracks, and the color must have drained from my face.

There was a shadow of a man standing in the window of my back room, staring out at me and watching as I completed my frantic run towards my house. He stood mannequin-still for a moment, a paper silhouette on my window, before stepping forward into the light of the sunless sky.

It was me, my face ashen gray and my hair matted black from water, dark rings around my eyes... but it was me all the same. We stared at each other, the panting me and the darkened me, each on our own side of reality.

I turned away from the window and shut the door on the lake, locking it out once again, as the me on the stairs started to scream. I heard him banging for some time, and then I heard him sobbing, but these sounds grew more and more dull the more boards I nailed over the frame. Eventually they were far enough away that one could be forgiven for mistaking them for the white noise of waves on a distant shore.

I packed up my car and drove back into the city with my crowbar resting on my passenger seat, just in case. At three different stops along the highway I stopped and cleaned the blackness out from beneath my eyelids and from underneath my fingernails and gums. I kept seeing it build there in my rear-view mirror, catching my attention.

I showered when I got back to my apartment and the blackness went down the drain in congealed wet clumps. No matter how much of it came loose, there always seemed to be more of it.

I wondered, as the sirens and horns and sounds of the city lulled me to sleep that night, if it ever turned night on the lake. I wondered if those hissing toddlers ever made it beyond that stone border... and I wondered how thirsty I would have to get before I dipped my hand and face into that clear water with the shadow in its center, and risked taking a refreshing gulp from the lake itself.

House for sale. Spacious, nine bedrooms, three baths. Secluded location, within driving distance to St. John's. Perfect for cabin. All new kitchen appliances. $1000 OBO, as-is, with all faults.

Lynn Reicker

A native of New Brunswick who currently resides in Nova Scotia, Reicker makes her publishing debut here in *Chillers from the Rock* with her chilling tale: *Extinction.*

Extinction

Eotriceratops. This ancient relative of the dinosaur, Triceratops, was recently unearthed in Alberta. I've always loved dinosaurs. I hadn't heard about this one, but my husband did when he went out west for a six-month job as a welder on a huge new construction project. After three months, he came back for a two-week visit and brought this little creation with him: he had made me a gleaming metal bookmark of the head of an Eotriceratops! The three horns had little snappy hinges on them so that they all folded over to grasp onto a book page.

I christened the bookmark Trippy. I don't know why, but I felt I had to call it something if it was going to share my bedroom – I always read in bed – with all the other named dinosaurs adorning the room. There were stuffed ones, plastic ones, clay, metal, rocks and driftwood that resembled them, and even paintings I'd attempted on the walls.

My husband was sympathetic to my dinosaur fetish, even encouraging it at times. Sometimes we would play 'dinosaur,' where one of us would be a big meat eater like a Tyrannosaurus Rex chasing a smaller, more docile herbivore such as a Brachiosaurus. And when the smaller beast was caught, the bigger one would devour it. Ah! All that gnawing and growling and wrestling. Very exciting!

While my husband was away, I fell into my own routine. I worked from 7-3, Monday to Friday at a diner, covering the breakfast and lunch rushes. I'd usually go to bed at 10, be up at 6. Tuesday nights, I'd often take in an early movie with my friend, Jordan, and on Fridays, it was girl's night out for a whole bunch of us, including Jordan and myself. Most of the rest of the time, I was on my own, except for occasional weekend outings with friends. I got quite used to the solitude and even enjoyed it.

At the six–month mark, the construction project in Alberta was complete. My husband made the decision to come back east and try to find work here. He had been given some good leads by other Maritime co-workers out there.

It was wonderful to see him again. I could hardly keep my hands off him when I picked him up at the airport. That first night we made love, sweetly and tenderly. My heart nearly burst with emotion. Afterwards, I laid my head on his chest as he quickly fell asleep. That's when it started.

When he had come home the first time, after three months, those seven days had been heavenly. I was so happy to have him home that nothing else mattered. But now, after six months of sleeping alone, the sudden roar of snoring under my ear was shocking. I rolled off his chest and on to my side, repressed memories resurfacing – sleepless nights, and going to work tired and cranky. I had missed my man while he was away, but I was always well rested.

Oh well, I reasoned, he's probably really exhausted from the trip home. It'll be better after tonight.

The next night it was worse. The politeness of the first night left me. I pushed his back and shook his shoulders. At last, he awoke and I asked if he could turn onto his side, that maybe that would stop his snoring. He turned, and was silent – for about ninety seconds. I tried reading, setting Trippy on the headboard cabinet while I flipped through the pages, but the volume of his snores kept distracting me. I tried for another twenty minutes, then replaced Trippy in his bed between the pages, grabbed my pillow, fiercely snatched the top blanket off the bed, and went to try and sleep on the couch.

In the morning, my husband came out and shook me awake. "What are you doing out here?" He slipped his arms around me. "I was cold without you, baby." He held me and nuzzled my neck for a moment before letting me go.

"I gotta have a shower. I think I've got another job lined up, locally this time." He smiled, thinking that would make me happy. "But I gotta meet the guy at nine. I better hustle." A peck on my cheek, then he headed for the bathroom.

As my bladder awakened and began to protest that he had gotten in the bathroom first, my mind clued in that he hadn't waited for my response to his question of what I was doing in the living room.

The days wore on.

My husband got the new job he was hoping for, working for a local sheet metal company in the business park, ten minutes from our home. My man would come home, we'd have supper, watch TV or play cards, then he'd go to bed around 9:30. I'd usually stay up till 10:30 or 11:00. I hoped if I was tired enough, I might fall right asleep.

The alarm would go off every morning at 6:00. My husband didn't start work till 7:30, but he always liked to be there early, having stopped for breakfast at Tim Horton's along the way. That meant early morning competition for the shower and other bathroom rituals. I started showering the night before so that I'd have a little more time in the mornings. Still, I was arriving increasingly close to my start time and becoming more tired and cranky every day. I was starting to forget customer orders, messing up on who got what, and was just being all-round crabby, followed by apologetic, with nearly everyone.

When the weekend came, I begged off going to the Saturday market so I could sleep in a bit, and Sunday afternoon I had a two-hour nap. I could tell my husband wasn't pleased. He wanted us to do things together, go out and have fun. I wanted that too, but all I could think about was getting some extra sleep.

The new workweek began. That Monday, my husband didn't come straight home after work like he had the week before. Instead, he stopped off at a bar for a few drinks with "the boys." Supper was cold by the time he got there, so I asked him to call me if he was going to be late again.

The next night he came straight home. We had a great evening together. We even made love before falling asleep. Yes, falling asleep! For some reason, there was no snoring that night, although he teased me next morning that I had snored and kept him awake!

Wednesday night, he was again a no show at suppertime. He came rolling in around seven o'clock. Apparently, it had been someone's birthday.

That night, back to the snoring and the sleeping on the couch.

Thursday night, he showed up at 8:30. I refused to even talk to him. I went in the bedroom and slammed the door. About 9:30, he came in anyway and got into bed. At 10:30, I kicked and punched at him to try and wake him, but he just wouldn't wake up.

It wasn't fair. Why should I always be the one to leave, to sleep on the couch, to never get any sleep? I screamed – a scream of anger and frustration. I felt like a wild animal; I was full of hatred for this human intruding in my territory. I grabbed my book and swatted his head with it. Still no reaction, but Trippy came detached with force of the blow and ricocheted with a clatter off the headboard.

I picked up the thin, metal dinosaur. It felt like more of a friend and caring being at that moment than did my snoring, stinking, drunken, selfish husband. I placed Trippy against my cheek, his coolness calming me a bit. I extended his horns and gently caressed my forehead. As I did so, a thought began to form in my brain. My pulse slowed as a steely determination took hold of me. I held Trippy close to my mouth and whispered, "Thank you." Then I grabbed my little beast in my hand and thrust my arm downward with all my might.

I let go. The three prongs of the Eotriceratops were buried as deep as they could go into the neck of my husband, blood spurting everywhere. His eyes sprang open, he gasped and spluttered. He felt at his neck, stared at me in shock, and then, miracle of miracles, was silent at last. As blood continued to trickle down to soak the blankets, I rolled onto my side, curled into the fetal position, and had a great night's sleep.

In the morning, once I was well rested, showered, dressed, and filled with a hearty breakfast, I called the police. They took us both away – in separate vehicles – to different places. I was quickly sent for a psychiatric evaluation and at my trial was found not guilty of murder by reason of insanity.

Eventually, I ended up here. The rooms are small but clean, someone else cooks the meals, and they're always at the same time every day. We even have arts and crafts. I've drawn and coloured many pictures of Trippy and have them posted around my room. Before the lights go out for the night, I always say a special prayer of thanks to my three-horned friend, then close my eyes and sleep like the dead.

Maggie Carroll

Carroll is a St. John's native with over a half-dozen credits to her name, including "When They Turn On You," in *Demonic Visions*; "Spring Heeled Jack" in *Demonic Visions 2*, and, "Falling Like Flies" in *Demonic Visions 4*.

In 2013 she received Honorable Mention for the Writers of the Future award.

Falling Like Flies

3:34pm.

Chelsea eyed the clock over the door, blew her bangs out of her eyes, and returned her attention to her work. Sick butterflies crawled in her gut as she bent her head to the microscope. She couldn't remember what slide she'd loaded, but it didn't matter. She couldn't concentrate on it anyway.

Her gaze went up again. 3:37.

She squeezed her eyes shut. *Get it together.*

Other doctors, her co-workers, moved around the lab. Chelsea was hyperaware of each and every single one of them, tensed and primed for one of them to notice something was wrong. Her eyes flicked to her lab coat, slung carelessly over her desk chair, but she dragged them away. *Don't draw attention; don't draw attention.* It was a steady mantra in her head. The back of her neck was cold. Her face was hot. Her hands were clammy.

Don't draw any attention...

At 3:52, she couldn't stand it anymore, and made a beeline for the bathroom. She huddled in one of the stalls, hunched over her knees, and did her level best to keep her lunch down. She forced herself to draw deep, steady breaths through her nose. They hissed out between her teeth. Cold sweat soaked her hair, trickling uncomfortably to pool on her collarbone.

Oh god, was she really going to do this?

She raised her head, stared blankly at the stall door for a moment, then jerked her gaze down to the lab coat at her feet. She reached a shaky hand down and fumbled in the pocket for the vial she'd snuck out of cold storage.

It was an innocuous little thing, a glass vial in a hard plastic tube. The liquid in the vial was clear, and looked as harmless as water. She popped the lid off the plastic tube and carefully slid the vial into her palm, twisting it with her fingers until she could see the white label. On it was a CDCP logo, and a string of letters and numbers and dashes. The important ones were at the end.

H1N1/1918

It wasn't too late. She could go back to cold storage, sneak it in just like she had sneaked it out, forget the whole thing, call it all off. But staring at the little glass vial, one crack, one chip, one scratch away from the deadliest flu in history, Chelsea knew it was already far too late.

She took one deep, centering breath, slid the vial back into the plastic case, and stuffed it into her bra. It fit under the curve of her left breast, nestled against the underwire. Random pocket and bag searches were common at security checkpoints, but she'd never heard of security groping a woman's breast. It was the safest place.

She could do this. She *had* to do this.

She took one final breath and let it out slowly. She straightened her hair, smoothed out her skirt, flushed the toilet for good measure, and left the ladies' room.

The back of the limousine was much warmer than the parking lot had been. Chelsea sat back against the uphol-stery, hands on her knees, doing her level best to present a cool, collected front to the man sitting across from her. She knew him only as Mr. Chin, a bland-face Asian of indeterminate ancestry, her first and only contact with the consortium that promised her the world.

"Were there any troubles?" His English was very good, with no trace accent Chelsea could detect.

She shook her head, and tucked falling locks of hair behind her ears. "No," she said, and cleared her throat. Her voice sounded strangled. "They checked my bags and pockets, but I had it hidden elsewhere." Absently, she rubbed the underside of her breast with the back of a hand.

Mr. Chin's lips curved faintly. "Clever girl. You have it with you?"

"Yes." She reached into the pocket of her skirt and pulled the plastic case out. Or, at least she tried to; her hand, clenched around the tube, refused to come out of her pocket. The absurdity of it all struck her. She was sitting in the back of a black limo with a man she didn't know, preparing to hand over a deadly virus with no idea of where it would end up or what it would be used for.

Her breath caught in her lungs, black spots swam before her eyes. Hysteria bubbled up in her throat until she thought she might start laughing uncontrollably. *What am I doing? This isn't me!*

Mr. Chin watched her with his dark, dead eyes. His face didn't shift once. "Ms. Bourne, if you are entertaining second thoughts, I might remind you of what is at stake."

The first laugh died in a hiccup. Yes, the stakes were very high. She closed her eyes and pulled her hand out of her pocket. Eerie calm settled over her, the fatalism of knowing she could only do what she was going to do. It was too late to do anything else.

"It's a reconstituted virus," she heard herself saying, clinical tones like she was presenting a lecture. "As I told you before, the original virus went extinct shortly after the end of the 1918 epidemic. This is an accurate re-creation, based on tissue samples and historical research."

"I assume it was tested?"

She nodded. "The macaques exhibited the classic symptoms. Their autopsies revealed they died from cytokine storms, massive overreactions from the immune system. This tracks with what we know. It's as close as we can make it."

"And this particular vial?"

Chelsea swallowed, feeling that chill in her bones again. "Is live."

"Very good." Mr. Chin held out his hand. Chelsea stared at it for a moment, then put the vial in his fingers. He whisked it away, snapping open the briefcase beside him. He carefully slotted the vial into a slot carved in the foam interior, and closed the case. There was a hiss of gas, and a digital readout lit up. Temperature control. As he worked, he spoke. "Under your seat, you will find a briefcase. It contains your payment. Two million dollars, the bills both unmarked and non-sequential. This concludes our business, Ms. Bourne. Have a nice day."

Chelsea knew a dismissal when she heard one, but that was fine with her. She wanted out of this limo. She reached awkwardly between her legs, feeling around with her fingers before finding the handle of a briefcase. She pulled it out, opened the door and stepped back out of the vehicle.

She hurried back to her car, heels clicking against the pavement. Behind her, she heard the limousine engine turn over, and the sound of wheels crunching across rock-strewn asphalt. She didn't look back. If she looked back, the enormity of what she had done might hit her, and there would be no recovery from that.

Chelsea drummed her fingers on her knee, her leg bouncing nervously as she waited for the hospital administrator to return. She was so tired of this office, tired of visiting it, tired of fighting in it, tired of the bland peach walls and lacy yellow curtains. But this was the last time she would have to come here, the last time she would have this conversation. That alone might have been worth—

No, can't think about it. Just forget it happened.

The door opened, and she turned in her chair. She was quick enough to catch the consternation and impatience on Hugo Reyes' face as he recognized her. His expression quickly smoothed out to a smile as bland as the walls, and he shut the door. "Chelsea," he said, and his tone was just condescending enough to make her want to scream. "What can I do for you?"

She watched him walk around the desk. Her eyes felt hot and dry, burning in her head. "I'm here to talk about the treatment plan," she said, and twisted her fingers together in her lap.

Mr. Reyes' smile faltered, and he sighed. "Chelsea, we've been over this. The HMO coverage has run out, and—"

"I can pay." Her hands were so tight, she might never get circulation back.

He hesitated, then shook his head. "It's an expensive procedure. You're a doctor, you know what's involved."

"I can pay," she insisted, leaning forward. She was so close, *so close...*

Reyes sat back in her chair, swiped a hand down his face. "Okay," he said slowly. "How much can you pay up front?"

Chelsea reached into her pocket, and pulled out the brand new chequebook the bank had issued her that morning. Euphoria and triumph surged and pulled at her body. "All of it," she said, and started writing. "Start the treatment. Right now."

Chelsea stuck her head in the room, mindful of the sleeping woman tucked in on the bed. Nancy, the regular nurse, bustled quietly around the room, clearing away dinner trays and checking the readouts on the machines near the head of the bed. She paused, then glanced over her shoulder and offered Chelsea a genuine, welcoming smile.

Chelsea waited at the door for Nancy to finish what she was doing, then stepped into the hall outside with her. "Hey," Chelsea said, glancing through the door. She could barely believe how much color and life the woman had regained. "How's she doing?"

Nancy's smile brightened. "Really well," she said. "She's responding beautifully to the protocols. She's regaining cognitive function, motor control. There are more good days than bad lately. She's even reading again. *Wuthering Heights.* She says it was your favourite."

It was the best news Chelsea had all week, and she had to swallow past the lump in her throat, the tears in her eyes. "It is," she said. "We read it when I was home sick from school. Is she plateauing at all?"

"Some," Nancy admitted, "but that's expected. Chances are, she's got a lot more healing to do before she hits the final one." Nancy put a hand on Chelsea's shoulder, rubbing her bicep comfortingly. "The treatment is working. I prayed for you, asked Jesus to send you a miracle. I guess

He was listening."

Chelsea had a flash of Mr. Chin's face, half-shadowed in the back of that limo, and a cold chill shuddered through her. Jesus never had eyes so dead. She forced a smile. "Yeah," she said, with cheer she no longer felt, "I guess He did."

Chelsea stared at the internal memo in her email, and her blood turned to ice. All week, she had been overhearing snippets of conversations, concerns about some new outbreak in India and Asia. She hadn't paid it much mind; outbreaks happened all the time. It was a conversational hazard of working where she worked.

But this...

Chelsea couldn't process it. Her brain refused to see more than two-word phrases at a time: *overseas travel, China and Thailand, fever, myalgia, sore throat, respiratory distress, morbidity, mortality, cytokine storm, rapid spread, Spanish flu, quarantine protocols, masks and gloves, avoid infected...*

Oh god. Oh *god*. Bile swirled in her gut and stars swirled in her head. Her vision went grey, then white, then spotty. She pulled the wastepaper basket to her in time to vomit her lunch into it.

She straightened up, dragging the back of her hand over her mouth, the cold, shaky post-puke sensation trembling through her. Clammy sweat beaded her forehead, and her stomach lurched again. She scrabbled for a bottle of water, and lost the cap somewhere under her desk as it bounced away from her leaden fingers. She drained it in one continuous swallow, and sagged back in her chair.

The entire office stared at her. Some were reaching for masks, faces full with fear and worry. On the monitors around her, the same memo was open. Her eyes burned with tears, but she gulped them back and reached for a mask in the emergency stash in her drawer.

When it was secured behind her ears, shaped against her nose, she reached for her purse and stood up. "I'm going home," she said faintly, and her co-workers nodded encouragement.

The facility was in lockdown. Chelsea had been trying for three days to get in, but staff was adamant. Quarantine protocols were enacted; there were no visitors allowed in or out. Chelsea didn't stop trying, though. The news was full of outbreak stories, talking heads shrieking that the end of the world was here. Ninety percent morbidity.Forty-three percent mortality.

The young and old and already sick were falling like flies.

The church down the street from Chelsea's townhouse was filled past capacity every day. The faithful prayed for a miracle, for God and Jesus and the Virgin Mary to save them from the devil. Chelsea never went in. She knew that God wouldn't save her, because the face of the devil was the one she saw in her mirror.

"Please," Chelsea begged, near tears and clinging to the doorknob. "Please just let me see her."

Nancy's forehead creased above the mask, and her eyes shimmered with sudden tears. "I'm so sorry, Chelsea." The bottom dropped out of Chelsea's stomach. "Your mother passed yesterday. This flu was just too much for her compromised system."

Chelsea stepped to the edge of the building and looked down, tucking her wind-whipped hair back behind her ears. The pavement was eighteen stories straight down, peppered with bodies. Plague victims or suicides, Chelsea didn't know. The world was filling up with the corpses of both, stinking in the streets, piled in parking lots.

Every one of them was her fault.

It wasn't Chin, or the shadowy group he represented. They had manipulated and tricked her, played off her desperate need to pay for her mother's treatment, but it wasn't their fault. She had let them. She had made the choice, and these were the consequences.

She had thought about pills, thought about slipping away from life wrapped in slumber, but she didn't deserve peace. She deserved screaming terror and violent pain.

She spread her arms, tilted her head back. Slid her foot forward. Open air beneath. Leaned forward. Gravity tugged at her… tipping over, falling to death.

A hand closed on her wrist and jerked her back. Confused, Chelsea stared at it without comprehension. It was enormous, wrapping halfway down to her elbow. "No," she breathed, and the hand lifted her, twisted her snapping and snarling, and she howled and clawed at it. "Let me die! Let me die!"

"You will not," said the man holding her. He dropped her into the gravel on the rooftop, and she gaped up at him. He was massive, scarred, scary and looming. His two companions were smaller, but no less terrifying. As Chelsea stared at them, stark realization sank in. It was impossible, insane, but she knew it in the marrow of her bones it was true.

"Let me die," she whispered, broken.

"I will never reap you," said Death. He was bland, with the kind of hair and bottle-lens glasses that made Chelsea think of the 1940s. "You're not done."

"It's your fault we're short a Rider," Famine said. Chelsea couldn't look at her. Nobody could be that skeletal and still live. Her voice was incongruously rich, with the light lilt of Ireland.

"My fault?" Chelsea squeaked.

"Your virus killed Pestilence," War rumbled.

They stepped apart, showing Chelsea the other side of the rooftop.

"You will take his place," Death said, with finality.

Chelsea couldn't think, couldn't move. Her stomach churned, her mind whirled. Her eyes locked onto the horses. Red, brown, pale. The white one, the one buzzing with flies, turned an eye to watch her, and Chelsea fell to her knees.

Come, it said in a voice like thunder. The first fly landed on her cheek.

Matthew Daniels

Matthew hails from the mythical village of St. John's, where he gave up his youth in exchange for a quiver of ghost arrows. They include short stories written in local collections such as *Paragon* and *Sci-Fi from the Rock*. He has since misplaced them, but he has really nice slippers. It is rumored that his beard sometimes volunteers with Sandbox Gaming. Long story.

Matthew is one of only a handful of authors to have his work featured in each of the three modern *From the Rock* anthologies.

Grow Gold Together

Crone learned that day that everything can have teeth.

The grass was tall; they could not see what their feet might find with each step.

The lion watched.

They had to turn their neck slowly to see the lion. Crone's lips trembled. There was spittle, white and clinging to their dimples like hoarfrost. Their hands, spotted and slightly curled even when Crone did their best to straighten them, shook with the frailty of their bones.

"Leave me!" they implored.

A mistake.

The lion dashed forward and back-pawed the aged form. Crone did not roll through the grasses so much as rail against downwardness. When spinning and hurtling, everything was downward and so you could fall in any direction. Briefly, the sky was a vast blue maw. Its clouds: teeth.

Desperately Crone crawled. By some kindness of the ancestors, they had landed in a thinned area of the turf. They could crawl without disturbing the grasses. Crone had been told about lions, had learned about them with the tribe. It was the lionesses that hunted.

When lions struck, they looked for nothing more than

rule. Or for the simple pleasure of the strike.

Crone crawled. The grasses did not move much. There was little wind. Their heartbeat was in their skull, and hid the animal's movements from them. It hurt to move. Their ribs echoed where the paw had struck. Their arms, ebony caked in dirt and sweaty sunlight, slowly raked the earth beneath them.

They wet themselves. It was summer and barren of movement. Crone hadn't known the lion was there until they'd blundered upon it. They left the urine behind, and only then registered that their meagre loincloth had been parted from them. Never before had they been this far away from the lake, but those were tribal days. Both days and years ago, probably.

They made their mind wander. A choice -- to forget the lion.

They couldn't hear the lion.

They couldn't see it.

Mostly their nostrils were filled with the notes of grass. Ahead was a new smell. A different kind of lake. Thin, moving in one direction. No wind to stir it. They'd never seen such a lake. Touch they tried to ignore. Their skin told them nothing they wanted to know.

When they could no longer smell their own urine behind them, when the question of the lion needed answering, they stopped. They struggled to make no sound, to breathe shallowly, so as not to be heard by predatory ears. Swallowing air and terror, Crone waited a moment, then lifted themselves to look up over the top of the grasses beside them.

They stared into the eyes of the lion.

Nearly nose-to-nose, elder looked at beast and beast at elder. In its savage gaze, Crone saw neither pupil nor sclera. Not even the lids, as the Lion did not blink.

With a shudder, Crone returned to the present. They were hugging their knees to their chest.

"Again?" Ashmother demanded.

Crone's eyes were wide. They looked around at the others, who ran the gamut from barely five to their own geriatric form. They glanced at every hillock, shrub, or whistle of the wind. "Eyes…" they croaked.

She was gathering everyone's pouches, mostly made of the bladders of various animals. Before her was a pile of seeds. Black with a stripe through, like the eyes. They'd all seen the eyes. But Ashmother huffed with frustration as her hands, scarred on the backs as from a great burning, worked their way through the numbers and the bags. Dividing seeds.

"Sharp killed it, Crone." She didn't look at them as she spoke.

Sharp was tall, even for a fifteen-year-old, and his only flesh was muscle. Some said he was less born than carved out of something. He held a spear tipped at each end with either a bone or stone blade. Around his waist was a string tying the animal skin he wore and holding additional tips and lengths of string, should he need to secure a lost tip.

"It's true. I did not miss." He shook his weapon as he spoke.

"Lion dies not. It seeks me," Crone whispered.

"Did we not all say that we've seen the Monster?" interjected Leaper.

"Which one?" Crone asked. They shifted, head facing left almost without transition. "It's here! In the corner of my eye, past those bushes!" Jabbing the air with a finger, they looked around at the others, desperate and trembling.

Leaper, who'd been facing that direction, shook his head. He laid a hand on Crone's shoulder. "It's all right.

Listen, I saw the Monster in the sunrise."

"I miss the sunrise," Sniff remarked. She heard everyone's gazes. She heard them in the stopping of hands, the silence of the seeds, the click and clack of shifting spearheads, the twisting in the dirt. "I smell no lion, I hear no lion. It's gone, Crone. Sharp killed it. For the Monster there is no spear."

"We've already seen three lionesses and the Lion since we all met," Crone retorted with a hard swallow. Sniff heard them stand. She heard the seeds dancing again as Ashmother returned to the sifting.

"I saw it with the rising of the sun," Leaper continued. "I looked and the night was broken. A sliver, a sideways eye, yellow in the darkness. Staring as I lay with woman before the gatherers stirred. It stared and I stared, and I knew because I knew. So I followed the gatherers that day, and much was strange. But I found it; I found the one seed. And so every morning, I stared for the sunrise, and the Monster showed me."

"I tell you…" Crone began.

Sniff had sidled up to Crone. She was the least old of the five gathered there. Much too young for hair in new places. Old enough to know that it means something for man or woman to lay with one or the other. Old enough to have questions, but not old enough to ask them. She was clicking rocks together. Crone took her hand when she reached out. In her hand were stones, little more than pebbles. Sometimes they clacked a little while the pair shifted.

Sniff's eyes looked alive, but they were empty.

"I learned to jump," Leaper continued. "Over gaps thin but deep, over places people feared to go. I built a raft to leave my island. Leaping, they say, over the water. I had only one seed."

Sniff turned her head in Leaper's direction. She stopped Crone from bolting by grabbing their arm and pulling them to her. They sat with her, quivering and silent. "I wondered," she said to Leaper.

He looked at her. There was a pause, and he flushed when he realized she couldn't tell he was looking at her. Hoping no one else noticed, he said a little too quickly: "How I found you?"

"How you found them," she corrected, tilting her head at Crone whose hand was still in hers. "Especially just in time. Do you not understand? They stared death in the eyes."

"Is the Monster not death?" Leaper asked.

"No," Ashmother spoke up. She cinched closed one of the bags, and held it toward Sharp. He was pacing to and fro, ever alert. In case Crone was right. "No," she said again. "We do as Dragon asks. I won't obey death. Not after the fire."

Crone frowned. Briefly, they were distracted from their thoughts of the Lion. "What is Dragon? This is a new word."

Ashmother stopped with the seeds. She scratched the back of a hand. Nothing of her came off, and she did not know the words to lament that. "There are lots of monsters. But this, this thing that gives us seeds and teaches us to trade. It is something else, and needs its own name."

"Have any of us been near it? To touch it or smell it or know its… its wind?" Leaper struggled the most with this. He did not like a thing he could not pounce upon, and had no word for presence. Not a presence like what this Dragon had. It was like wind. Invisible, untouchable, but it could push you at its whims.

Crone was lost again. They turned about, shoulder to shoulder, and Sniff did all she could to soothe them and keep them in the group. Ashmother watched them, except for Sharp. He was behind her, and her thoughts went back as she looked down upon her hands. Everyone's voices faded as she remembered…

"Brother!" her voice shredded into the night. Trees, tall and thin, tore at the fire around her. Only when people – hers or theirs, she couldn't tell – were slammed into the trees did she realize that the trunks were not the fingers of great shadowed hands.

"Flee!"

"Hope fo-"

"HELP ME!"

An arrow whizzed past her. She knew it should have thunked on the ground beside her, because she was so young that it had to be aimed downward to hit her. But she did not hear it land.

"Brother!" The smoke. Thin, cruel, it took the life and thickness out of her voice. Friend and foe looked alike. Spears shattered. Rocks clattered, thudded, or bit into flesh with that tell-tale sucking crunch of everlasting night.

Fire made the shadows real.

A man, full-grown, pulled her up by one hand and hauled off with the other. In it was a stone tied to a stick as a crude hammer. Then she was on her back on the ground. She didn't see what ended the man, and didn't wait to learn.

"Chase them! Let none live!" someone shouted.

"Where's the hides?" shouted another.

She crawled, coughing and sobbing, toward the wall of the nearest hut. But even as she reached it, it crumbled inward. Sparks puffed outward like shooting stars too young to leave the earth. A pyre splashed into the darkness around her. In it was a shape.

Eyes.

Long of face, with many teeth, and she thought it might have a skin that was not a skin. Like a snake and yet like stone, beautiful and pitiless. Her arm and the side of her face ached with a resonant searing, and she remembered being kicked into a campfire earlier during the attack.

She stared.

Stone still but not frozen, she watched the creature and thought, Will it help us?

It spoke to her: "I am the Dragon."

If this is all to kill, then kill me.

"Darkness is another kind of light. Faster because it needs not move. I am not here to kill."

It can hear the words behind my eyes?

"I hear many things. Fight for your people, and come back to this hut when there is no fire."

The forest is ever fire.

"I am forever," it corrected, shaking its head. "Now do battle with forever in your heart. Trust your hands as my voice."

She did not entirely understand. As a six-year-old girl, she was looking at too much and not seeing enough. But she found that it spoke truly.

She could fight. There were seeds in the ashen remains of the hut. When the sun rose, it showed her who she needed to bury. She tried to make fires and none would catch. Her skin rang with rising light, and its pain was too great to be hers.

Much later, Sniff tilted her head in Ashmother's direction. "Is everything okay?"

Ashmother regarded Sniff only briefly. "Can we talk now? About how we've changed?"

Sharp gripped his double-ended spear more tightly. He remembered his time before leaving his village. He said nothing.

Leaper stood a little straighter. "Why does the Dragon not appear like the sun? Every day?"

Crone shuddered. "I've only seen it in...in..." They started weeping softly.

Sharp stepped over to Crone's right. On Crone's left, Sniff held their hand. "I saw its eyes when I killed it, friend. I did not see Dragon."

"Then you did not kill the Lion!"

"But I did," Sharp insisted. "And the Lion was afraid. But not of me."

Ashmother cinched the last of her pouches.

Crone wiped their eyes. They let go of Sniff's hand. She dropped her rocks and took a few whiffs of the air. Like a fern in the wind, each of Crone's limbs seemed to shake and jostle in their joints as they struggled to move. They met at eye level with Leaper. "I am the oldest one here. You should listen to elders. Everyone says so."

"But that's my point," Ashmother butted in.

Most of the others turned their attention to her. Sharp watched Leaper.

"You're the oldest one here," she continued. "And how old are you?"

Crone drew themselves up and regarded Ashmother sternly. "Eight."

Everyone looked at everyone else. "Six," declared Ashmother.

"Five," said Sniff.

"Seven," said Sharp and Leaper together. They looked at one another.

"How old do I look?" asked Sniff.

"This is nonsense," Leaper declared. "Everyone ages differently. None of us could stay with our tribes. We've all travelled, seen different tribes. By the moon, even last time we met our ages weren't as different. What's the big deal?"

"Something to hide?" asked Sharp. He stepped half a foot closer to Leaper.

Leaper blinked, but said nothing.

Sniff fidgeted with alarm, opening and closing her mouth in rapid succession. It was Crone who helped her to stand. They dusted her off. "You look how I expect a five-year-old to look," they said.

Sharp looked at the pair. Leaper watched Sharp warily.

"How did Leaper find you?" Ashmother asked Sniff.

Sniff wiggled her nose. "I was feeling my way in the bushes, looking for berries."

To Leaper, the memory was like lightning in his chest. "I thought you were on someone's hunting grounds. You walked past three sprung animal traps. Fresh kills."

"I knew I smelled animals, but I thought they were leaving me alone." Sniff shrugged. "Not that it matters. It's not like I could see the ropes. Or find a tool for skinning them."

"Why are you blind?" asked Sharp suddenly.

"It's how I saw the Dragon," Sniff replied.

"That doesn't answer his question," Crone pointed out. "None of us were harmed by the Dragon. It is frightening like thunder and lightning are frightening. We can see them and hear them, but they have not struck us."

"Then why do you fear the Lion so much?" Of all people, it was Ashmother who asked.

"Because it's a Lion." The obviousness of this was shocking to Crone.

"Daddy used to make war on me," Sniff said quietly. It took a moment for everyone to process that. Leaper opened his mouth, but she continued speaking: "It was his fists. For many days, in many places. Once, he hurt me and I fell. There was a rock. Then there was only light. Like a flash of lightning, but it didn't stop. It was a crack in the back of my head, and it throbbed and it burned, but always it was light. That's all I see now. White, bright white, bright with light. Even when the sun goes down."

Ashmother gathered Sniff up in her arms. It was Ashmother who wept. But she did not picture a man beating his daughter. She pictured burning woods. Even after many moons, she never found her brother. She thought, At least Sniff had her tribe. She thought, At least I have my eyes.

"I saw it in the rain," Sharp said. "It was not like with you, Ashmother, and very not like what Sniff lived. Bright morning spring rain. It was like an invisible thing, and only the glittering could hint to me its shape."

"What made you think the Lion was scared?" asked Crone.

"I have done much fighting," answered Sharp. "Many are the things and the people I have killed. I know when something is scared. And I know that what scared that Lion was not my spear. And I did not frighten it. Though I was the one to strike the killing blow, it did not fear me."

The sky cracked.

Everyone jumped.

Sniff clung desperately to Ashmother. She did not respond to the flash, but everyone else did. Crone's heart sank. "We weren't watching the sky…" they murmured.

Leaper rushed to collect the seeds while Sharp said, "To the cave!"

Sharp brandished his spear at the sky with one hand and with the other he braced Crone in order to help the seeming senior keep up. No mere beginning was there for the rain. It was as though rain had always been.

A short conversation's span, though they shared no

words, was all the time it took for them to get everyone into the cave. After setting aside the pouches of seeds, they all gathered in a circle. With each blast of thunder, they all shuddered because the very earth shook with the force.

After a double flash of lightning, Leaper spoke: "Is not the Dragon angry?"

"I don't think the Dragon causes storms," Crone replied.

"Can we know that?" mused Ashmother.

"It has not right to anger," Sharp bit out. "We've done as bidden."

"I haven't," came Sniff's tiny voice.

Thunder.

Everyone watched as she removed from under her animal skin a pouch of her own. It was smaller than the ones used for the seeds, and not of the same make. She held it in front of her and still no one spoke. In silence, she passed out from it four small white flowers with green bulbs. One she held for herself.

"What...?" Leaper began.

"All the Dragon told me was to get out," Sniff said.

Everyone except the blind one held their flower cupped in their hands, ensconced in their laps. Crone sat with their back to the wall and they were facing the entrance to the cave. If anyone – or anything – came in, they would know. They were the only one not shivering. "Get out of where?"

"Everything," the smallest member replied. She held her flower at chest level, so that her nose loomed over the scent. It had a spicy quality that was hard to place, and a more common aroma of the waxy and fresh traits of flower petals. "The hut, the tribe. Father. The Dragon told me, 'Follow my lead. Show others your endless light.' And I did not know what it meant."

"How did you see the Dragon?" Ashmother's voice was high and thin. Her instincts told her something was amiss.

"I came on a wandering group after I left my tribe," Sniff said. "They taught me about these flowers. They let you see things when you eat them."

"But why give them to us? We've all seen it." This came from Sharp. He sat closest to the entrance and farthest out of the circle of the group. His spear rested in his lap, which was why he needed the space.

Only when she looked at him did Sharp's shivers come from something other than the wet and relative chill. To him, a person's eyes should only be unseeing when there was no one left to do the seeing. When an animal gave its last breath, it looked to him as she did. His nose twitched. She answered, "I didn't see the Dragon through the flowers."

"But we've all seen it in light, haven't we?" asked Leaper. "Dawn," he said of himself. And he pointed: "The glint in the Lion's eye," which made Crone shiver. "Rain glitter," and Sharp nodded. "Fire," at which Ashmother rubbed her burns.

"Everything went white when I landed on the rock," Sniff replied.

She heard them all. Swift intakes of breath. The rustling that comes from straightening a back. Bare fingers sliding ever so slightly as grips loosened – or tightened – on flowers. "So you see it all the time?" Crone probed her.

"No," she said. "But I can. It comes and goes. It doesn't speak much. I've never had seeds. They're hard to find, hard to keep track of. When I let them go, they could go anywhere."

"I thought it was the seeds that brought us together?"

mused Ashmother.

"Why did you come?" asked Sharp.

"Aren't we a tribe?" she asked.

The sky boomed. Leaper flinched. He looked down at his flower and then around at the others.

Lightning flashed in the entrance.

They ate their flowers. Thunder rolled. Everyone watched each other and reached out to hold hands. Crone and Ashmother leaned over to grab each of Sniff's hands. She smiled.

Lightning flashed in the entrance.

"Why are we doing this?" Sharp asked. The rain was heavy and constant, but not as ravaging as it had been when they first ran in.

Lightning flashed in the entrance.

"I believe," Sniff answered.

Leaper frowned. "What" – thunder boomed – "do you believe?"

Lightning flashed in the entrance.

"In the people who gave me the flowers," Sniff said. "And in us."

Lightning flashed, and it was not alone.

Crone's eyes widened. His mouth moved to form words, but such was the rage of thunder that it was hard to tell; did he speak, or only work his lips?

With each flash of lightning now there was…something. It was more a crawling of surfaces than a true form. With each flash it moved further into the cave, which did not offer much more room than what the group used. With each flash, the children – for they were, by age, all children – found that more of the undulating nothing became intelligible. They thought they saw a head, a long neck, a lithe and horizontal body.

Wings.

When the lightning was gone, Sniff could see it. She could not see the walls, but she could see the Dragon. She saw how more of its body (so to speak) became revealed after a certain point. But for her it was simply surfaces shifting on a white background.

When lightning flashed, the others of the group saw the Dragon. Rather, they saw something that was not quite there. A will that made itself of shadows in a way that their minds might recognize.

"You look younger than you used to," Sniff said after a flash.

"Now that you mention it…" murmured Leaper.

"…it's smoother, smaller, less detailed," added Crone.

"It is my way," said the Dragon (though its mouth moved not), "to dwell in the earth. To make lair of cavern and wall and precipice. How come you here?"

"You know the answer to that," Sniff responded. There were gasps. Ashmother looked upon this small form with a new awe. Never had they seen the blind youth show such command.

"I am proud of you all," said the Dragon. "You have done well."

"Why do you look younger, while we look older?" Sharp asked. He gripped his spear fiercely, but his face was taut and his eyes danced over the formless crawling; he saw nothing he could pierce or smite.

"Our labours have begun in earnest," the Dragon said. "We must needs focus. For they have not yet borne enough fruit to be self-sustaining."

"I don't understand you," Leaper remarked. "Why send us all-"

"Do you know about the Lion?" Crone asked. They were the only one who took their attention away from the

Dragon every now and again. They were watching in case the Lion should appear behind.

In a flash of lightning, the maw and eyeless face of the shivering nothingness in front of them had moved to face Crone. The aged youth bounced with fright. "You speak as though there were only one." Its tone was befuddled.

Crone's face was affixed. As though it had become a part of the cave wall, contours of horror measured out in nothing more than a few cracks and the shifts of shadows. "Every time I have reached out to beasts, they have become dotards of dismay," the Dragon went on. "I turn to you, therefore, since people remain people."

"Surely the beasts could not understand what you tried to do with seeds?" Ashmother asked.

Sharp stood and stepped over to lay a hand on Crone's shoulder. In his other hand, his spear remained pointing at the crawling surfaces. The Dragon answered her, but continued to watch – assuming it could actually see – the face of Crone. "No, but they have their own ways. The storm is just a storm. It will pass."

"Crone was rejected from their village," Leaper thought aloud. Everyone – including the shifting shadows – turned their attention to him. "The villagers thought their stuff about boys and girls was madness."

Sniff frowned. "Boys and girls?"

"I chose each of you. You all know this," replied the Dragon.

"Exactly," Leaper pressed. "I get why you wanted me: I cover distances. I hunt and hide well. I run long and fast. And I have a talent for getting through to people. For closing gaps. Ashmother is a leader, good at plans and numbers. At making traps and seeing true shapes and telling plant from plant, seed from seed. Sharp, too, is obvious. Why Crone? Haven't they suffered enough? And we love

Sniff, but you bring her into danger."

"You are not far apart in age," the Dragon pointed out. "You are not an adult who protects the child."

"That's what he's saying," Sharp interjected.

"Why am I the youngest if we're mostly the same age?" asked Sniff.

"All will become clear," the Dragon said. "Most of the tribes you five have visited have begun to trade in seeds. It is representational currency, and promises great advances for you over bartering. I do this for you."

"Four," Crone managed through chattering teeth.

Ashmother glanced at Crone, of whom she was proud. She glanced down at the seeds. Each in different bags. A flash of lightning, and The Crawling had moved again. Now it was in a half-sitting, half-lying position much like a feline might do. They could not see its hindquarters, as its body (for lack of a better word) extended out of the entrance. She'd made four bags. "Sniff has never passed along the seeds. It is not safe," she added in support of Crone's point.

"The Lion is dangerous," the Dragon answered. "For that I am sorry. But you must spread the seeds. You are doing well." It faced Sharp. "Crone made up a game as a child."

Everyone looked at each other.

"We traded pebbles," Crone said to this. They were huddling their knees to their chest, and their eyes were downcast. They were glad of Sharp's hand on their shoulder. "Why are we spreading a children's game?"

Thunder.

Nothing was in the cave with the group. Except for Sniff, everyone was looking around for the vanished Dragon. Sniff's face was gradually moving in the direction of the entrance, and away.

"You can still see it," Ashmother pointed out.

"Yes," Sniff replied.

As the crashes and flashes of the sky became less frequent, the group shared what little food they'd had left. This was mostly fruits and roots. Instead of its previous deluge, the rain merely came in sheets. Which was something like progress. Leaper and Sharp fell into a deep sleep almost on command. Ashmother stayed awake long enough to calm Crone down. Crone slept fitfully. Sniff was the last to give in to the night.

First she watched the Dragon as it faded into the distance. Then she watched the others drop off, one by one. Because no one paid her any mind, she roamed the cave and sniffed everything out. She touched the walls where the crawling surfaces had been. Going slowly on hands and knees, relying on the shifts the others made in the dirt when they moved and the scent of their bodies, she managed to find the seed bags without disturbing anyone.

Taking heavy whiffs of each of them, she could glean no new information. She suspected that the Dragon was able to come to them all because she could see it when there was no light for the others to see it, and this somehow sustained its presence. But she did not know the words to put this idea forward to them. She felt it in her bones, but could not find the logic or the rules at play.

The next morning was wet and grey, but otherwise serviceable weather. Sniff awoke because the ground was bobbing beneath her. "Hm?" she said in confusion.

"Good morning!" Ashmother chimed as she walked beside Sniff. The little one opened her eyes many times, but did not experience much change. Still, she felt more awake when they were open.

The ground turned out to be Leaper.

Sniff sat up straighter and noticed that her legs were

hooked over Leaper's arms. Her arms had been loosely tied together over his chest. He was carrying her piggy-back. It was not hard to untie her own hands; they were bound together in bunny loops just so she would not fall. "What happened?" she asked as she rested her hands on Leaper's shoulders. She cocked her head for sounds around her and sniffed many times.

"We hoped you'd know," Sharp said from her left.

She could hear Crone's shuffling ahead of her. She whispered into Leaper's ear: "What's wrong with Crone?"

He didn't miss a beat: "We don't know. They've been like this since we started out a few hours ago. How did you know?"

"Their footsteps sound messier when they're bothered," she answered.

"I learned the songs of the herds before the tribes attacked," Ashmother said. Sniff heard the ragged rustling of the other girl's hands, middle-aged in appearance, as they slid over the burn scars.

"I will catch today's meal," added Sharp.

"But you know, don't you, Sniff?" Leaper asked.

She thought for a moment. "Other tribes know the songs, or have their own. They'll be going after the herds, too. Or looking for new herds.

"All we have to do is follow the water," Leaper confirmed.

Sniff frowned. "I don't-"

"It's in the distance," Sharp filled her in. "Just after this wall on our right. We saw it from the top of a hill."

Crone rounded the corner first.

Leaper set down Sniff when Crone made a high-pitched choking sound. He and Sharp ran forward. Ashmother took Sniff's hand.

She smelled a beast. And urine.

They all gathered to find Crone facing the Lion. Both were trembling, their breath coming in swift and shallow cascades. The Lion shifted its gaze endlessly, eyes bouncing and nostrils flaring. Crone was sweat-spangled and incoherent. As the four looked on, the Lion tentatively stepped forward. Crone stepped back.

Crone saw the Dragon in the Lion's eyes.

They also saw the kind of stark terror that steps outside of time. This was not the fear of losing a hand, or the horrors of seeing where the arm ended. Fear as it appeared in the Lion's eyes was the blinking moment before the pain set in, before seeing that the hand is gone, but after seeing the swing of the sword that took it.

Ashmother stepped forward. She did not take Sharp's spear. Opening her bag, she held up one of the seeds. This got the Lion's attention. Crone showed no sign that they even registered the Lion's shift in focus.

Carefully, the Lion approached. Carefully, it sniffed at the air. It stood before Ashmother and made a sound that Sniff knew. She'd never heard it before – not the way a beast makes it – but still, she knew it. It was the sound of a helpless child, blind after being beaten by her father, running and falling and picking herself up. It was the sound of the villagers casting her out, because surely she could only have earned such beatings. They had no name for his behaviour.

Most of all, it was the short, high-pitched cry of legless, hopeless fear.

The Lion nuzzled at Ashmother's bag. Blinking, she looked to Crone for some explanation. But they still looked forward, as if the Lion had not moved past them. At a loss, she untied it from her waist. Holding it forth, the Lion clamped its teeth gingerly upon the end of the bag. It was soundly snagged in a large lower tooth, and so the beast could walk away with the bag. Its back was too straight, its head forward but not high enough for pride.

Crone collapsed as the Lion passed and wept, shattered by phobia like frozen glass that has buckled under its own weight.

Sniff and Leaper rushed to Crone's aid.

Sharp slowly lowered his spear.

Ashmother turned to the others. "Does the Lion fight for the Dragon?"

"I didn't see the Dragon," Sniffed replied.

Crone opened their mouth, but their face was such a rictus of liquefied resolve that they took their silence for terror.

"Crone," said Sharp. When he got no response, he stepped forward and kneeled before the most heavily aged of the group. "You haven't told us about your tribe."

They closed their mouth and looked at Sharp. They licked their lips. They swallowed. "We haven't talked about any of our tribes. Not the ones we came from before Leaper left his."

"How did they handle you getting old, even though you're still seven?" Oddly, this question came from Sniff.

Crone looked at her and she did not look back. She simply looked. "When they realized that I am not boy and I am not girl," Crone replied, rubbing their chin with one hand, "they were confused. Some of us, they with wisdom, have gotten old quickly before. We thought it was because they were smart with numbers, or they'd travelled, or they could speak as with talent. But they did not think me wise for not being boy or girl. They thought me a demon, and chased me away."

"Do you think the Lion was chased out of its pride?" asked Sharp.

They all looked at him, puzzled.

"Well," he started, "I've seen many frightened beasts before. They were facing an enemy too powerful and they had nowhere to run. Usually, that enemy was me." With that, Sharp leaned on his spear, bracing it on his shoulder and holding it with both hands. "But none of us could harm him. And it was Crone he saw first. But that's not my point. What I'm saying is, we all came out of our tribes…"

"Yeah," Leaper objected, "but we saw the Dragon."

"So did the Lion," Sniff put in.

"Just now?" asked Ashmother.

"No, only Crone saw it just now."

"But how…?"

Sniff faced Sharp to answer him: "I can see – well, I'll call it seeing – something surrounding people who have seen the Dragon. I saw that in the Lion."

"So what do we do now?" Leaper asked.

"That cave," Sniff started, pointing in the direction of the one where they'd seen the Dragon together. "We should meet there at the next year gap." By this she meant the first new moon of the year.

Crone was horrified. "Y-…you want us…to split up?"

"We need to go back to our tribes," Sniff explained.

Ashmother caught on first: "To see what we've done."

"But the Dragon told us," Sharp said. "It explained that trading those seeds would help it clean the world. No more lightnings or lions."

Sniff put her hands on her hips and tried to fix Sharp with a stern expression. "How did we see it last night?"

"…"

Leaper looked at Crone and Sniff, the ones who looked too old or too young to travel alone. "Even if we could find our tribes," he said, "any one of us could die along the way. Or trying to get back here by the next year gap."

"We could waste many dances of sun and moon before we find all the tribes if we go as a group," Ashmother pointed out. "We'd be just as likely to do what we're doing now, and find new tribes to teach to trade."

"We all know the stories," Crone finally spoke. "The ones where the people split up. You know how they end."

"Then we need to make light," said Sniff.

"But you said all you see is endless brightness," Sharp objected. "And the sun's up right now. There's lots of light."

"I'm going to talk to the Dragon," Sniff maintained, "and it can only come out through light. You know that. We also need a way to destroy the seeds."

Ashmother put her hands on Sniff's shoulders and kneeled before the girl. "You don't know what you're saying."

"I do," she said, chin held high.

"We could wait for sunset or rain," Crone proposed.

"It breathes fire," Sharp said. They all regarded him. Sniff didn't move, but cocked an ear in his direction. "Only fire is sustained enough that we can call out to him. The lightning was hard on all of us, and unreliable. But we can make fire. And it could destroy the seeds without all the work of smashing them with rocks."

"Then we make fire," Sniff declared.

It had rained the previous night, so the group set out looking for the first opportunity to create fire. As the day passed, the sun's influence grew, and things began to dry. But it was distance away from where the rain was worst that really did it. In the meantime, they passed glittering water. Sharp did not see the Dragon. Sniff noticed clumps of additional seeds, but this time the group did not collect them. Leaper kept glancing toward the horizon, but the day was not far enough advanced for the Dragon to show itself through the sun. Ashmother kept nervously looking at and covering up her burn scars. She was usually the one who cooked for them, but bringing out the Dragon with fire made her uneasy. It was Crone who found the right materials for starting a fire, beginning with a cluster of bushes that were near a forest but not in its shade.

Five times they managed to get a flame beyond embers only to see it diminish. Only on the sixth try did it catch and last. Five times they tried calling out to the Dragon through the fire. On the sixth, Sniff simply threw in her bag of seeds.

"WHAT HAVE YOU DONE!?" roared the fire. It had eyes now and snaked over them.

Four of them scattered backward. Sharp stood before his friends, pointing his sharp stick at the horror story of fire. Black, reeking smoke blossomed out of the fire-feasted seeds and wrapped up the Dragon like an unholy summer. Something like starlight at daytime glittered in the festering air as it formed wings upon the blazing beast.

Though faint, the sound of crying babies leaked out of the ephemeral wings.

Sharp's muscles, sinewy and proven strong, made the smallness of Sniff's hands seem that much greater as she laid her gentle fingers upon the shaft. She pushed down upon it. She could not have forced it down, but he actually lowered it because this little girl was moving for him to do so. She stepped forward.

"If you have nothing to feed, you are nothing to fear," she said to it.

Crone found themselves profoundly disagreeing with their friend, but they said nothing.

"You have wasted precious seeds! There is much to do!" Though the fire took up the same amount of space, it intensified. It roiled within itself and shifted from red to a gleaming, unnatural gold. It was hard to tell if the wings were still smoke or if they were slashes made in the peel of daylight that revealed the endless starry blackness behind everything the world was.

"Tell us," Ashmother said instead, "what has come of our tribes."

"Why have you burned our work?" demanded the Dragon of Sniff.

She did not see it with her eyes, but she did see the Dragon. She saw the looming serpent, but not the wings. "To summon you," she answered. "Now, tell us about the tribes."

"Never make such waste again," it said.

"Tell us." Ashmother almost turned her gaze from the Dragon in shock, because it was Crone who now stood tall and joined in the demand.

"Tell us," echoed Leaper.

Sharp jabbed the ground with his double-ended spear twice. He said nothing.

"I could send the Lions upon you," it growled.

"We'll burn all our seeds," said Sniff, "and go back for more. We cannot hurt you with fire, but you cannot stop it if we send it against every seed we find."

It narrowed its eyes.

All five of them were filled with memories, like stars pinpricking them everywhere at once. To their very pores they were flooded with knowledge of the tribes they'd visited until now, and the other tribes those ones had met. Many fought, many traded, and a surprising number did both.

And they were all aging.

Not merely the passing of years, this aging was spread out over all the individuals. Every time someone exchanged an item or service for a number of seeds, a little youth was taken. It took many trades for the effect to show.

Sniff turned her head in Crone's direction. She was appalled by what that meant for them.

"It's the right thing to do," said the Dragon.

Leaper had twin streams running down his face. "Why didn't you tell us you needed youth?"

"You wouldn't understand. I have to break the cycle. There are so many worlds."

"We have only this one," Ashmother said.

"Give my friends back their youth," Sniff demanded.

"That cannot be," replied the hungerless fire. "A waterfall could go back up as easily."

"We will stop every seed! For the rest of our lives if we have to!" Sharp declared fiercely.

Lions roared in the distance.

"The tribes are already trading," said the fire.

Then it was gone.

Not only the smoke and the serpentine searing, but even the heat had vanished. Ashes and dry plant remained, but there were no embers.

Crone's hands trembled. Their lip quivered. But they stood and did not falter. "They won't stop trading," they said. "The tribes gain too much, and dislike to change their ways."

"They'd fight us if we demanded," added Sharp.

"Then we add more," Ashmother proposed. "We got them to believe in the seeds, and the Dragon stole that belief. Let's give them other beliefs. Like swarms in a troubled nest. There's one of the Dragon, but many of us."

Leaper swallowed and looked toward the horizon.

The sun was setting.

Chantal Boudreau

A Toronto native currently living in Sambro, Nova Scotia, Boudreau is an avid and prolific author with over fifty credits to her name. She is the author of the Fervor series of novels, as well as the *Masters & Renegades* series and *The Snowy Barrens Trilogy*.

Boudreau is likely best known for her work in short fiction, and the anthologies she has appeared in have been shortlisted for both the Bram Stoker award and the Aurora award.

Her extensive short-fiction bibliography includes fantasy, dark fantasy, and horror.

Territory

Samantha Cook had been a realtor for much of her adult life, and was one of the better salespeople at her realty firm. That was why she had been assigned the Berman Street house. The house had gone through five owners in the last three years, and was now recognized in her firm as a "problem property."Considered a hard sell, management had made the executive decision to add it to Samantha's portfolio. They believed only a few of their realtors were capable of unloading it for a fifth time. Samantha happened to be one of those realtors.

Not that there was anything physically wrong with the house. The building was in fine form, and it came with a reasonably sized and well-tended estate. Inspectors could find nothing wrong with the place, and as long as a potential customer didn't know the house's history, Samantha had no problem seeding their interest, especially with an unusually low asking price. The problem was that Windsor had a small town mentality and that meant that everyone knew everybody else's business. Rumours had already infiltrated the community as to why new owners were so quick to abandon the place. As a result, Samantha could only hope for a sale involving an outsider. Nobody local was even willing to go anywhere near the place, let alone take ownership.

Samantha glanced over at the file folder on the passenger seat. Fortunately, her next potential buyer was such an outsider – a single woman, a divorcee actually, from a neighbouring area. Samantha liked divorcees. They often had the urgent desire to change their surroundings and compromised much more quickly than the average married soul -- anything to escape a place haunted by memories.

Haunted -- Samantha chided herself for thinking the word. She didn't want to jinx this sale from the get-go.

Her cell phone rang.

"Allen's Realty. Samantha speaking."

"Heeeey, Cookie. She run off screaming yet?" The voice on the other end belonged to Scott, a rival realtor at her firm. He had phoned to taunt Samantha, a little disgruntled that management had chosen her to handle the Berman Street challenge over him, but also somewhat relieved that it was her problem and not his.

"I'm still waiting for her to get here, Scott. Now bugger off. I don't want your kind of bad luck to rub off on me. I've got a good feeling about this one. As long as she doesn't get wind of what the previous owners believed they saw, I think she may be a sure thing."

"Bah! No such thing. Not that it matters, and no extra pressure, but we've got a betting pool going at the office. I say she bolts." Scott sounded cocky.

Samantha knew better than to play these games with Scott. This was his method of trash talking her, trying to throw her off in hopes that she would fail and, in the process, make him look better. She wasn't about to let him spoil a positive vibe, so she decided it was time to get rid of him.

"Oh, look at that. She's driving up now. Got to go, Scott. It's time to work my magic."

Samantha hung up without giving a chance to answer. She had no compunctions about lying to him. Stretching the truth was a big part of her job – the trick was in not going far enough to cause a fraud lawsuit. The Berman Street property was going to require some expert exaggeration and adept omission of fact. Considering that the prior owners' issues with the house could not be scientifically proven made the latter fairly simple. Nobody could accuse Samantha of failing to disclose something that didn't legitimately exist.

Samantha glanced at her watch, aware that time was of the essence. The potential buyer, a woman by the name of Natalie Raymond, was already a few minutes late. Much longer, and the delay would throw off Samantha's entire schedule for the day. With an impatient sigh, she slung her purse over her shoulder and stepped out of the car.

The well-primped woman stood, straightening her company-standard blazer before approaching the front of the house. Her high heels clacked against the pavement as she hurried up the paved driveway. Once standing in front of the door, hands on hips, she eyed it as if facing down an opponent on the battlefield.

"If you give me a hard time on this sale, I'm bringing in an exorcist – I swear. You behave or else," Samantha threatened.

The house didn't respond in any way, but it felt to Samantha as if the building were returning her stare with eerie resistance. She just may have a fight on her hands after all. However, this house, from all accounts, was a bully and bullies were essentially cowards. Samantha didn't get where she was by being a pushover or by backing down, especially not in the face of a bully. While not worried about her own ability to cope with the unruly property, her concern was the nature of her client. All she needed was for the presence in the house to keep quiet until the showing was done.

Drawing her from her confrontation, the sound of gravel crunching between tires and pavement caught Samantha's attention and she turned to see a car pulling up behind her own. A woman, probably in her early thirties, emerged looking harried and in a foul mood. She tossed a cigarette butt onto the shoulder of the road and ground it into the dirt with her heel.

The newcomer wore dishevelled clothing, as if she had dressed in a rush, and her hair, pulled back in a haphazard ponytail, escaped in small wisps in places, fluttering around her head in the slight breeze that brushed past her. The most unpleasant part of her appearance was her facial expression. Samantha had never had a client arrive at a viewing with such a terrible scowl on their face. She noted that this would add an extra level of difficulty to an already challenging situation. It was always a struggle to get someone with a negative attitude to see a property in a positive light.

"Ms. Raymond?" Samantha asked with a bright smile, extending her hand in greeting.

Very careful about how she addressed her clients, she was always professional, never calling anyone by their first name unless invited to do so, and never addressing a divorcee as either Mrs. or Miss. They were quick to take offense, their marital status often a touchy subject.

The client ignored the gesture. She nodded in response, pushing the loose hair away from her face as she glared at the house.

"Don't call me that. It just reminds me I've been too busy to get my name legally changed back to my maiden name. Call me Natalie. And don't waste any small talk on me. Just show me the house and tell me what you can about it."

Samantha was taken aback. Natalie offered none of the pleasantries one might expect upon meeting someone for the first time, and no apologies for arriving late. She had a harshness to her, rough around the edges, that Samantha had certainly not been expecting. From the client's file, based on her financial information, she was well educated and decently employed, so Samantha had been anticipating a certain level of social etiquette. She had to wonder if Natalie's demeanour was all the result of her involvement in a bitter divorce, or if there were something more to it.

Natalie gave her a dissatisfied look.

"Well, are we going to stand here all day, or are we going in?"

"Of course, of course," Samantha acquiesced, her tone apologetic. "Please, follow me."

She led Natalie into the foyer and turned on the light there, although it was mostly unnecessary. The house had plenty of southern facing windows and the foyer was bathed in sunlight.

"It's big and bright," the unhappy woman remarked. "I was hoping for something smaller... and less friendly. I would have expected it at the asking price."

"It is large for one person," Samantha agreed as she swept into the next room. "But that presents the opportunity for boarders. With that as a means of income, this house could practically pay for itself. What a wonderful investment!"

"I don't work well with boarders," was Natalie's sullen response. "I have every intention of living alone. I need peace and quiet for a change."

Samantha wondered if this had anything to do with some sort of tumultuous relationship with her ex-husband. The file had indicated that Natalie had no children.

Based on the woman's temperament, Samantha doubted she had much in the way of friends either.

"Well, there is plenty of space between you and any neighbour, so they certainly won't be bothering you, and there is very little traffic on this street. I suspect you would get an abundance of peace and quiet here, if that's what you're looking for."

"That's not what I meant," Natalie told her, but she did not elaborate further. Samantha knew better than to pry.

The realtor noted that Natalie was unusually quiet as she toured the house, barely glancing at any of the preferred features pointed out to her. That didn't bode well for a sale; a truly interested potential buyer always asked questions. Experience told Samantha that much.

It wasn't until they arrived at the final room, one of the smaller bedrooms upstairs intended for a child, that Natalie broke her silence. The room also happened to be the one Samantha dreaded showing the most. If there was going to be trouble, it would likely happen there. After a quick once over, Samantha was ready to usher her out. Natalie stood her ground, however, and posed her first question.

"So what can you tell me about the ghost that lives here?"

Aghast, Samantha searched her mind for a way of answering that without assuring the loss of a sale. She had been hoping this out-of-towner would have no idea why the prior owners had left the place in such a hurry, willing to forego a sale price that matched what they had paid, just to be rid of the house. Until that moment, Samantha had considered herself fortunate. While they had walked the circuit of the rooms, there had been no phantom sounds, no transparent visions, and no upsets of any of the staging decor. She had considered herself spared of any such nuisances, ones that would require explanation.

Samantha gave Natalie a nervous smile. "What, the old rumours and wives' tales suggesting this place is haunted? Those are just spread by the locals to scare off outsiders. Everyone knows ghosts don't exist. There's no point to those stories."

Natalie's expression hardened, something Samantha thought wasn't possible.

"Humour me," she said.

Her worst fears realized, Samantha resigned herself to considering this showing a lost cause. She took a seat in one of the chairs that had been used to stage the room. This would probably take some time, and her feet ached after rounding the house in particularly uncomfortable heels.

"Alright, I can give you an abridged version of the tall-tale I have heard. Apparently, this home once belonged to a local couple who had a couple of sons. The eldest, a boy by the name of Alvin, was reputed to be a bit of a town bully. In particular, he considered this house and the surrounding area his 'territory' and any other child he caught passing through here, he would charge a toll. If they didn't pay, he beat them up. Apparently one day, one of his victims snapped, and decided he wasn't going to take it anymore. He stashed a weapon in his pack, a knife, so he could defend himself against Alvin's bullying. When Alvin jumped this child, the smaller boy fought back with the knife, stabbing Alvin and killing him. The stories claim that Alvin has never left here. He still haunts his 'territory', roaming the house, yard, and street to torment those who haven't paid his toll. They say he's even meaner now that he's dead – that he's still angry at the kid who killed him. He haunts children more so than adults."

Samantha hoped this last fact might lessen the blow, since Natalie had no children of her own.

Natalie stood there, so placid and exceptionally quiet that poor Samantha found it horribly unnerving. Although she had given the potential buyer only half of the story, the realtor knew the tale well. The last family who lived in the house had deserted the place after their youngest child had been hospitalized when a heavy vase had launched itself off of the mantelpiece of the living room fireplace striking the girl in the head and knocking her unconscious. No one could claim that it had merely fallen on her after it had toppled by chance, since the girl had been more than a metre away when it had happened.

That had been the last straw for the parents, having already been subject to a series of similar occurrences, escalating in severity. They had moved out later that week, putting the house on the market at a price that allowed for as big a loss as they could afford to take -- anything to be rid of it.

Waiting for such a long time for a response from Natalie made Samantha uncomfortable. She gave a nervous little laugh before speaking. "Of course, the rumours are just that, a way for local folks to scare away outsiders. They're not all that fond of strangers, but they do warm up to you once you've been here for a little while. It really is a nice neighbourhood once you've settled in."

The air in the room seemed to chill as quickly as the look in Natalie's icy blue eyes. She crossed her arms and pursed her lips.

"That's a pity," she said. "I was counting on the stories proving to be true. I guess I'll have to keep looking."

This statement confused Samantha. She couldn't fathom the idea that someone would actually want a house that was haunted, specifically *because* there was a ghost present. It didn't make any sense.

Before she could wrap her head around the notion, she was forced to change her train of thought abruptly. If she hadn't redirected her attention, she wouldn't have managed to duck in time to avoid the die-cast metal airplane that was suddenly winging its way at her head. Samantha barely avoided being struck by the nasty projectile, which instead crashed into the wall behind her.

Natalie smiled for the first time since Samantha had met her, an expression that bore an air of the Machiavellian.

"Never mind," she said. "I'll take it."

Natalie pulled the last box from her car and rested against the vehicle's cold, hard metal surface. She would find a place to stash the box along with the others, but she wouldn't be unpacking right away. She had some preparations to make first, ones she hoped would cure her of her greatest blight.

"This isn't home. I need to go home. You have to tell them the truth. You have to set me free." The disembodied voice that echoed around Natalie's head had the pitch of a small child.

"Shut up, Annette. This is my home now. If you don't like it, get lost. You know you're not welcome to hang around with me. You never were and you never will be." *That's why I'm in this mess,* Natalie thought. "You ruined my life, you ruined my marriage, and I'll be happy to be rid of you after all of these years."

She hoisted the box up onto her shoulder and lugged her tired body up the front steps. When she opened the door, she made sure to give warning, glancing around the empty foyer.

"This is the last of my stuff, Alvin. I have your toll and I intend to pay it. Let me just put this down and I'll go get it from the car. I think we're going to be friends, you and I. I'm willing to play by your rules." Natalie spoke out loud, even though she appeared to be alone. She didn't wait for a reply. Once fully inside the house, she haphazardly shoved the box she carried into a random corner, before heading back towards her car.

More words from nowhere: *"It's all your fault, Nattie. All you have to do is tell them. Confess, and I'll leave you alone."*

"I've told you a million times, Annette. You can't be my conscience and I don't have one of my own. You are wasting your time and mine. This is your last warning. Go away, or suffer the consequences," Natalie said. She pulled a cigarette from her purse and lit it before grabbing the plastic bag that rested on her passenger seat.

Preparation – it was all about preparation. In fact, this was the last stage of her preparation. Natalie had begun with a search for a house reputed to be haunted, and then she had done her research. This house had held the most promise for what she had in mind. Once she had assured herself that the story wasn't a hoax, Natalie had dug a little deeper. A trip to the local tavern where she made herself friendly by buying a round of drinks had yielded results. She had managed to locate Stanley, the great uncle of the legendary Alvin, and a few more drinks had netted Natalie the tale in its entirety, with all the gory details. Uncle Stanley had been even willing to tell her everything he happened to know about Alvin, once the alcohol had loosened his tongue. He admitted his nephew, Alvin's father, had been a bully as well and had beaten both his sons on a regular basis. It was likely why Alvin had taken to bullying in turn, a transferral of his rage to someone weaker than himself

The discussion with Uncle Stanley had led to another revelation. The answer to her problem of how to cope with Alvin was jellybeans. That had been Alvin's favourite treat, Uncle Stanley had told her. Natalie realized that a phantom child couldn't eat candy, but it was the offering that counted, not the consumption. She gave the bag in her hand a shake as she started up the front step. The rattle of the candies within brought a smile to her face.

"What are you doing, Nattie? Home, I want to go home. Let me rest. Tell them. Tell them the truth."

"Mind your own business, Annette," Natalie said between puffs on her cigarette.

She paused long enough to dig a bowl out of one of the boxes labelled "kitchen" and started up the stairs, bag in one hand, bowl in the other,and cigarette held between clenched teeth. Once she had arrived in the room where the toy plane had almost taken the realtor's head off, she placed the bowl in the middle of the room and filled it with jellybeans. She addressed the room in general.

"These are for you, Alvin. I'm paying your toll, so that you leave me in peace. I'll check the bowl daily, and if you need a refill, consider it done. But I want this to be especially clear – this toll is for me and only for me. It doesn't cover anyone else who happens to be trespassing into your territory, and you may have noticed that I didn't come here alone."

"Nattie – why are you doing this? You set this up on purpose," the ghostly voice whispered. *"This isn't fair."*

"Neither is haunting me for fifteen years, you little witch," Natalie snarled, sealing the bag with the jellybeans. "I don't know how many more times I have to tell you. It was an accident! – An accident!"

She stood up, slinging the bag over her shoulder and

flicking ash off of her cigarette.

"Do you want to know who else is here, intruding in your territory, Alvin? This is my little sister, Annette. The little brat used to follow me everywhere. Just like now, she wouldn't leave me alone. I told her I would give her trouble then, but she wouldn't listen anymore than she does today. Well, she's going to pay for that now. You hear that, Annette?"

Natalie's voice reverberated around the mostly empty room. This time there was no response.

"Oh, so now you get quiet on me. Do you want to know how it all went down, Alvin? I told Little-Miss-Tag-Along not to follow me, as per usual. I was going to meet a boy – one I wasn't supposed to see because he had a bad reputation. I was meeting him in the park, but I had to walk the long trail along the ravine. She walked up behind me while I was on my way, and said that she knew who I was meeting and that she was going to rat me out. I told her to get lost and I gave her a shove. I wasn't *trying* to make her fall, just push her back. But she rolled down the side of the ravine and hit her head on a rotting log. When I went to check on her, she was already dead, so I just left her there. I pretended like I didn't know where she had gone when she didn't come home by nightfall. It was no big deal; a man walking his dog found her three days later."

The jellybeans rattled in the bowl. Natalie took that as a sign that Alvin was paying attention.

"I'm sure you know what I mean, Alvin," she continued. "You were a big brother once. You probably remember how much of a pest your younger brother was. The whole thing was her fault. She shouldn't have been following me. She shouldn't have harassed me. But then, Annette kept haranguing me, long after death, probably the most persistent of pests. She said I had to confess so she could rest, but I didn't kill her on purpose so I'm not about to confess to a murder I didn't commit. It's not like what happened with you. That little boy brought that knife planning to use it on you. He was most definitely guilty."

Natalie had no intention of mentioning the fact that Alvin's killer considered it self-defence. She wanted to rile the phantom bully up as much as possible, but convince him that she, personally, was on his side. She was also hoping to generate some sympathy towards her own situation. She allowed her shoulders to sag and gently nudged the jellybean bowl with her foot.

"I'm tired, Alvin. I'm really tired. Day and night, I have to put up with her, and her nonsense. She thinks she's better than me and she hardly ever shuts up. She's driving me crazy. I barely made it through school, but I had an easier time ignoring her then and I resorted to drugs to get me through the worst of it. Her constant pestering destroyed my marriage – sex sucks when you have a voice hounding you about how she wants to go home the entire time – and now it's even threatening my job. When she forced me to go on stress leave, I realized that I was going to have to take some desperate measures. That's why I'm here, Alvin. That's why I'm paying the toll... just for me, not for her. I just need a little peace, after all these years."

That was when the noises began. The room started shaking, windows and jellybean bowl rattling like there was a minor earthquake. The swirling winds within the room and the howling followed, guttural sounds of rage and whimpering noises, as if a battle had commenced within those walls. But it wasn't an even fight. Odds definitely fell in favour of the violent bully, enraged that another had invaded his territory without paying the toll, and taking out years of frustration on the lost soul that had accompanied Natalie as she had moved into the house.

Despite the chaotic struggle that she left within the room, Natalie wore a large smile as she stepped into the hallway and closed the door behind her. Perhaps Annette was right. Perhaps in her heart of hearts she had been trying to hurt the girl that day alongside the ravine, but she'd never admit to it. The way she figured, Natalie had done her penance: fifteen years of torment and suffering seemed like a reasonable sentence for her crime. She now had a refuge and all it required was remaining in Alvin's territory and paying his toll – like transitioning to a half-way house. Natalie could handle that.

The noise wasn't all that bad the farther away she moved from the room, and in the farthest reaches of the house, the shaking could only be felt as a mild tremor. Once she was far away within the house as she could get, Natalie pulled a book out of one of her boxes and sank happily into a chair. She relaxed, wearing an expression of pure bliss.

"Ahhh," she sighed. "Peace at last."

Teresita E. Dziadura

Dziadura has steadily been making her voice heard in the Newfoundland writing scene more and more over the last two years, making her presence known at NaNo-WriMo writing events and seminars as a force to be reckoned with, bringing wit and insight to every conversation she's a part of!

She makes her first mark in the world of published fiction with her short story "Beyond No Man's Land," a chilling take sure to cement her as one of the fresh new talents in the industry.

Dziadura describes herself as a sci-fi and horror nut, but is also a longtime fan of British comedy. She has studied Marine Biology and has four children with her husband of twenty-five years.

Beyond No Man's Land

Day 1

Today I died. Not in glorious battle, defending King and country, but from a short blade in the back. I didn't see my killer. He didn't stand before me and fight me like a man. No, he was a coward. A thief. It was an enemy within that unjustly stole my future.

Now I drift and float above the trenches of no man's land. I can see everyone, my old comrades and enemies alike, lying in the trenches, cleaning their weapons or huddling for warmth around the small stoves. I see the dead, strewn across no man's land, waiting for the front lines to change so they can be collected. I miss the warmth of blood in my veins, of the breath exhaling from my mouth, a cup of tea. I miss the smells. The earthiness of the Somme mud, the corned beef on a bit of bread. I even miss the smell of death. An odd thing to miss, but when you could smell it you knew you were still alive.I see other spirits, wandering lost and aimless along the muddied and bloodied fields of France. They look as lost and hopeless as I feel. Neither they, nor I can rest. Not while our killers remain free, our deaths un-avenged.

Day 2

Another day is dawning. The men in the trenches are awakening to a blood red sky. The pallet of the horizon is a flaming brilliant red, washing all below it in shades of grey. An irony since the land below should be red and the sky grey.

A fellow I met, John Tolkien I believe. He was an odd fellow. Always jotting down bits of poetry and speaking rather wistfully of home; had some very fantastical views as well. He was with the Fusiliers and we met in a camp near Amiens in the summer of 1916. Just before we were both to be sent to the front, he and I sat watching a sunrise and he looked at me and said, "Tom, old fellow, this is a poor start to the day. My father always said that when a red sun rises, blood had been spilled the night before." I didn't wish to seem put-off by this, though his words disturbed me, so I laughed as I replied, "Then every morning should have a red sunrise and sunset as well!" I acted cavalier, but it was an ominous forewarning of many dawns to come during this bloody conflict. The next day we headed out on our separate ways. I wonder where he is now.

Day 10

The time is interminable. To any who think that the dead do not feel the passage of time, you are wrong! Each day is the same: sunrise, watch a battle I can do nothing about, sunset, then darkness. I cannot leave here. I am tied to this infernal place! I do not sleep. I drift between the British and German front lines. If I could impart knowledge to my comrades, I could tell them of each enemy movement, each machine gun and rifleman emplacement! How many could I save? It burns at my soul! I cannot abide this helplessness! I see the same anger and frustration on the faces of the other souls who drift with me here, constrained to this place by sudden death and unfinished business. Business we can never attend to!

I saw the spirit of a man I remember killing. It was about six months ago, I suppose, when we met on the field. We'd gone over the top in a surge to retake the German lines. I'd run into him on the field as I weaved my way through the artillery craters and dead bodies. Out of the smoke he appeared before me. I remember him very clearly. He had a bright red floral scarf tied around his neck. Perhaps it had been a lucky charm from some lover. Without thought, as we had been taught in basic training, I rammed my bayonet home and took his life. The blood staining his faded grey woollen tunic matched the red in the unlucky scarf. It didn't haunt me like my first kill had. I'd not even spared him a second thought, but now each day we drift past each other and his blank expression and stained tunic haunts me like no other kill ever has.

Day 14

I must find a way to act! Is there a heaven or a hell? Is this purgatory? If this is purgatory, it certainly lives up to its name! I feel as if I am doing penance for the sins of every man ever born! I'll soon go mad! Can the dead go mad? Perhaps that is how hauntings happen. Hauntings… this makes me wonder…

Day 17

Ha *ha*! I did it! I turned over the inkwell on my commander's desk! You should have seen his face! He was penning the letter home to my mother full of sorrow and apologies. It would be delivered by a priest and an officer. They'd see the pair of them walking up Patrick Street in Olde St. John's and know that another son was gone. But whose son? Old Mary Brown's perhaps? Joey, well, he enlisted with me and lives still. Or maybe it would Mother Annie Stamp's child, Robert, two years my senior. Nay, it's Kitty Molloy's little boy who won't be coming home this time! Poor Private Thomas Alfred William Molloy. Killed to death by murder most foul, ending his sad little life at the ripe old age of seventeen,though they all think me to be twenty-three.

The lying prat is saying my death was a tragic accident! No war hero am I! My family will receive no medals for heroic acts or meritorious valour, just a Union Jack and the standard war medal. I see my mother's name, scrawled in his hen's scratch across the salutation: "Dear Mrs. Malloy, It is with great sadness and regret that I must inform you of the accidental death of your son, Pvt. Thomas Molloy in a training exercise."

Dammit! It was no accident! I was murdered! They must know it to be murder. How could they not? A man does not die with a knife in the back, not inside our lines in our very trenches, without it being murder, but they could not be bothered over the life of a simple private from Newfoundland! My death was an inconvenience to them, nothing more. My Mother and sweetheart will never know the truth of it! I'd weep if I could shed a tear.

I may not be able to cry, but my heart burns with anger upon reading his words! A fury I'd never felt before possessed me and when I reached out to swipe the lying pen from his hand, I struck the inkbottle and it flew! Lord, but it flew! There was ink running everywhere. Spatters of the black ink cover the front of his meticulous uniform, staining the olive brown of his woollen tunic and his broad leather belt. It ran over the letter and pooled on the page, like my blood from the knife. My rage fuelled this. I'm sure of it!

The pompous ass has finally left, stripping his clothes as he goes. Some poor orderly will be given orders to get that ink out. Can I touch the ink? Will this work? Yes... yes, I'm writing! The ink, it slides across the paper under my fingertip. I can spell -- M-U-R-D-R – I've done it! Will they see? Will they care?

Day 18

The stodgy old fart is trying to pen another letter to my mother. He balked a little when he saw MURDR drying on the paper, but ultimately scoffed. Brushed it off as one of his aides playing a joke. What a dark joke that would be.

He's a lying bastard. How could they see it as an accident? There was a dagger in my back. I can still feel the cold steel sliding into my flesh. It didn't hurt at first as the thin blade sunk into my kidney. I let out a single startled cry. No one heard though. There was artillery going off and my cry was lost on the wind. With a push, I fell and was left there in a side trench. Left alone to bleed to death, my blood soaking into the ruddy earth, staining it black.

It was then that the pain hit. I couldn't breathe. I couldn't cry out.

I'd tried to crawl for help through the thick French muck, but each movement brought a wave of agony and with each beat of my heart my strength flowed out with my blood, blackening the red earth. He must have hit an artery. I lay in the cold mud for what felt like interminable days in a haze of pain and weakness. The coward didn't even have the courage to face me and end my suffering! My last vision was a pair of brown boots and puttees before my eyes. The puttees were torn and darned with bright blue wool like a lightning bolt tracing down his leg. Then there was nothing.

Nothing! No hailing of the medics. No cries of 'man down!' No one yelling that a murder had been done to me! No outrage that one of the men -- our men, a comrade! -- could be so slain behind our own lines. No inquiry or investigation! Just a letter home on plain paper and signed by a fat old man who didn't know my name until I was an inconvenience to him!

There he sits. Captain Benjamin Mayhew. An officer of the Great British Empire! Sitting here smoking his pipe and sipping his tea and biscuits while I lie mouldering, un-avenged, in the ground! A flatulent, pompous old man pretending sympathy for a woman he'd never met!

Send him to hell! I have to get through to him! He was never a cruel commander. I cannot believe that he would allow this if he knew the truth. Is this a wilful ignorance?

I cannot abide this! This farce! This injustice! My eternity will be spent wandering the green fields of France. Floating through farmers' fields and watching rabbits running and hiding from foxes and hawks! No rest.No meeting with lost loved ones. I will not be forgotten! I am not some inconvenience to the bureaucratic process of war! Darn you! Listen to ME!

The light? Did it flash? I wonder. Can I control the lights like I did the ink?Staring at it is ineffective. Can I touch it? If I close my hand around the light, it goes out! Open my hand and the light is on.

Ha ha! He did not enjoy that at all. He sits there now staring at his light, pen dripping drops of black ink onto the paper. Let me try something. We'd been trained in this new type of code. Marse, Mash, Morse! That's it! Morse code. Dots and dashes! I can close my hand briefly for the dots and longer for the dashes. Let me try and remember… H: dot dotdotdot, E: dot, L: dash, L: dash, O: dot dot. Hello!

Did he get the message? He sits there blinking rapidly at the light. I wonder…

Day 21

I've been trying for days to reach him! Is he an imbecile? He is the one who had us taught Morse code. The idea was that if something happened to our communications men, we could all get a message out, regardless of how rudimentary. Did they not train the officers?

I truly hope that is not the case. If it is, my cause is lost!

Unless I wait until he has someone else with him! Someone who might know! But who can I trust? I can remember the names and face of each man in my unit and many of the others around me, but I cannot remember a thing about them as men! Were they good and honour-able? One of them is my killer! I can't even remember the hours before my death! Days and weeks before, yes, but the hours and minutes right before… nothing. If I do reach them, how am I to tell them who the killer is? What proof is there? Why did he kill me?

Day 23

Being dead is not what you would expect and noth-ing like the clergy would have us believe! I was taught that when you died, you went for judgment, then de-pending on your sins you'd be sent below as the devil's sport or to purgatory until your sins were absolved, then you'd join the heavenly host. So far I've seen neither angel nor demon,and I don't remember judgment. Regardless, living like this is more akin to a torture of hell, than any punishment Icould envision. I do not wish to fall into the despondent madness of the other souls I see around me -- wandering aimlessly or screaming mad. If the sounds that they make can pass to the living world, I know where the legend of the banshee originated! A shrieking howl, like a wind blowing viciously through a crevasse.It would freeze the soul of someone living. It would vibrate in my bones if I had any!

Day 25

I've all but given up hope that my old commander will recognize the flashing light for what it is. I suppose it was only to be expected. The lights flicker, wax and wane all the time, or stop working altogether. I am beginning to despair that my fate is to walk these fields for all eternity, never to ascend, be reunited with my family. To see Gran or Mum again. Da will be awfully disappointed as will my brother, Matthew, and sisters, Jenny and Sadie. Would my old dog, Carlo, be there? I'd like to think so.

I feel that there is something else. Something beyond. I sometimes feel I can almost touch it or see it, as if it's just behind a thin veil that slips from my grasp like fine silk. Slithering away on a breeze. Then gone. Something is holding me back, tying me to this place of death. Not just my death, but the death of thousands. There are men in full suits of armour, roman legionaries, kilts, and animal hides. Women in gowns that I've seen in picture books from the Middle Ages, and wee babes and children. No animals though. Not a deer nor dove. Either the churches are right and they carry no souls, something I find hard to believe, or they live without the regrets that we humans carry with us.

Regardless of these musings and my despondency, I will keep trying to reach my commander. As useless and insipid as he is at times.

Day 26

His clerk! The bloody clerk! Corporal Ralph, whatever his name is! He was bringing Captain Mayhew his coffee and biscuits and saw the flashing light. He asked old Mayhew about it and he said it'd been happening every day for a couple of weeks now! When Ralph looked at the light for a few minutes, I could see his lips counting the dots and dashes! He was so excited he spilled the coffee over Mayhew! I believe Mayhew thinks poor Ralph to be losing his mind. Perhaps shell shocked. No, my good

Commander, he's perfectly sane and my personal hero!

I need to let them know it's me! That I was murdered! Mayhew may think Ralph mad, but he's giving him the benefit of the doubt as they are both staring at the light expectantly. Though Mayhew looks more irritated than expectant. What to say? My name, that I was murdered and my date of death?

M-O-L-L-O-Y pause M-U-R-D-R-D pause A-P- R- 8

Ralph is scratching madly at his little notepad, marking down the dots and dashes. Looking for a pattern. If I were alive, I'd say my heart had stopped beating with the anticipation! Will he get my message? Will he understand? Will Mayhew believe him? Look! The colour is draining from his face! I guess that he's understood at least part of it!

Ralph and I knew each other. We were not close acquaintances, but we did know each other's names. It must be quite the shock to be contacted from beyond the grave, perhaps more so if it's someone you know!

He's showing his notes to Mayhew. He looks equally shocked; but will he believe him, believe the words in print before him? Mayhew has sent Ralph at a run from his office! I'm believed! I think. I'll not get my hopes raised. Not yet!

Interminable minutes pass since Ralph dashed from Mayhew's office, but another man has brought a brown folder with my name on it and "Deceased" written across the front in bold block letters. Mayhew is reading everything in it from cover to cover. It's my military biography. My entire three years of military life summed up in a handful of paper.

Day 27

Things are happening fast now. Mayhew is meeting with other officers, the medics that found me and the doctor who, I believe, signed my death certificate. They have my small box of possessions and my "diary", something most of us kept with daily musings, little anecdotes and often a last letters of goodbye to loved ones in the case that we fell in battle.

I can hear them, but things do seem far away, as if I was listening through a wall. Mayhew is incensed. He's slammed my service folder down no less than six times now!He's yelled about incompetence, stupidity, laziness, and ineptitude. What did he find? I know he spent what seemed like forever going over and over my final medical report and death certificate (how easy that phrase comes to me now!). There was one section that he kept tapping with his pen. There are ink spots up and down the entire margin. They look like black tear drops. Perhaps they are mine.

I did try reading it over his shoulder, but he was discourteous enough to not hold the paper steady for me and kept shifting it about. The few words I did see meant nothing to me. "Penetrating trauma, severed renal artery and exsanguination." I also saw "shock", but I could have told them that myself. I thought that Mayhew might be covering my murder up to protect his reputation, but I think the "official" report he received may have been falsified. I heard him yelling at one of the clerks, a Corporal Smith if I heard correctly, that he'd been lied to and he "had better have an explanation on my desk by 0800 hours tomorrow morning or you'll go from being an administration clerk to clearing barbed wire in no man's land!" His round face was florid with anger. I was fearful he'd have an apoplexy! If he falls ill, my advocate will be gone. I cannot face an eternity walking these fields.

Day 37

So I wait, then wait some more. I'd not have thought to experience the passage of time after death, but it does drag on. Interminably so! The living hashad a few battles and the fate of my soul has been put aside for the moment. I see a few more souls wandering the fields after each battle. Some wear the spiked helm of the Hun,while others wear our colours. Thankfully I've not seen anyone I know. That's not to say they haven't died, just that they aren't stuck here with me in this forsaken place.

There hasn't been any massing of men in the communication or side trenches since yesterday. I am hoping that Captain Mayhew can see fit to look further into my death.

Day 38

I cannot believe it! My last vision was a pair of poorly mended puttees! Blue wool used to sew the tears. I'd not ever thought to see it again, but I have! In the good Captain's office no less! I have to let them know! The light....

"Darn that light! Will it never stop flickering?" Captain Mayhew growled under his breath.

"Captain, I think it's our *friend* again."

"What the blazes is he saying now?"

"It's hard to say! The light is flashing so quickly. It's

like he is panicked or excited over something. How panicked or excited can the dead get?"

"You know, I still find it difficult to swallow that a dead man is trying to tell us he was murdered. "

"Yes, sir."

"I'm a practical man. I find it difficult to believe in spirits or ghosts. Especially those haunting my office!"

"I know, sir."

"If it's true and we find the killer, no one will ever believe us. Can you imagine the Brigadier General's face? We'd be carted off to the funny farm! Discharged as being shell shocked!"

"Quite true, sir; however it's about the only explanation, as farfetched as it may seem." Corporal Ralph Morrissey glanced at the flickering light. "Slow down, man! If you want me to get your message, *slow down*!"

The flashing light, hanging by its thin aluminum wire, ceased its rapid blinking. After a moment's pause, it began its erratic flicking, the flashing light painstakingly spelling out its unearthly message through a series of dashes and dots. Both men shared a brief look and a shiver ran down their spines raising gooseflesh along their bodies.

He'd heard Morrissey's plea.

"Dear God, help and protect us," Mayhew sighed as he crossed himself and cast his eyes towards the sky. Not much scared the old soldier, a veteran of the Boer war and other skirmishes and now a captain in the current conflict, but messages from the dead? Ghosts wandering the trenches? Coming back to send messages of murder behind the lines? Mayhew's heart was beating far too quickly. He feared, for the first time in his life, that he'd suffer a heart attack or an apoplexy.

"Sir... I think you need to see this!"

"What is it, Morrissey? Speak!" Mayhew growled as he stepped behind the young man and looked at the paper he was scribbling on.

Kill... Smith... Kill... Smith... Kill... Smith... Smith... Smith... Kill... Kill... Kill... MURDR...

"What in God's name? He wants to kill Smith?"

Morrissey stared intently at the flicking light. "Sir, there's more..."

"On with it, man!"

Smith... Murdr... Kill...Me...

"Dear sweet God!" Mayhew felt his legs weaken. "Smith? CorporalAlbert Smith? Brigadier Garfield Montgomery's aid? That effete little man? A murderer? How? Why would he want to kill Private Molloy, a simple soldier from Newfoundland, while he is a commissioned soldier with a promising career ahead of him? I can't possibly go to the Brigadier with this! The word of a dead man. A message sent via a faulty light!"

"Sir, I don't presume to know why Smith would want to kill poor Molloy, but I do not doubt these messages or my interpretation of them! Tommy was a friend of mine and a good and honourable man."

"Morrissey, friend or no, Molloy will have to be left a casualty of war. Collateral damage, if you will! We cannot make a charge of murder against one such as Smith without hard proof! It would be the end of our careers and possibly a court martial."

"Sir, could we not, at the least, inspect Smith's bunk and belongings? Perhaps a clue will be there. Maybe they were both after the same woman. We've all been to these villages and more than one man has taken to the local girls. Only days before Molloy's death, the men had been allowed a leave in town."

"Very well, Morrissey. I'll make sure that Smith is kept occupied. You take two men of your choosing and search his bunk. Make sure they can be discreet if nothing is found! I don't want this getting back to the Brigadier! If it does, you are on your own!"

A grin spread across Morrissey's moustached face. "Yes sir!"

And with that plans were made.The next morning, Mayhew would request Smith to come and review the plans for the upcoming assault. They'd been bogged down in the Somme for months now, gaining a few feet before losing a few feet more. Spinning their wheels and going nowhere. A massive assault with the Scottish Highlanders as the van was being prepared for later the fall and it was not unusual for these meetings to happen somewhat spontaneously.

Day 39

At 0800 hours, Smith walked in to Mayhew's office with a stack of documents in his hands and rolls of maps tucked under one arm. For such a short and thin man, he had a swagger and arrogance about him. He had a perpetual condescending sneer. Officers overlooked it because of his relationship with members of the royal family. Smith's uncle was a duke of some renown with strong ties to Parliament and some said he had the ear of the King himself. No other would be able to get away with such blatant insouciance to senior officers.

Today Mayhew found further meaning behind that smug grin. Perhaps the grin of a killer who thought he'd gotten away with cold-blooded murder. He saw the cunning in Smith's eyes. The hands he had earlier thought small and delicate looking now seemed to be lean and long fingered, perfect for holding a knife and driving it into the back of a man. The small touches of fortune that adorned Smith -- a gold ring, an expensive pocket watch -- now screamed an affluence that could pay off men to not tell the truth of things seen, even that of a military doctor.

Mayhew, a man not unaccustomed to death and killing, felt dirtied by being in this man's presence. It was a feeling he could not shake, regardless of how often he chided himself for it. The man was innocent until proof was presented! However, the feeling would not abate.

"Gentlemen, I need your sworn word that anything we do now will go no further! If you cannot follow this, please step away now and nothing will be asked of you!"

Neither of the young men moved. Both were friends of Molloy and one had grown up with him. They had always felt that the "stray bullet" to Molloy's back that the camp doctor had said was the cause of death was a bit suspect. Now they had a chance to perhaps find their friend's killer. A man who'd they'd lived with for the last year or more. Morrissey hadn't told them whom he suspected; they'd find that out soon enough.

When both men nodded their agreement, Morrissey led them to the small dugout room that acted as the bunkroom for six of the camp's aids. It was nothing more than a room dug out from the side of the trench and it was as damp as any other, but being commissioned soldiers, they had a few luxuries. There was a good stove for heat and boiling a kettle, lanterns, and a small table to use for eating or as a desk. Smith's bunk was up against the far wall in the corner.

Morrissey assigned Private Brown to watch the door and ensure they were not disturbed, while he and Private Donaldson searched. Donaldson stripped the bed and checked for any tears where something may be hiding inside the straw stuffed mattress. He also checked under and around the bed and checked the clay walls for any nooks. Nothing. He then proceeded to remake the bed while Morrissey checked through Smith's personal bunk box. Of course Smith's was far a more ornate box than the others, made of solid mahogany. It was a "gift" he bragged, from his grandfather who'd brought it home from his service in India.

Morrissey carefully removed each item: clothes, letters from home, a few small prizes like a Hun knife and helmet, things common amongst the men's possessions. There was nothing to raise an eyebrow over. Even his diary was filled with the usual, stories of day-to-day life, battles, friends lost. Morrissey's heart fell. He'd not be able to prove Smith's guilt, a guilt Morrissey had felt certain of since he first decoded Molloy's message.

With the box empty, the rich smell of spices, leather, and exotic lands filled his nose. They were the scents of the small trunk's travels. A frustration built inside him. The bastard would get away with it! How many more had he killed? How many more would he kill? As the rage and anger built, the small kerosene lamp started to flicker on and off, the staccato flashing a painful reminder of Morrissey's failure. With a rage he'd never felt before, he slammed his fist into the trunk's empty bottom and it burst clean through.

A false bottom! Was this some penny dreadful he was now living in? Morrissey's heart still raced, but with excitement, as he pulled back the shattered wood exposing papers, a long thin blade, with flakes of dried blood crusting around the tang.

"Sloppy!" Morrissey thought. "The blade will rust!" But as his eyes flicked over the contents, it wasn't the blade that drew his eye, but the epaulettes. There was a pair laid ever so carefully next to travel documents and identification papers. With trembling hands, Morrissey lifted the papers and gasped as he thumbed through letters, an additional journal, and the epaulettes. He scooped the entire works up and with his heart pounding against his chest he said, "We have what we came for! We need to get to the captain's office!"

The men dashed out the door, faster than they'd ever run before.

Captain Mayhew and Corporal Smith were bent over his desk going over a map showing existing lines and fortifications. They were in a heated debate over the best place to breech the enemy lines when Morrissey and his two assistants burst into the office. With a tone of command that Mayhew had never heard before, Morrissey bellowed to his companions, "Hold that man!" as he pointed directly to Corporal Smith.

Without hesitation the two men roughly grabbed Smith, pinning his arms behind him.

"What is the meaning of this?" Smith snarled. "I'll have all your heads!"

With a calm he didn't know he could feel, Mayhew stood tall and looked at Morrissey. "I take it you found something?"

"Yessir!" he blurted. With that, he dropped all the items taken from the bottom of the trunk.

Smith's face went white with terror and he began to struggle against his captors. It was in vain, however, as both were strong front line soldiers and Smith, while an adept assassin, was, ultimately, a very unassuming person with limited strength.

Mayhew looked down at the papers, knife, and other personal possessions now covering his desk and picked up a single sheet. He took his time reading it and slowly lifted his head, his blue eyes boring into Smith's brown ones. "Well, it seems I will be speaking directly with the Brigadier today about your service in His Majesty's Army, Mr. Smith. Or should I address you as Herr Schmidt?"

Smith fainted and the light in the captain's office flared to a blinding phosphorous brightness just before the bulb burst, scattering glass over the ground and desk, and speckling the back of Smith's neck in tiny shards.

As blackness descended, those present heard a whisper of a voice...

"Peace."

Chelsea Bee

An Ontario native currently residing in Newfoundland, Bee released *London Calling* in the summer of 2017 to critical praise for its unapologetic examination of violence against women, set against the backdrop of a Newfoundlander touring the London theater world.

Tommy

"Tommy?"

"Tommy!"

"Thomas Jones!"

A crowd of over one hundred men and women are combing through the woods, calling out my son's name. My wife, Julie, and I clutch each other's hands and call out for him. Tommy has been missing for three days.

I know the odds.

Tommy isn't coming home alive.

Julie and I haven't spoken about it. I don't know what her reaction will be when we find his body. *If* we find his body. I can still see hope behind the pain in her eyes. I want her to hold on to that hope. I need her to hold on to that hope.

We search with our eyes to the ground. Julie is looking for a footprint or an entrance to a secret hideout -- somewhere she can rescue her little boy. I'm looking for an abandoned bike, or a blue baseball cap lost in a struggle to fight for his freedom. Even a body. Anything that could lead us to Tommy's remains. Yes, he was mine too, but he was his mommy's boy. He and I liked playing catch in the park and watching Star Wars late into the night on the weekends, but I didn't have the deep understanding of him that Julie did. She could diagnose an ailment with a kiss on his forehead. She knew in her gut that something was wrong the day he went missing. I thought he just got distracted on his way home from school. But she knew it was something else. She knew it was something he couldn't control. She knew it was something much more sinister.

We search until it turns dark. Only a dozen or so of us stay in the woods searching all day. People have lives. They have their own kids to take care of. We cover a small fraction of the couple hundred acres of land that surround our American Midwestern town.

At the end of the day, Julie and I sit down on the couch, each with a plate of casserole that one of the neighbours delivered to us. I can't remember which neighbour. Pyrex containers filled with casserole cover the surfaces of our kitchen.

I don't know how people think that a casserole will make our son's disappearance hurt any less. I guess it means one less thing to worry about. Though I wish I could get lost in the monotony of domestic life again. That's a privilege I never thought I would lose. I don't want to look at the casseroles any more. There are people starving in this country, and they bring food to us? Julie won't eat a darn thing.

Julie turns on the news when we get home, just like she has every day since Tommy's been gone. The screen fills with a picture of our Tommy wearing his white and blue baseball uniform, holding his bat for his team pictures last season. The screen changes to a picture of a chain-link fence covered in blue ribbons, photos of Tommy, and signs asking Tommy to come home, telling him he's missed.

"The boy is described as Caucasian, light brown hair, slender build, eight years old. If anyone has any information on his whereabouts, please contact police immediately," the young woman delivering the news says in a voice over on the photos. The screen cuts to a stranger standing next to the fence, being interviewed by a reporter.

"To me, it has to be the parents. I think the police need to look in to them a little more. Who lets a kid bike home from school alone in this day and age, you know? To me, there's more going on here than just a random stranger. This is a tight-knit community, random crime doesn't happen here."

I hear Julie let out a wail and begin to sob at the accusation and I quickly turn off the TV. She shouldn't have to hear that.

"They think it was us, Paul. They..." Julie trails off, pressing Tommy's baby blanket to her face. She hasn't let go of it since he was reported missing. I know she blames herself for letting him walk home alone, and for waiting for so long to report him missing. She had told herself that he had gone to a friend's house after school and forgot to call. It took hours for us to call everyone in the neighbourhood to realize he hadn't been seen since he left the school. Someone saw him passing the chain-link fence that has been transformed in to a Tommy shrine, but after that it was like he had vanished.

I pull Julie in to a tight embrace. She presses her face

in to my neck and breathes deeply, Tommy's blanket trapped between our chests. I glance out the window and in the corner of my eye, I see a small figure walk pass the large living room window and quickly hide behind a tree. Before I know it, I'm yelling Tommy's name and charging through the house. Julie follows close behind me. We run, barefoot, out into the backyard and I begin frantically searching behind the couple of trees behind our house.

We don't see anything.

"Paul..." Julie says, and I see the last bit of hope fade from her eyes.

"I saw him. I swear, I..." I run my hand through my thick brown hair, trying to make sense of what I had seen.

Julie turns, shoulders slumped, and returns to the house. I look back once more, and see no sign that anyone was ever there.

"I saw him," Julie says, as she bursts in through our front door.

"What?" I turn to face her, wondering if she's lost her mind.

"I mean... it looked like him..." she trails off.

"Dammit, Julie. I thought you really found him." I sit back down, disappointed.

"No, Paul, listen," Julie sits down next to me. Her face is lit with hope and excitement at her supposed breakthrough.

"What was it, Julie?"

"I saw him. I saw Tommy," she says with relief. "He was with a bunch of other kids. They were hanging around in a parking lot by that coffee shop Tommy used to like going to for hot chocolate. He was there, and he was safe."

"If it was him, then why isn't he at home right now?"

"I got out of the car, and started walking up to the kids. I called out to Tommy. He turned and looked at me. We made eye contact. It was him, but it wasn't him. He looked just like himself, except for the eyes."

"What was wrong with his eyes?" I ask, voice quaking.

"They were black. Pitch black."

I purse my lips. She's seeing things. She has to be. I don't want to traumatize her any more than she already is, but she can't continue like this.

"Then one of the other kids took his arm and they started running toward the woods. I started sprinting toward them. As soon as they reached the edge of the woods, I blinked, and they were gone. They all just...disappeared."

Another two weeks pass, this time with no sign of Tommy. The community support has dwindled. Tommy's shrine on the chain-link fence has stopped growing. The news has moved on to another tragedy. A school shooting a couple of states away. More grieving parents. More fingers pointed. More denial that it will happen again. Julie has stopped crying, but still won't let go of Tommy's blanket. I'm planning on going back to work on Monday. We could live off of our savings for a few months longer, but I need to do something again. The police still have no leads. I need some sense of normalcy again.

There's a snowstorm beginning, so Julie sends me to the grocery store to get a couple more items just in case we get snowed in.

I finish up at the store and quickly put the couple of plastic bags of groceries in the trunk of my car. The snow has started to pick up and it's sticking to the ground now. I get in the driver's seat and scroll through the music on my phone, trying to pick something to listen to. I hear a knock on the window and look up. There are three children, who look to be about twelve. Their breath doesn't make a fog like mine. They don't leave any footprints in the snow. A fourth child, a smaller boy, moves forward. I look in to his eyes. Dread starts to fill my heart. His eyes are pure black. Not the rich brown that I've known for eight years. Not the same rich brown he got from me. But it's him. I know it's him. I reach for the door handle.

"Tommy?"

Kelley Power

A native Newfoundlander, Power's work has won the *Newfoundland and Labrador Arts and Letters* competition (Digital Multi-media) and the *48-Hour Novel Writing Marathon* (Engen Books). She is currently working on the manuscript of her first novel, for which she recently received a project grant from ArtsNL. She currently serves the betterment of Newfoundland culture as the vice president of the Writer's Alliance of Newfoundland and Labrador.

In February 2018, Power was nominated for a *YWCA St. John's Women of Distinction Award*.

In early 2018 her short story *F*%$ Jesus* is set to appear in *What's Written in the Ladies*, an anthology collection.

Power is a member of the *Naked Parade Writing Collective*; and likes to recharge her creative batteries taking pictures of rocks, collecting rocks, and making her dog hang out with her while she does it.

Treatment

Joan wakes to the heavy stink of rancid meat. Her head lifts when she gags, peeling her cheek off a cool, smooth surface. In the small circle of light sagging from a single shaded bulb hanging above, she sees it's a table, no bigger than a manhole cover. On its other side is an empty arm-chair with supple cushions.

The smell comes again. It rolls across her tongue, coats her mouth. A dry urge starts low in Joan's belly. She tries to stand, to put some space between her and the stench, but is pinned to a metal stool by a weight: no source, no substance.

A soft shuffle skirts the light.

"Time to start treatment."

The reek in the air shifts. Joan can feel it pull away, sense it licking the edge of the lamplight. It's faint enough that she can take a breath without retching, that she can swallow and clear her throat.

"Who's there?" she says. The words are shaky, not much more than a whisper. She clears her throat again, trying to exorcise the weakness from her voice.

A girl, not much taller than the table, pads out of the

darkness on bare feet. Smooth blond hair swings across the shoulders of her pale blue nightdress as she hoists herself up into the cushioned chair.

"What's happening to me?" Joan asks.

"I told you, this is treatment." The child's light, girlish voice is at odds with the adult words and inflection.

Joan searches for an explanation for where she is, what's happening. She catalogues the symptoms: sensory hallucinations, racing heart, overactive fear response. Maybe she's suffering a severe fever. Or last night's cocaine could've been laced with PCP or psilocybin. She'd have to tell Steve his product was turning to heck.

Her training tells her the right approach is to disengage from the hallucinations, try to ground herself in familiar reality. But the child's assumption of authority is like an electrified needle through her skull, sending sharp shock bursts to a point buried in her brain. She can't help herself.

"Child, let me off this stool." It's a command, but offered in the soft, even tone Joan uses on the pediatric ward. She tries to make eye contact, a show of confidence and sensitivity, but the girl keeps her head bowed, smoothing her nightgown down over her knees as she settles into the chair.

"Treatment is more effective if you sit," she says. No deference. No fear.

"Let me off this stool!" Joan explodes. Thick muscles, built over hours prowling hospital corridors, bunch and flex in her legs as she strains to stand. She shifts from side to side, gripping the table edge. She's rooted to the stool and the stool is rooted to the floor.

"Joan, you're going to hurt yourself." The reproach floats above the rough fury of cursing and movement across the table.

Joan freezes mid-lunge, panting. "How do you know my name?"

"I'm Anna's friend. She's told me about you." The child's head is still bowed. She's scratching small bits of lint off the lace cuffs of her nightgown.

Anna. Thin, pasty Anna, wheezing her way through the ward, always messing her pajamas. A twelve-year-old waste of bed space. Her constant wet cough thrummed Joan's nerves.

"Anna has no friends. The only people that visit her are her parents."

"You're wrong, Joan." Tilting her chin up, the child looks across the table through light-reflecting obsidian eyes. "Anna has me."

The hairs on Joan's arms stand at attention and her heels pound out a back-peddle beat. Still trapped. She lunges forward, fingers curled into claws, raking the air in front of the child's face.

"It took me a long time to find the right word to describe you, Joan." The child doesn't blink. Her wide eyes stare into Joan's, her face relaxed. "What word suits a person children look to for help, but who does everything she can to hurt them?"

The child tucks her legs up under her on the chair. "I try not to use labels in my treatment, but you're special. The more I found out about you, the more I needed an anchor to help me understand you and frame these sessions. Evil. Vile. Any of those would work. Smearing a bacteria culture onto Anna's lip balm, watching the girl use it to salve her dry, cracked lips – pure sadism. I was observing you by then. I could see how hard you worked to keep your mask of concern in place. You're very good at hiding your satisfaction; one of the best I've seen."

Joan is sweating now, her arms tiring. The girl's face remains just out of range of her swiping hands.

The child continues, "I decided the best way to think of you was as a predator. A predator has cunning and persistence. She blends into her environment and waits. You're very good at hiding. A predator targets the weak, the solitary. Like Wendy and Mark and Peter. And now Anna. The problem with a predator is she gets comfortable when she thinks she's at the top of a food chain. She gets careless, loses patience; stops worrying if she'll be seen."

Winded, Joan leans on the table. Its surface softens and her hands sink into it like two brands melting plastic. She screams and throws her weight from side-to-side. The table holds tight.

"Anna saw you, Joan. You rushed things, didn't take your time with Peter. The air in his IV tube was a risk as it was, but you didn't even check over your shoulder before you pressed the plunger on the syringe."

Joan's screaming morphs into a snorting grunt of rage. Flecks of spit gather in the corners of her mouth.

"That's how I found Anna, because of your mistake. She knew nobody would believe her, that she'd be trapped with you as her nurse, watching her and waiting. She curled on her bed that night, cringing in a dark pit of fear. She spoke into that empty void for help. I heard her.

And I came – to show you you're not at the top of the food chain, Joan."

Joan's mind races on adrenaline, trying to outpace the terror, and looking for an explanation for the trap she's in, for the child's knowledge. A thin wedge of rationality pierces her panic. Hallucinations. She has to remember that she is hallucinating. She nurtures the idea with deep breaths, feeling her heart rate slow and the blood return to her extremities. She tests a small laugh; it helps her settle.

"This isn't real. You're not real. Nobody knows." Tension unwinds in her shoulders.

"Would you be able to smell that putrid stink coming off you if this wasn't real?"

The gut-roiling stench surges back into Joan's nostrils. She feels the bile rise into the back of her throat.

"But you've seen patients with phantosmia. You know smells can be imagined. But if this isn't real, would you be able to feel pain, Joan?"

The woman's trapped hands tingle. She watches as the flesh of her fingers splits and tiny maggots crawl out. The slits spread along the backs of her hands, up her forearms. The skin turns green and gelatinous; patches of bone peek through. She rears up in panic and agony.

"But maybe it's pain disorder: your brain telling you there's pain when there's no physical cause. Because obviously your body isn't really rotting off your bones. Is that what you're thinking?"

Joan isn't thinking. Terror is lighting her nervous system on fire, flushing every thought from her head except the single, wailing imperative she can't obey: Run! Run! Run!

The girl leans across the table. Her eyes grow wider, the pitch-black orbs distorting the features of her face. Her mouth, curved into a crescent by flattening pressure of the nose above it, barely opens when she says, "You're wrong. It's real. This is treatment."

The slick smell of decay slides down the back of Joan's throat, cutting off her scream. It's a palpable presence in her belly, expanding and pushing out on her stomach until it has to come back up. A gush of thin yellow fluid spurts from her mouth. It covers her hands and forearms and seeps into the open fissures.

She's gulping air. Her lungs can't produce oxygen fast enough to meet the demands of her brain. A dark ring creeps around the edge of her vision, shrinking her focus to only the child's face: the black eyes have merged into a solid inky circle, the skin around it stretched so thin that her nose and mouth have disappeared. The single eye no longer reflects the light; it devours it, like a deep, empty crater. A maw. Coming for her. It meets the diminishing range of her vision until everything is black. She is consumed. A deep pressure starts behind her breastbone and pain flares across her back, spreading down her ruined left arm, into her neck and jaw. The scream finally tears through the constriction in Joan's throat; a wailing siren devoured by the dark.

Joan is lying down. Her head and body are supported, cushioned. She's in a bed. Her eyes snap open, but blinding brightness forces them closed. She tries squinting, to let them get used to the light. Shapes are indistinct splotches of colour. She takes a deep breath, inhales the soggy smell of cold green beans and mystery protein. Hospital food. The knowledge strikes as a light pain spreads across her chest and presses into her breastbone.

"Be careful. You've had a minor heart attack. Your chest is going to be sore for a while."

Joan can make out the words, but they're fuzzy. They're coming from a small form fiddling with a dark square box next to her bed. The box beeps. A heart monitor.

"There," says the shape, a pink blur walking around the bed to tug closed one of the curtains on the window. The pink clothing darkens to magenta in the dimness. Nurse's scrubs.

Tears well up in Joan's eyes and her hands clench the coarse blanket covering her body. Thank god. Thank god. It wasn't real.

"Most people recover from their first heart attack no problem," says the shape.

A woman. Joan's eyes are adjusting. She can make out a petite form with long blond hair tied up at the base of a delicate neck.

"A bit of activity, a better diet. That usually takes care of it," the woman says as she takes the edge of the second curtain in her hand and flicks it closed with a little jump to give her extra momentum.

"But rest is the most important. A good night's sleep, napping during the day."

The words are right – Joan would say the same thing to a person recovering from a heart attack – but there's something wrong with the voice delivering them. It's high and light. Like a child's.

Joan's heart starts to hammer. Uncontrolled, no care or caution to the flare of pain creeping out from the centre of her rib cage. The tiny woman turns. In the dim light, Joan can make out her black eyes, shining like glassy marbles in her pale face.

"There won't be any rest for you, Joan."

Joan is crying again, tears of relief flushed out by those of dread and panic. The smell of hospital food fades and a rank rot creeps into Joan's nostrils.

"You said this was my treatment," she croaks. "You're going to kill me trying to make me better."

The girl-woman giggles.

"Joan, I said this was treatment, not *your* treatment. I'm here to treat Anna. To cure her. Of you."

Sifting

My sister was born on the second day of the new moon, in the sixth month, during the seventeenth year of the occupation. I remember because that was the day my mother and brother died, tethered to one another by a limp grey umbilical cord in a bed of fluid and blood. Maggie, the midwife, was shrunken and haggard by the end, trying to clean her sticky red hands on her stained apron. My father and I sat on the floor, his chin pressed to the top of my head while he rocked back and forth. Sometimes there's bleeding, he told me. Sometimes it doesn't stop.

The men came four days later.

My father told me to go to my room when the knock fell on our door. He kept my baby sister in his arms. I closed myself in the bedroom and sat on the side of my bed, wondered if they'd come for an inspection. I was never sent to my room during inspection; we would sit together in the kitchen while the Inspectors opened their small grey notebooks and took long, slow strides through our house. The only sound allowed was the scratching of their pencils as they recorded compliance. Or lack of compliance. We prayed for a good inspection – one where the

Inspectors left without speaking.

A scrape and squeal told me my father had lifted the wooden bar out of its bracket and pulled the front door open. I ran my fingers over the coarse wool blanket on my bed. Maybe they had come for an inspection. But our inspections only happened on a Saturday. This was Thursday.

There were murmurs at the door. Inspectors didn't speak when they came; they just walked inside. My hands started to tingle and my dangling feet bounced in time to the tip-a-tap flutter in my chest.

The voices were muffled, as if spoken from under a pillow. I slid from the bed and went to my bedroom door, neck tense as I strained to hear.

"Yes, on Sunday. She died giving birth to our daughter." My father's voice was clear, but the reply was muddled.

"...fortunate...child..."

"Maggie deserves the credit. She's—"

When my father stopped, I pressed my eye to a sliver of space between the door and its frame, close to the floor. He was stepping backwards to avoid two men. They weren't Inspectors.

One was thin, the bones of his face sharp peaks under his pasty skin. He was dressed in the black and brown uniform of a soldier, a scarred wooden club holstered at his waist. He scanned the room from under the shadow of black peaked cap – a fox looking for the scramble of a mouse.

The other man was thickset and squat, round in the face. His small bright eyes peeked over full cheeks stained with a light pink flush. He wore a belted, thigh-length brown leather vest over a white shirt with billowed sleeves, its tight cuffs tucked into tan gloves. His beige pants settled around his ankles and over the laces of a pair of shined shoes that matched the vest. When he turned to order the soldier to close the door, I saw his belt buckle: a rectangle of naked hammered steel engraved with a circle split in half by a vertical line.

It was the first time I'd seen a Sifter up close.

The thin one stayed on the grey hooked mat by the door, legs apartand hands behind his back. The Sifter stepped around my father and moved into the sitting room as he picked up where my father left off.

"Maggie. The midwife." He pulled at the fingers of his gloves. His voice was light. "A useful woman. A busy Sunday for her, wasn't it?

My father turned to follow the man's path through the house, but kept his eyes on my sister, Clara, sleeping in his arms. "I wouldn't know," he said.

The Sifter walked to the kitchen, to the table I'd set for dinner. He laid his gloves on one of the plates and picked up the spoon next to it. He held it to his face, breathed on it, and wiped off the fog with his thumb.

"Indeed. You wouldn't have heard, I suppose. The Brewers did live a ways outside of town. And you've been busy. They had a baby the same night as you."

The face of a tall man, younger than my father, came into my mind. Black hair matted to his head by rain, intent eyes -- that's how I remembered Mr. Brewer. I'd never met his wife.

The Sifter continued his walk around the table. He

set down the spoon and picked up a meat knife; ran his thumb across its sharpened edge, then pressed the tip into the table, leaning on the handle with one hand. He faced my father with a small smile.

"They must be very happy to have a child," my father said. He kept looking at my sister.

"It's dead." He let the knife go. It clattered onto a plate. Clara stirred. My father shushed her and swayed her side-to-side, his eyes now following the squat, smiling man.

"Did you know the Brewers?" the Sifter asked. Behind my father's back, the thin soldier standing in the doorway moved a hand to his worn club.

"No. I don't know them."

"You never met them?"

"Yes, I've met them. You asked me if I knew them. I don't."

"I see. So you didn't know that Mrs. Brewer was a Cerula."

"What…" My father hesitated. His body was stiff and straight. He opened his mouth. Closed it. Clara offered a gurgle. He looked down at her, found his voice. "No. I didn't."

"I see." The Sifter continued to aim his small smile at my father.

My mother had told me stories about the Cerula when she put me to bed. She told me how they were all descended from a small group of children who appeared in the fields of a town outside our own, hundreds of years before, at harvest time. They were hungry and sick. They had no memory of how they had gotten to the fields. Their hair was dark as pitch and their skin was tinged the same

bright blue as the clear autumn sky. Despite their odd-
ness, they were taken in and cared for by the people of the
town. As they aged, their skin took on the same soft pale
tones of the people around them; they married men and
women from that town, and the ones beyond, and had
families.

My mother explained how, now and then, someone
would spring from the bloodlines rooted in those first
children: a black-haired man or woman who could grow
things – anything, anywhere - in shades of blue she tried
to explain but I could never imagine: lush indigo vines
that crept around doorways and windows; flowers with
spiral cobalt petals and teal leaves curved like sickles; per-
iwinkle plants that made medicines I'd never heard of. The
people who shared this gift called themselves Cerula.

She told me how they were despised by the occupiers
who hated everything they couldn't understand or find a
use for. She told me how the ones that survived the war
were hunted by the Sifters and how none had been seen
in years.

In school, they never told us about the Cerula at all.

The Sifter huffed – a sound like the light laugh my father made when he let me have my own way, but empty;
without the warmth. He picked up his gloves from the
plate and waved them in my father's direction.

"Of course," he said. "Yes. If you had known a Cerula,
you would've reported it."

He walked to the far side of the kitchen and stopped. I
couldn't see it from where I was, but I knew he was looking at the photo on the wall. It was a flat, colourless por-
trait of my parents standing in their formal clothes with

me, an infant, held up under my arms by my mother, to face the camera. It was the only image we were allowed to own, the only thing allowed to hang on the walls besides tools and utensils.

"This photo is expired," the Sifter said. The family unit photo hadn't been updated in almost a decade.

"I'm sorry," my father said. "We were waiting. There were miscarriages. Coin has been tight since the drought. When the pregnancy—"

"Why can't you people follow simple laws? Have it by the end of the week." The Sifter pointed. "How old is this one now?" I imagined his finger pressed against the glass of the frame, weighing on my tiny grey breastbone.

"She's ten."

"Where is she?" He surveyed our small house, eyes scanning the two bedroom doors across the sitting room. I slunk back, scrambled, and leapt onto the bed.

"She's sleeping," I heard my father say. I closed my eyes and curled onto my side.

"Call her."

I waited for my father's voice before sliding off the bed and opening the door. I rubbed my eyes; it seemed like something a person who'd been sleeping would do. I looked around the room as if seeing the strangers in it for the first time. The soldier near the door still had his hand on the wooden baton, his palm resting on the butt of its handle. He was focused on my father. The Sifter watched me.

"Tell her to come here."

"Eva, go to the captain." It was his firm voice, the one he used when he bartered at the market.

I did as I was told. The captain – the Sifter - was standing between me and my father. He tucked his gloves into his belt and squat down, blotting my father out of view. He put his hands on my shoulders. They were soft, but heavy. And damp. The moisture seeped through the fabric of my light cotton shirt. My heart beat so hard I could feel it in my fingers and toes. I hoped he couldn't hear it.

"Such pretty eyes. A perfect shade of grey." His own were pale blue, almost white. They made me think of the belly of the dead shark one of the fishermen had dragged in last summer and hung by its tail at the wharf.

He kept looking at me, but tilted his head to throw his voice over his shoulder. "She was from the low plains, you know. Mrs. Brewer."

"I thought she was from Harriston," my father said.

"Before that. She grew up a rock crawler. Living in the dust. Probably learning her filthy creeling plantcraft."

I'd never heard a grown-up say "creeling" before. Some kids at school used it when they were pushing around the boy that sat alone at lunch or knocking around the few people who shot their hands up in class to answer teachers' questions. When those kids said it, it was mean, but it sounded easy off the tongue, like they never gave any thought to what it meant. When the Sifter said it, the word came out bitten and chewed, like he hated the sound of it coming from his own mouth.

"The Cerula have almost died off," the captain said. "Why can't you people let nature take its course?"

His fingers tightened on my shoulders. It hurt, but I didn't let on. His eyes narrowed. His smile dropped and the bead of sweat it had been holding on his upper lip slid down to the corner of his mouth. The pink flush on his damp cheeks deepened and he squeezed harder. I flinched. I couldn't help it. His lip lifted at one corner and he stood up to face my father, holding me in front of him with one hand on my shoulder. Heat radiated off his heavy frame through the back of my shirt and pants. Sweat seeped out of my pores, warm and wet where it met the heat from the Sifter, cool and sticky where it dried on my skin in the room's chill air.

"But Brewer was a different sort anyway, I suppose," the Sifter said. "He was a seditionist, you know; had real talent for spreading conspiracy and heresy. Apparently, the fever outbreak in Tonstay last year wasn't random. It was the government secretly testing a new productivity enhancement drug by dumping it into the town's wells. His pamphlets were high entertainment." He gave another of his hollow huff-laughs.

"A rare imagination," my father said.

"Naturally, you haven't seen these pamphlets, because…"

"Because if I did, I would have reported it." My father straightened to his full height as he said the words, as if coming to attention.

The Sifter pinched my shoulder again and air hissed between my lips. I couldn't help it. He gave me a light shove, propelling me forward. I turned to face him and walked backwards the few steps to my father.

"For a man with a family to be involved in seditious activity, with so much at stake…" The Sifter shrugged. "Not that it matters to the Brewers. They won't be printing any more pamphlets."

I looked away from the Sifter to glance at my father. His skin was like a tanned hide from all the time he spent working outside. Only someone who knew his face, like me, would notice the darker flush across his cheekbones. I could see the soft, smooth curve of Clara's cheek and forehead peeking out from the swaddled bundle in the crook of my father's left arm. I slid my fingers into his free hand. He squeezed it and kept his eyes on the man in front of him.

"That's the way of things," my father said. "Recklessness is selfish. Isn't useful to the unit."

The Sifter captain looked at my father without blinking. I was glad I didn't have to face that stare – it invited a person to fill its emptiness. I knew I would start talking and never stop. Not my father. He was strong. He stared back; took on the yawning silence emptying the room of everything except the strained vibrations of two wills colliding, squeezing out even the air between them.

The subtle glide of wood against leather split the quiet of the room. I'd forgotten about the soldier. We all turned to look at him. He'd pulled out his club and was spinning it slowly in his palm, fingers fluent in the grooves in the handle.

"The private is impatient," the Sifter said. He sighed when he spoke, but there was irritation in his voice and the hand he waved at the soldier, who slid the club back into its holster.

To my father he said, "You're a plain-speaking man, Mr. Hewood. I like that." He pulled his gloves from his belt and tugged them on as he walked to the front door the soldier was holding open. He stopped on the nubby hooked mat and turned back.

"You're also a useful man. I was told you provide some of the best swine in the county to the government stores. A solid service. Take an extra week to get that photo taken care of."

He loped off the doorstep and headed to the garden gate. The soldier followed, rapping the handle of his billy club so it snapped against the doorframe with a crack when he crossed the threshold.

When they were both through the gate and the growl of their car engine had dwindled to little more than a faint buzz, my father walked to the door and closed it. He dropped the wooden bar into place. His knees buckled as he turned and he let his weight sink onto the door, sliding to the floor. I ran to him and he tucked me under his arm and drew me and my sister tight to his chest; it was heaving, the breath being gulped in and gushed out.

"It's okay. We're going to be okay."

He said it against my hair, then kissed the crown of Clara's head.

My sister was born on the second day of the new moon, in the sixth month, during the seventeenth year of the occupation. I remember because she had come to our door that night in the arms of a tall man, black hair matted to his head by rain, eyes intent.

"You have to take her, James," the man had said. "They found out and they're coming for us. Less than a day away."

"Brewer, I —"

"Kara lost too much blood. She's too weak to run. I can't leave her, but I can't let them take the baby. Please."

"I don't…it's too—"

"Maggie came straight to us after she left your birthing this morning. Told us what happened. Does anyone else know yet? She'll never tell; she hates them more than anyone. You can take the baby as your own, you can give her a life."

My father had looked down at the child, his features drawn with grief and hurt.

"Please!"

"Eva, take the baby," my father had said. He'd left me at the door and went to his bedroom. Mr. Brewer had bent and laid the infant in my hands so I could fold her against my chest.

"I hope you'll love her as a sister." The man's eyes were shining when he'd cupped the back of the baby's head, stroking with his thumb.

Father had come back carrying a bundle the size of a bread loaf, wrapped in a tight layer of white homespun. I knew what it was. I'd helped wash the bodies of my brother and mother hours ago; rubbed myosotis oil over their foreheads with shaking fingers; stumbled over the words of the transition incantation as my father recited it in his firm voice; wound the rough, lye-smelling fabric around their stiffening forms as my father lifted them; prepared them for the next day's communal funeral pyre.

My father had held my brother's cloth-wrapped body tight against his chest, then handed it to the man. Nodding at my father, he'd tucked the bundle gently under his jacket and run back into the rain. I'd watched him until the door swung closed.

Kneeling, my father had squeezed my shoulders and pinned me with sad eyes.

"You can never tell," he'd said. "Not your friends or your teachers. Nobody. No matter what. Can you keep the secret?" I was ten. I could do it.

"Yes, Daddy."

"We'll keep her safe, the two of us. What will we call her?"

I'd looked at the tiny sleeping face crowned by a mop of dark hair.

"Clara?" My mother's name was Clara.

My father inhaled sharply and cleared his throat. "Yes. Clara."

Mike Hickey

A bestselling author & award-winning filmmaker with a love for all things spooky, Mike created *Fright Hype* for Crypt TV in 2015 and has hosted the popular web series since along with press and event coverage for major films like *Halloween* (2018) and *IT* (2017).

Recently, he wrote and directed the short film *That Halloween* (2021) which premiered Halloween night 2021 on SuperChannel through the Blood In The Snow Film Festival and is currently collecting laurels and awards on the festival circuit. He's also produced several shorts including the Telefilm Picture Start films *Matchstick* (2017), *Fishbowl* (2022), and *False Light* (2018) which was selected for Not Short on Talent at Cannes. He is currently in development on a number of feature projects.

Through Engen Books Mike helmed *Terror Nova*, an anthology of Newfoundland inspired horror stories, which was released to great acclaim in 2020. The series continued with *Terror Nova Writers Retreat* in early 2022.

Mike currently lives in St John's, Newfoundland with his wife, Maria, and their dog, Samhain (who responds to "Sam" and doesn't respond to requests to stop pooping in the kitchen.)

Stephen King & The Dungeon of Nightmares

I was always one of those people who would just do something to have a good story to tell, so when I read "Shoeless Joe" by W.P. Kinsella — and, of course, by "read" I mean listened to the audiobook in my car because my overactive mind doesn't allow for me to sit down with an actual book — the journey of Ray (also Kinsella) hit a little close to home.

The only difference between me and Ray, who most people know from when he was played by Kevin Costner in the film adaptation "Field Of Dreams", is that I don't really need a disembodied voice encouraging that "if you build it, he will come" to do something as ridiculous as plow over my family's income source to build a baseball field; I just need a "y'know what'd be cool?" thought to strike me.

But listening to the story of Iowa farmer Ray's journey to bring reclusive writer J.D. Salinger to see the ghostly Black Sox play retribution baseball on his backyard field, it started brewing something different in my head. Then, either through divine intervention, a psychotic slip, or my phone glitching and playing the audiobook from my pocket, I heard it.

"Ease his pain."

This voice came to me while I was watching Kubrick's "The Shining" which I do surprisingly frequently considering that I stand firmly in the King camp that it's a bad adaptation of his book.

Considering this, when I heard those words during the film it donned on me: I was supposed to go to Maine and convince Stephen King to come with me to the Stanley Hotel in Colorado.

I didn't know to what purpose. I didn't anticipate we'd remake the movie to appease his displeasure with Kubrick's film — he had already done that with Mick Garris to mixed reception — but I was sure once I had him in the car with me, I'd get another sign to tell me what the next step would be.

I expected the hardest part of my quest wouldn't be the days of driving to get to the US border, or crossing the border while doing my best not to tell a border agent that the purpose of my visit was to kidnap the most prolific author of our time and take him to the inspiration of one of his most contentious and frightening stories, but that it would be getting the gun.

In the book, Ray managed to get a revolver from a pawn shop. In the movie, he just fakes it. I thought I'd make the attempt to get one and then settle for faking once I failed. But like so many things, once I actually started the task, I resigned myself to completing it.

I figured getting one in Bangor might raise some flags, so I decided to try Benedicta, a town not far over the border. There were a few other towns between there and Ban-

gor I could try in case of failure, but sadly and convenient-
ly, getting a gun in the States is alarmingly easy.

I threw it and the box with a dozen loose bullets in
the trunk of my car and buried it under a coat hoping I
wouldn't need to call the items into action.

The drive from Benedicta to Bangor is short but a pretty one. Living in the northeast, I've grown accustomed
to picturesque autumnal scenes, but Maine in the fall is
something else. Warm tones speckle the rolling hillside,
and you understand the droves of northbound vehicles
with their plates from increasingly southern ports of call
all flocking to partake in the time-honoured tradition of
"leaf peeping".

After about an hour I arrived in town and, ever
stealthy, googled "Stephen King House" which promptly
resulted in photos and the address, allowing me to make
my way to my literary hero's home with an easily pur-
chased gun in my trunk.

Modern society is incredibly flawed.

King lives in exactly the house you expect him to. It's
a giant, spooky mansion complete with batwing fretwork
on the cast iron gate. I was surprised it didn't come with a
built-in thunderstorm backdrop.

Sitting in the long shadows of Stephen King's mansion
on a late afternoon I started to second guess this whole
"kidnap Stephen King" plan I had concocted.

I felt the colour drain from my face. What the hell was
I doing? Was I really going to try and get Stephen King to
climb into my beaten down Toyota and then drive across
the country to Colorado with me? What was I – OH MY
GOD IT'S HIM.

Shuffling down the sidewalk towards my car was the lanky septuagenarian. Broken-in jeans hung off his thin frame, as did a polar fleece pullover jacket. Wispy grey and white hair flipped out from a tattered Red Sox cap. The cap seemed like a sign. I was ignoring the fact that King is a renowned Sox fan and probably had worn the same cap every day for the last twenty years. No, this was a sign from the voice. After all, it was a Red Sox game that Ray had brought Salinger to in the book. King wearing that cap as I first laid eyes on him had to mean something.

Of course! A ball game! That's what won Salinger over. I'd invite King to a Red Sox game. How could he say no? From there I'd make my pitch for the trip to Colorado to visit the Stanley Hotel he based the Overlook on. This all seemed so obvious now.

All the second guessing flooded out the door of my old Corolla along with me. I jammed my right hand into the pocket of my jean jacket to make a fake gun with my knuckle and made my way towards the icon.

"Uh, Mr. King?" I stammered out. King turned to me, first with the forced smile that comes from entertaining admirers while trying to simply walk home from some mundane task, then his eyes caught my pointed pocket and the smile flattened.

"Yes?" His voice carried more annoyance than fear.

"Uh, hello Mr. King. My name is Mitch and I'd like—"

King cut me off.

"You'd like me to come to a ball game with you?"

"Uh…"

"Kid, you're not the first to pull this stunt. Reading "Shoeless Joe"?"

"…Audiobook."

"Right. Look, it's late October. The Sox missed the playoffs. Even if I believed for a second that that was a real gun and not a candy bar or something, I couldn't go to a game with you if I wanted to."

"I have a real gun."

"In you pocket?"

"…in my trunk."

"Right. Well, if you were going to use it you would have gotten it out of the trunk and like I said there's no baseball to see."

I hadn't thought about this. It was late October. I hadn't been following baseball that closely this year, so I hadn't been paying attention to the standings or playoffs. It hadn't occurred to until he said it that the Red Sox were eliminated.

Crap.

"How do you feel about the Bruins?"

"Hah!" King laughed despite himself. "Where are you from, kid?"

"Newfoundland."

"Newfinlund?" He echoed back to me while somehow still ignoring my pronunciation and butchering the word. "You came all the way from Newfinlund — took a ferry ride, I guess, crossed a border, all that — without realizing the Sox haven't played in three weeks and now want to change your whole plan to a hockey game on the fly?"

I froze. Embarrassed by how nonchalantly my literary idol was calling out my lack foresight.

"I did come all this way. Honestly, I didn't know what I was doing. It was only when I saw your cap that I thought we'd go to a ball game. Besides, I like hockey better anyway."

"Of course, you're Canadian."

"I guess. Either way, I heard the voice, and it made me want to come here."

"You actually heard the voice?"

"Yes, sir."

"Have you heard voices before?"

Before I answered a car drove by with a gaggle of college-aged kids honking and waving at the author. He smiled and waved.

"No, this was the first time."

"And what did the voice say?"

"Ease his pain."

"Like in the book?" He suddenly seemed fascinated. "And what made you decide it meant me? Kinsella is convinced Salinger has an unrequited love for baseball. What about your voice saying 'ease his pain' made you want to come here?"

"Well, I was watching Kubrick's version of The Shining at the time."

This made him chuckle, which I took as a good sign.

"Alright, Mitch from Newfinlund. I'm not committing to a Bruins game, but if you promise to leave the gun in your trunk, you can come in for a cup of coffee and we can talk about this."

All things considered, he was being more than reasonable. It was surreal. I had heard a voice, driven to Maine, and now somehow was following this literary icon through a batwing gate — with actual batwings — into his home for a cup of coffee.

I was shocked. This was crazy. This was… wait, this was actually crazy. What the hell was going on?

"Uh, Mr. King?" I started to ask as we walked into his foyer.

"Please, call me Steve." He said, turning and pulling on a golden rope hanging from the ceiling.

My heart plummeted — and so did my feet. I dropped down a long shoot and slid into Stephen King's dungeon.

Not unlike his house, Stephen King's dungeon is exactly what you'd expect. Moisture runs over rock walls lit by open torches. Rats scurry across the dirt floor. Shackles hang from the walls of the cells, some of which still have portions of arms attached.

I'll give the guy credit: he knows how to stay on brand.

I had lost track of how long I may have been down there when I heard a door creak and footsteps descend the stairs.

"Mitch, I'd like you to meet someone," the author said as he stepped into the light and from the darkness behind him, the Thing of Evil emerged. "This is Molly."

King's corgi panted at me, winded by the the trip down to the dungeon on such short legs.

She waddled forward and licked at a wet spot on the floor.

"Molly, no." King urged and gestured toward me.

"Him."

She looked up to me and came forward again.

When she reached the narrow bars of my cell, her body seemed to contract like rubber to easily squeeze through.

I retracted and pushed myself against the far wall as I watched the dog's eyes begin to glow red.

Then, like a snake dislodging its jaw, Molly opened her mouth revealing rows of teeth receding into a void blacker than my mind could conceive. Her jaws expanded wider until they stretched to match my size and Molly, known to King's social media followers as the "Thing of Evil", shuffled forward on her short legs and consumed me whole.

But at least I got a great story to tell.

Afterword
Matthew LeDrew

"Never Look Back" is the Engen Books motto and we stand by it with everything we do, but what most people don't realize is that it's a double-entendre. It's meant to evoke not only our commitment to being a forward-looking publisher that triesto predict future trends and business norms... But it's also meant as a callback to the warnings yelled by many a slasher-movie victim when a killer is fast on their tail: "Don't look back!" that added dimension to our motto is because Engen Books has its roots in horror, thriller, and chiller publishing.

As much as I adore all the *From the Rock* volumes, there's something about this genre being the first one to come out after our ten-year anniversary that feels like... coming home, somehow. And this was an amazing collection. I love what Ellen Curtis and Erin Vance have done with this title, turning it into the must-read book of every spring season sinceits inception. I love that even after three volumes, we can still find bold, fresh, new talent -- like Anastacia Hopkins, Jon Dobbin, and Eryn Heidel– and put their work alongside award-winners like Kelley Power and authors with multiple books in the genre under their belt; not just because that was part of our mission statement, but because they *deserve* to be there. *From the Rock* is a title where the fiction, not the name attached to it, comes first, and that understanding has allowed us the pleasure to break in some remarkable talents for your reading pleasure.

'Chillers' is an amazing genre to break into, because – and this will shock some – it's a valuable tool in learning how to tell a good story. I believe that there's a reason I started in chillers and can now break away from them. Think of all the great directors who started in horror and went on to greater things: Peter Jackson, James Cameron, Sam Raimi, and Stephen Spielberg to name a few (there are dozens). I believe this to be because at the core of good storytelling is an understanding of human emotion. That ability to elicit an emotional response from the reader is at the key to understanding what makes good fiction -- and horror stories are a good stepping-stone into that. It's hard to get romance right, or nostalgia, or awe... but fear is something basic, something we can all agree on. If you can master the art of conveying a story through fear, then you've learned how to tell a story using emotion, and you're well on your way to learning how to use those tools in the future for other emotions and stories.

Once again, thank you to everyone who submitted-- and to those who got into this collection, you've made it genuinely something to be proud of. Pat yourselves on the back; I look forward to seeing what you do in the future.

Matthew LeDrew
Publisher, Engen Books
"Never Look Back"

ON THE COVER

The amazing new cover of this collection was provided by Mike Hickey, and award-winning horror film producer!

A bestselling author & award-winning filmmaker with a love for all things spooky, Mike created FRIGHT HYPE for Crypt TV in 2015 and has hosted the popular web series since along with press and event coverage for major films like HALLOWEEN (2018) and IT (2017).

Recently, he wrote and directed the short film THAT HALLOWEEN (2021) which premiered Halloween night 2021 on SuperChannel through the Blood In The Snow Film Festival and is currently collecting laurels and awards on the festival circuit. He's also produced several shorts including the Telefilm Picture Start films MATCHSTICK (2017), FISHBOWL (2022), and FALSE LIGHT (2018) which was selected for Not Short on Talent at Cannes. He is currently in development on a number of feature projects.

Through Engen Books Mike helmed TERROR NOVA, an anthology of Newfoundland inspired horror stories, which was released to great acclaim in 2020. The series continued with TERROR NOVA WRITERS RETREAT in early 2022 and with TERROR NOVA LURKING IN DARKNESS in 2023.

Mike currently lives in St John's, Newfoundland with his wife, Maria, and their dog, Samhain (who responds to "Sam" and doesn't respond to requests to stop pooping in the kitchen.)

DARK STORIES FROM ENGEN BOOKS

THE HOWL BECONS

Growing up without his father, Tyler had no way of knowing the horrible secret that has plagued his family for generations. To free himself and find the cure, he will have to look beyond himself and into his dark history.

"A very ambitious novel… the horrors of everyday life can be worse than anything in fiction. The idea of using werewolves as a metaphor – to me this pushes the book a bit above much of what is out there… Brad [Dunne] is a very good writer and obviously has a deep background."
— Andrew Peacock

WESTON'S WAR

Something evil grows in the heart of Colorado. Bill Weston was a man of the West. He knew it – its land, its people, its stories. It was where he plied his trade, hunting men for money. His life wasn't easy, but it was predictable. That all changed when he captured Faraway Sue and he was led on a trip through the Colorado forests

"Take a little Zane Grey. Add a little Penny Dreadful. Read with Sam Elliot's voice. Discover Jon Dobbin's masterful The Starving."
— Darrell Power,
Great Big Sea

CHILLERS FROM THE ROCK

A COLLECTION OF SHORT STORIES
EDITED BY ERIN VANCE & ELLEN CURTIS

Twenty-six short stories written by a diverse mix of some of the best suspense and horror authors in Atlantic Canada, including both award-winners, veterans of their craft, and brand new talent.

Edited by Erin Vance and accomplished genre author Ellen Curtis, this collection features the thrilling, creatively charged, astonishing fiction that showcases the talent, imagination, and prestige that Atlantic Canada has to offer.

Featuring the work of Paul Carberry (*The Gray Chapter*), Kelley Power (*Tombstories*), Matthew LeDrew (*Coral Beach Casefiles*), Ali House (*The Hunters and the Hunted*, a new story by Mike Hickey (*That Halloween*) and more!